W9-BZO-895

# DRUNK ON A PLANE

## THE MISADVENTURES OF A DRUNK IN PARADISE: BOOK 1

### ZANE MITCHELL

Drunk on a Plane
The Misadventures of a Drunk in Paradise: Book #1

*by*
*Zane Mitchell*

Copyright © 2018 by Zane Mitchell

**ISBN:** 9781792646454
**ASIN:** B07MKFW4G7
**VS:** 01312019.05

All rights reserved. No part of this book may be reproduced in any form or by any electronic or mechanical means, including information storage and retrieval systems, without written permission from the author, except for the use of brief quotations in a book review. This is a work of fiction. Names, characters, businesses, places, events, locales, and incidents are either the products of the author's imagination or used in a fictitious manner. Any resemblance to actual persons, living or dead, or actual events is purely coincidental.

*To my grandfather,*
*The OG that made AI real.*
*I miss you.*
*Kiss Grandma for me.*

# CONTENTS

## SNEAK PEEK - DRUNK ON A BOAT

# 1

ALRIGHT, SO LET ME PREFACE MY STORY BY SAYING—YOU'RE NOT going to believe it. Even if I told you the whole goddamned story, you'd still say that I made it up. But haven't you heard the saying that truth is stranger than fiction? Alright, then. Repeat after me. *Truth is stranger than fiction.* Okay. Got it? Good.

Now, I'm gonna start with the basics. This is where your brain's gonna start telling you you'd be better off putting your money on Blockbuster stock than on me. Hey, who knows, VHS might make a comeback someday, right? I mean I hear vinyl's making a return, so you never know.

My name is Drunk. Daniel T. Drunk, Jr. if you wanna know what it says on my MasterCard. I'm T or T-Bone to Mikey, my best buddy since the second grade. My mother calls me Terrence, which, if you've got half a brain, you've figured out is what the T stands for. Pops calls me Junior. You? You can just call me Drunk.

Lemme start by telling you the benefits of having a name such as Drunk. First of all, no one expects much out of you. In fact, they expect you to be blitzed eighty to ninety percent of the time. When you go to a bar, or a wedding, or hell, a bar mitzvah, and you introduce yourself as Drunk, everyone wants to buy you a drink. So, there's that. That's a pretty decent perk. When I hang out with buddies, I rarely get asked to be the designated driver. Even though my initials are DD. I mean who wants a Drunk driving them?

But best of all?

The chicks.

They dig it.

Here's the deal with that, though. I can get all the pieces of ass that I want. I can get the hot ones. The skanky ones. The downright virginal ones. What I'm having problems with is finding the till-death-do-you-part ones.

Most women would consider me attractive. Does that make me cocky to say that? Fine. Call me cocky. A cocky Drunk. I'll take that. Mostly because there's some truth to it. I can't help it. When I look in the mirror, a sexy-as-hell man looks back at me. Now, I'm completely aware of the fact that I didn't do anything to *earn* these good looks. I was born with good genes. I got my mother's thick dark brown hair and bone structure. Pops gave me his height and these massive paws that can grip a bowling ball like no other, and *his* pops gave me his Grecian nose.

I get lots of people telling me about the significance of my nose. Yeah, it's a little oversized. But that seems to attract the women. If I had a dollar for every time some random chick in a bar asked me, "Big nose, big hose?" I'd be a very rich man. Sorry, was that offensive to someone out there? We might as well part ways now, then, because I not only have a big nose, but I tend to have a big mouth as well, and this is only the beginning of my story. Things are sure to get worse.

So what was I saying? Oh yeah. Most women think I'm attractive, and I agree with them. They look at me, hear my name is Drunk and then promptly think I'm perfect for that one-night stand their girlfriend said would cure them of their broken heart. Or they want me to be an outlet for their over-worked, overstressed little bodies. I mean, orgasms cure every-thing, right? Eh. I might be a little jaded right now, so I'm not gonna be the one to answer that question, because I'd probably tell you that meaningless sex is overrated, and you'd call bull-shit faster than I could get down on one knee.

Here's the thing about getting down on one knee, though. You can't do it when the only women you meet are out for only one thing. Back in my twenties, meeting women who were out for only one thing was awesome. Maybe awesome is an understatement. It was downright majestic. Ma-fucking-jestic, okay?

But I'm thirty-five. No one wants to be thirty-five and a man whore. Nah, that's not me anymore. About three years ago I decided to do my mother a favor and knock that shit off. I tried to lay off the sauce for her too. I cleaned up my one-bedroom apartment and went down to the Furniture Mart out on the interstate and bought me a living room set and a new mattress with a frame.

Yeah, figure that. I sleep eight inches off the floor now and I'm a fucking adult or something. But, that new Sealy Posture-pedic did something even twelve years of Catholic school couldn't do. It inspired me to save myself for marriage from that point forward.

Yeah, see, you're starting to pull out that bullshit card, aren't you? I knew it. Come on. Have a little faith, will ya? No. I'm not kidding. I am a born-again virgin. Get out the black lights, check my mattress if you don't believe me.

Oh wait.

On second thought...you probably better not. I'm claiming born-again virgin status, not saint status.

Anyway, a little over a year into my vow of chastity, I met Pamela. I'd let my mother con me into going to church with her one Sunday, even though I'd warned her that Father O'Hare would likely cast me out what with all of my wicked sins and everything. But she'd decided to slap a suit on me, polish me up real nice, and we'd chance it. Her and I had gone and left Pops home alone to watch the Chiefs kick the crap out of the Patriots again. It was an epic 2014 game, which Pops was keen on rewatching over and over again. By now I was pretty confident he knew every play by heart. Anyway, after church my mother and I stood out on the church steps with all of her book club gals. She'd introduced me proudly to all of her friends as her "single boy, Terrence."

Yeah.

*Her single boy, Terrence.*

I'd wanted to slip into a black hole. How had thirty-three years of life been reduced to my mother referring to me as her single boy, Terrence?

*Fuck!*

It took about five shakes for someone's sister's cousin's niece's friend to make a beeline back inside the church, and they'd come back outside with Pamela.

Oh sweet Jesus, Pamela. She was blonde. Stacked. And oh my God, that ass. Like *twelve* on a dime scale. That woman looked at me like I was a god, too. I was used to that. And let's be real. Between my Grecian nose and the suit I was wearing, I looked like a god.

I couldn't believe my luck. Who knew all the good girls were hiding in church? Had I known that, I probably would've started going to church with Mom when I'd turned thirty.

"Pamela, this is Terrence. Terrence, Pamela," introduced one of the women my mother vaguely referred to as a "friend" of hers.

The old me would have corrected the woman and told Pamela just to call me Drunk. But the new, looking-for-a-wife me said, "It's a pleasure to meet you, Pamela," with my best George Clooney swagger.

She'd taken the hand I'd offered, and I kid you not, sparks flew.

My mother had actually been the one to suggest I take Pamela to coffee after church and she'd catch a ride home with her friend. That had been the day I'd met my future fiancée. The woman was sweet, smart, and did I mention stacked? Those first few weeks of our relationship, that woman had me hotter than a Carolina Reaper, complete with tears and all.

Of course, I'd been open with Pam right from the beginning in telling her about my vow of chastity and how I'd wanted to find a woman I could settle down with before giving myself away again. She'd told me she understood and valued my principles. But if anything, that had made her want me more. You want to talk about blue balls? I left her house so fucking hard, so many times, her next-door neighbor probably thought I owned stock in Viagra.

Now, just so we're clear. Holding out until marriage with a woman like Pamela had been the hardest thing I'd ever done in my entire life. It was even harder than giving up alcohol, and that had been downright painful.

Now, a man can only last so long under those circumstances, so I did what any red-blooded, born-again-virgin man would do and I got down on one knee. Holy shit, you'd think I'd scored tickets for my mother to see Oprah or something, the way she screamed when I told her I was getting married. It was as if I had done something right for the first time in my entire worthless life. Just by getting down on one goddamned knee.

Of course, Pops didn't care. He only wanted to know how much a wedding was going to set him back. I told him I had it covered. My job at the station earned me a decent enough salary. I'd never had a serious girlfriend, I rarely had to pay for my drinks, and I lived in a one-bedroom apartment over a bowling alley, so I had a hefty savings account. That was enough to warrant a toast out of him.

"To Junior and the new Mrs. Junior," he'd said, holding up

his can of Budweiser, but not bothering to get out of his Barcalounger.

As for Pamela, she didn't seem to care that her new last name was going to be Drunk. Mrs. Pamela Drunk. I should have known then that shit wouldn't last. What woman wanted to be known as Mrs. Drunk? Pops always claimed he'd had to pay off my mother's father to convince him to let his daughter marry a Drunk. Mom said Pops was full of shit, and Granddad died before I could ask him, so who knows which family member was the most full of shit.

Now, if it had been up to me, Pam and I would've gotten married as soon as we could hook up with a JP. But it wasn't up to me. It was up to the women in my life. And the women in my life wanted an old-fashioned Catholic wedding with all the bells and whistles.

Apparently bells and whistles meant forcing ten of my best friends to wear penguin suits and hiring an orchestra *and* a DJ.

Fuck.

Do you have any idea how long it takes to set that kind of shindig up? Twelve fucking months. That's how long. I was beginning to think my balls were gonna fall off. I literally went home one night after a particularly long and agonizing make-out session, went to piss and threw up on my penis. True story.

Yeah, so here's the interesting thing. As much as I was having problems keeping my *system* in check, apparently, so was Pam. The night before the wedding, I was instructed to make myself scarce. She swore up and down it was bad luck for the groom to see the bride before the wedding. I suppose I should have told her it was also bad luck for the bride to sleep with her ex-boyfriend the night before the wedding, but I just didn't think I needed to say that to my loving bride-to-be.

FUCK.

A belt saved me from the worst mistake I'd ever made. Yeah, a fucking belt. I forgot it at the apartment, and when I went to go grab it the night before the wedding, I saw things that would make James Deen blush.

Yeah, so there I was, holding a belt with my fiancée and her sleazeball ex naked in my apartment, screwing on my virginal Sealy Posturepedic, imprinting her goddamned footprints onto the headboard.

Dammit, that hurt.

In retrospect, I should have put that belt to good use. I should have whipped one or both of their asses with it, or I should have used it to hang myself back at the hotel, where my bags were packed and ready for the honeymoon to Paradise Isle, which at this point was a complete and total waste of money.

Instead, I'd done neither. I'd blown the two folded-up hundies I was going to use to tip the priest and equipped myself and all ten groomsmen with a few bottles of semidecent bourbon, and we'd gotten plastered in my hotel room. I woke up two days later with the hardest fucking erection, the most massive hangover, a packed suitcase, and two tickets to paradise. So I did what any spurned-not-in-his-right-mind man would do: I took a cold shower, stuck a piece of Doublemint in my mouth, and headed to the airport.

So here I sit. On a cold-as-hell Monday morning, February nineteenth, two thousand and fucking eighteen, still partially drunk, on a plane, and on the way to what was supposed to have been my honeymoon. I didn't even take a minute to text anyone to tell them where I was going. I just bounced. Maybe when I get to the five-star resort Pam booked us with my money, I'll let someone know where I am. Until then, bring on the in-service flight drinks.

## 2

OKAY, SO I LIED. IT PROBABLY WON'T BE THE FIRST TIME, SO TRY not to get too riled up. Instead of boozing away the flight, the minute the plane took off, I fell asleep and I didn't wake up until the woman sitting next to me tapped me on the shoulder, told me we'd touched down in Atlanta, and asked me if I wanted my Doublemint back.

After deboarding the plane, I made a beeline for the terminal bathroom and then spent the rest of my layover stuck inside a stall with the worst case of whiskey shits I'd ever had. Apparently, my three years of sobriety had taught my innards to become accustomed to what normal life was like, and now they revolted against my weekend of binge drinking with the most rancid-smelling liquid black sludge I'd ever been a party to. I heard several sets of men's shoes clicking in on the freshly mopped, shiny bathroom floor while I sat silently wishing I'd used that belt the day before and ended my agony. Of course, the clicks had gotten no further than the sinks before I heard them get progressively quieter as the owners of said shoes walked back in the direction they'd just come. *I don't blame them*, I thought as I wallowed in the stench that hung in the air around me like a thick malodorous fog. I was making *myself* sick by inhaling my own putrid odor.

After mopping myself up the best I could with the eight remaining squares of one-ply paper in my stall, I stood up and immediately felt fifteen pounds lighter. The empty stomach combined with the slight tremor in my hands gave me an overwhelming urge to find something to eat.

Preferably a burger.

With bacon.

Why I always craved bacon after a boozefest, I'd never really understood. But it was as much a Drunk family tradition to eat bacon after a night of drinking as it was to eat smoked weenies bathed in barbecue sauce while watching football at my folks' house on Thanksgiving Day.

So I stood in line at the terminal's burger joint and kept one eye on the Smith & Wesson watch my mother had given me when I'd graduated from the academy. I was cutting it close, but I had no choice. It was either refuel here or get the shakes on the ride across the Atlantic, because a chintzy bag of pretzels and a plastic cup of soda on the plane wasn't going to cut it.

The line seemed to take forever, and I peered over the white-haired couple in front of me twice, wondering why they weren't moving. In the meantime, I stared down at the little old man in front of me. He had two islands of white hair around the backs of his ears and a sea of chicken-like speckled skin in between. I'd been playing connect the liver spots in my mind when at last it dawned on me that maybe they weren't waiting in line. Perhaps they were simply discussing the weather in Omaha while standing in the vicinity of the line.

"Are you in line?" I finally asked.

The husband, whose shoulders were so rounded and hunched over that he would've been lucky to register in at five feet tall, wore a pink-and-blue Hawaiian shirt that hung down low over the back of his khaki chino shorts. Pale, birdlike stems poked out of the hems, and his white nylon socks were pulled up just below his knees. His legs ended in a pair of all-white New Balance sneakers. When he turned to look up at me, his entire torso turned as a unit. "What?" he asked, cupping the back of one ear.

"Are you in line for burgers?" I said, louder this time, slouching over to get my mouth closer to his ear.

The man looked at his wife. She was shorter than he was and wore a floral beige cotton dress and a pink sun visor that said "World's Best Grandma." "He asked if we're in line, Al," she hollered into his good ear.

His eyes opened wider, showing a pair of watery greenish-blue eyes sunken into his wrinkly face. "Oh!" His mouth formed the letter as he said it. The combination of the wide eyes and mouth suggested that somehow my question had surprised him.

"Go ahead, go ahead," he said. He hobbled several tiny steps to the left while scooting his wife and their small silver rolling suitcase covered in bumper stickers over with him.

"Thanks," I said, giving them the kind of smile where my lips mashed tightly against my teeth and my cheeks squished up into my eyes. It was a fake smile, but I didn't care. I rolled my suitcase with me as I lowered my head and cut in front of the pair of senior citizens.

*Budging in front of old people. Mom would be so proud,* I thought as I ran a hand self-consciously through the dark mop of hair I hadn't bothered to put product in that morning.

Even cutting the elderly couple out of the equation, the line seemed to take forever. Glancing at my watch didn't seem to make it go any faster. In fact, after staring at the second hand, I discovered it took exactly seventy-three seconds for me to move the distance of one fourteen-by-fourteen-inch square tile.

At long last, I was at the front of the line. I ordered a triple bacon cheeseburger and a bottle of Dr. Pepper for the flight. I was going to need some serious caffeine if I was going to make it, and I'd never been a coffee drinker.

The three cashiers behind the counter stood, seemingly, with their thumbs up their assholes. There was a whole lotta kitchen and not enough cooks, apparently. But they dutifully stood their ground at their stations with uncomfortable looks on their faces, trying not to make eye contact with the angry faces of the people waiting for their food so they could make their connecting flights.

Once my order had been filled, I shoved my bottled soda into my bag, grabbed my burger, and took off on a dead sprint for the gate that I was now surely late for. My long legs helped me pass about six other runners, and then I heard the announcement over the loudspeaker. Delta Flight 661 to Paradise Isle, final boarding call.

*Fuck.*

I ran even faster, just about knocking a little girl over with my suitcase along the way. The crash spun me around and I arrived at my gate even more disheveled than when I'd begun the day.

"I'm here!" I shouted at the young black woman at the gate. Her hair was tied back in a little fuzzy ball at the crown of her head making her appear to be about fifteen. "I'm here!"

"Boarding pass?" she asked in a thick Georgian accent.

I shoved my burger into my mouth to hold while I patted myself down. I'd stuck that damn thing somewhere. A crinkly piece of paper in the back pocket of my trousers stopped the patting. I tugged it out and handed it to the girl.

"Thank you, sir." She flattened out the paper and held it against her scanner. It beeped appropriately and she handed it back to me. "Enjoy your trip to Paradise, sir."

I shoved the paper back in my pocket, pulled the burger from my mouth, and steered my suitcase towards the waiting door. As soon as I'd stepped onto the gangway, I heard the girl closing the doors behind me.

# 3

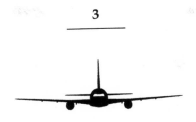

BECAUSE I'D NEARLY MISSED MY FLIGHT AND I WAS THE LAST TO board, I'd been in a rush to find my seat. Which must have been why I hadn't noticed the woman in seat 23B until about halfway through the inflight movie.

Staring up at the ridiculously stupid comedy playing on the televisions fixed to the plane's ceiling, I grinned with my mouth hanging half-open like a douchebag with sinus problems, all the while pressing the airline's cheaper-than-shit free earbuds into my ears with my thumbs in an effort to hear the movie over the roar of the engines out my window.

So it wasn't until she was right upon me that I finally noticed her. Heading to the restroom at the back of the plane, no doubt, she took a slight pause to stare down at me with the sparkliest pair of crystalline blue eyes that I'd ever seen. Her spicy scent, which immediately turned my testosterone up to a low boil, was more intoxicating than the twelve-year-old bourbon I'd wallowed in the night before, and in that split second, I realized that I'd never seen anyone like her before. The woman could have been a movie star, she was that fucking gorgeous. She had a certain Megan Fox quality to her.

Her shiny black hair was straight and fine. My imagination immediately started thinking about how it would feel to run a hand through it and maybe give it a little tug. Chicks dug that. I was sure it would be soft and silky, like smooth satin sheets, and if I closed my eyes I could almost feel it slipping across my shirtless torso. She had an exotically tanned flawless complexion, as if she'd just come from a vacation instead of heading off on one, and she had a perfectly shaped little turned-up nose. It was the kind that a butterfly might land on in a Disney movie. As I stared at her, I could almost hear the little fairy sparkle noises in my head.

My heart stopped beating in my chest for the length of time she paused next to my seat, and with my mouth hanging open like an idiot, I was forced to quickly snap it shut. When I did, I nearly choked on my dried-out, oversized cotton-mouthed tongue. The hangover I was fighting made my brain go limp— the complete opposite of what my penis was doing at that exact moment. And because of all that, all words escaped me, and I'd only managed to croak out a raggedy, "Hey," before she'd moved on down the line.

I thought I caught a glimpse of the pale pink corners of her mouth quirking up, but ultimately, she passed by without so much as a hello.

"The force is strong with this one," I said in an exaggeratedly deep voice, and my urge to follow her kicked in like a salmon's instincts to swim upstream.

Curious to see if my Darth Vader impression had garnered a smile out of my seatmate, I shot a glance over my shoulder. His greasy brown hair was plastered to his forehead in clumps, and a small pool of drool soaked the pillow he clutched between his head and the window frame.

I lifted my eyebrows and pulled my lips to one side in a frustrated sigh. *I should be sleeping like that guy right now,* I thought. Instead I was wide awake and now horny as hell.

My mind raced back to the plan I'd made on the nine a.m. flight from Kansas City to Atlanta. It wasn't a complicated plan. Quite the opposite, in fact; it was a fairly simple plan. I was going to fly to Paradise Isle, a tiny British territory in the Caribbean Sea. I was going to maneuver myself to my all-inclusive resort. I was going to take advantage of the free drinks. And then I was going to screw the first woman that would have me. If I was lucky, I'd find myself a *pair* of females on a girls-only getaway, and I'd end my virginal streak with the biggest fucking bang I could.

I scratched the scruff around my chin. What had begun as a five-o'clock shadow the day before was now practically a full-on beard. I looked down at myself. My grey polo shirt, made of some type of polyester that wasn't supposed to wrinkle, was wrinkled. It had a certain satiny sheen to it, which wasn't my usual style, but I only wore it because it was the least offensive shirt in the suitcase of clothes that Pamela had packed for me.

I knew I wasn't exactly looking my finest, and yet, I felt like I had to try anyway. I owed it to myself. Hell, the universe owed me something, too. I'd fully committed to a sexless relationship the way my mother said God had intended, and then I'd been fucked in the ass as a reward. I was owed this. I deserved some mile-high sex with a random hot stranger, goddammit.

I straightened my collar and smoothed out my shirt. Then I stood up and opened the overhead compartment, while casually turning my head to stare towards the tail end of the plane. The Megan Fox lookalike had her hip propped up against the last seat before the restroom. That was when I noticed the S-curve of her body. Her cropped black leather jacket allowed me to see not only her narrow waist, but also her heart-shaped bottom.

I felt a definite constriction in my pants. What I wouldn't

give to… I bit my lip hard. *Baseball, Drunk. Baseball,* I chided. I couldn't very well walk towards the back of the plane sporting a teepee in my pants. I had to get things under control. *It's just that it's been so long,* my subconscious whined back.

I reached up and unlocked the overhead bin, pulled my generic-looking black carry-on out, and dropped it onto my seat. Unzipping the front pouch, I extracted a fresh stick of Doublemint, jammed it into my mouth, and then made a beeline for the sexy thing at the end of the plane.

Ignoring the fact that I probably reeked of whiskey shits and bacon, and ignoring the fact that I was feeling somewhat swampy in the nether regions, and also ignoring the fact that I was using gum to hide the fact that I had yet to brush my teeth, I pressed on. I'd smelled, looked, and felt worse and had still managed to score tail in my past.

This was on.

On like Donkey Kong.

I passed several rows before a pink sun visor on my left caught my eye. World's Best Grandma, it read. I winced as I passed the little old married couple I'd cut in front of at the burger joint and kept walking. There was no time now to think about how my mother would smack me with a rolled-up newspaper if she knew I'd cut in front of an elderly couple. I heard the toilet flush in the lavatory. Soon the door would open. Megan Fox was on deck.

I heard the smooth slide of the lock. The door opened and a big meatball of a guy tried to pry himself out. I wondered how he'd gotten himself in there in the first place. By my estimation, it should have taken a shoe horn and a can of Crisco to wedge him into such a tight spot.

I was right behind Megan Fox now. I caught another strong whiff of her spicy perfume, and I wanted to lean over and give her a love bite on the neck, but big beefy guy was headed our way. She turned her body sideways so that she was flat up against the side of the seat, and I stepped into the row beside me, nearly squatting on a twelve-year old's lap while her father shot me the stink eye.

Big beefy guy pushed past us.

I sprang into action.

# 4

I'LL GIVE THE WOMAN ONE THING.

She's fast.

No sooner had big beefy guy planted one of his stretched-out navy-blue sneakers directly on my sandaled foot than she was gone. My head had literally lolled back in agony for all of two seconds, during which time I'd had to fight the overwhelming urge to scream, and when I lifted it, big beefy guy was gone, my foot was throbbing, and the bathroom door had slammed shut.

*Dammit.*

While waiting outside the door, I cupped my hand to my mouth and blew, inhaling immediately. What blew back at me vaguely smelled like mint but had undertones of bacon and booze. It wasn't as bad as I'd imagined it would be, so I was feeling pretty positive. Now I just had to have a good pickup line. She looked like the sexual deviant type. In my experience, that type responded best to shock tactics. I had to make it sizzle.

When I heard the water shut off, I put one hand against the door frame and leaned forward. The lock sign went from red to green and folded opened.

Go time.

I rubbed a hand against the bristles on my chin. "Excuse me, miss. Sorry to bother you, but did you happen to see any airplane keys laying around in there?"

She blinked her long black eyelashes at me, looked back in the bathroom and then back at me. I was pretty sure I saw a smile quirk one corner of her mouth. Making a woman smile was half the battle. Getting her to drop her panties was the other half.

I was close.

She lifted a brow and shook her head. "Nope, no keys." Her pillowy lips parted and her head tilted forward slightly, almost challenging me to keep going. I could tell I was on the right path.

I leaned in a little closer, and my voice lowered an octave, hitting that raspy range that I liked to reserve for one of two good causes: the preliminaries or the Olympics. "You know, in case you were wondering, I'm federally licensed to go down your landing strip."

Whatever joviality I'd seen in her eyes disappeared, her face sobered slightly, and she tilted her head to the side. "Excuse me?"

Some guys might be shaking their heads right now, palming their foreheads, even, saying, "Buddy, you didn't read the signs!" But I wasn't one of those guys. I'd been taught to commit. Once you commit, you don't back up. Only fucking pussies back up, and I'll tell you one thing right now.

I ain't no fucking pussy.

So I pressed on, rubbing my jaw like someone might rub a genie's lamp for luck. I grinned at her then, thinking, of course, that would make her swoon. My crooked, stubbly smile tended to do that to women. So even at this point, I'm still feeling confident, right? Can you believe that?

Yeah.

Neither can I.

"So, uh, how about you and me join the mile-high club?"

I'll give her credit. Megan Fox kept her cool. She smiled at me patiently and touched her fingers lightly to her lips. In that split second, I thought I was in. I thought we were headed into the lavatory for a little airplane Q&A.

But then things took a turn. And I'm gonna be real here. It wasn't a turn in my favor.

Megan Fox popped that hand forward in a sharp right jab, punching me squarely in the esophagus.

*FUCK.*

Now I've been punched in the face before. Loads of times. Jealous boyfriends and bar fights, mostly. The occasional criminal. My buddy even punched me in the face once after a particularly bad disagreement over the outcome of a fucking video game of all things. But I'd never taken a throat punch before.

I'll tell you this.

It fucking hurts.

It felt like a Lego was now wedged in my jugular.

I was immediately incapacitated. My shoulders rounded, my chest caved in, and my head rolled forward as I began to gag. Psycho Megan Fox gave me a shove so she could go back to her seat, and I stumbled back against the bulkhead. At that point I didn't care that I'd struck out. I only cared about the fact that I couldn't inhale.

Yeah, so there I am, writhing about in the back of Delta's flight 661, wishing once again I'd hung myself with that belt, when my seatmate of all people comes strolling down the aisle. His hair was still matted to his forehead, and his cheek was red and indented from where he'd been smashed up against the plane's window. He took one look at me and gave me a nod and a thumbs-up signal.

"All good, then?" He paused for a split second while I barked out some unintelligible seal verbiage. "Right," he said and walked right past, into the lavatory, where he promptly shut the door.

*Fuck my luck.*

# 5

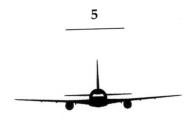

You'd think a punch to the throat would wear off at some point, but it really doesn't. No. That kind of shit sticks with you.

I'd actually been kneed in the nuts by a woman before, and while I'll wholeheartedly agree that it hurts, eventually the pain goes away and you can go about your day. Getting throat-punched is like the gift that just keeps giving. It hurts to swallow. It hurts to breathe. And at that point, I didn't even want to know what it felt like to eat.

So as I'm reclined back in my seat, struggling to survive, my seatmate, who's fully awake, decides now's the best time to reach over, shake my hand, and introduce himself.

"Ow ya goin', mate," he says in jolly fashion and what could only be described as the language of kangaroos from the land down under.

I'm sitting next to him quietly whimpering and wishing for a stiff drink and a Vicodin. I might have been happy to have shaken his greasy mitt pre–Megan Fox, but after, I wasn't feeling quite as congenial. I managed to give him a blink.

He pulled his hand back and nodded before wiping his nose and giving a sniffle. "Right. Tough day?"

I gave a stiff nod. I still didn't feel like talking.

"No worries. She'll be right," he said cheerfully. "Where you from?"

Holding my crushed windpipe, I sat up and looked at him. The Aussie wanted to chat. "Missouri," I croaked.

"Missouri. That in the US?"

I nodded. "Midwest," I whispered.

"Right. I'm from Straya, if you couldn't tell by my accent."

*Get the fucking hell out of here*, I wanted to say.

He pointed at my neck. "A lady do that?"

I looked away. It was too embarrassing to admit to a total stranger that a woman had just assaulted me in the john. Not only was I ashamed at my lack of game back there, but I was further ashamed at my inability to dip, duck, or dodge. The guys at the station would have had a field day with that one.

"Fuckin' cunts," he said, taking my unwillingness to answer as an affirmative. "Hey, man, you goin' to Paradise too?"

I nodded, wondering where in the hell else he thought the plane was going to drop me off. Pit stop in the middle of the Atlantic, anyone?

"Where you stayin'?"

"Seacoast Majestic," I whispered hoarsely.

"No fuckin' way," he said, grinning. That was when I noticed he'd slicked his hair back in the bathroom and removed his brown leather jacket. Now he was wearing a plain white t-shirt and a silver Rolex with a black face. In that split second, I wondered how a guy like that afforded a watch that was probably worth more than the shitty Acura I drove back home. "I got a room there myself."

*Brilliant.*

"Maybe you wanna meet me for a drink later? A couple of single blokes on the prowl ought to do quite good with the ladies, eh? Better than drinking alone, I always say."

From my seat, I watched Megan Fox adjusting herself in her aisle seat four rows ahead of me and considered his offer for a second. He was right. I did my best work with a wingman, and despite my present condition, I was still bound and determined to find the sweetest piece of ass Paradise Isle had to offer and fuck it until the wee hours of the morning. "Maybe."

"You got a number or something?"

With one hand, I reached into my back pocket and pulled out my wallet. I had a wrinkled business card tucked inside. It said Officer Daniel T. Drunk, Jr., Kansas City Police Department. I flipped it over to show him that my personal cell number was written on the back and handed it to him.

"Crikey. You're a cop?"

"Yep."

He pursed his lips and nodded his head a bit. "Well, good onya, mate." He leaned over, putting the brunt of his weight on his right elbow rest, and then flicked a hand against his chest. "Name's Jimmie."

"What were you doing in Atlanta?" I asked him, not really caring, but feeling pressured to make conversation and wishing he'd fall back asleep again so I could try and do the same.

He nodded. "Right. Well, you see, I have a friend who needed a little help. Just finished up, and now I'm headin' out for a little R&R. You know? What's got you headin' to a remote island all alone?"

I looked at him. My face was somber. Was this douche canoe really gonna make me say it out loud? Nah. Saying it out loud would be like admitting that aliens existed. Who knew if that shit was real or not, but whatever you did, you just didn't say it aloud. It's like it made it official or something. I wasn't in the mood. "Just a trip I booked. No reason," I grunted, salty that this guy wasn't getting the hint.

"No lady waitin' for you there?"

I shook my head and then leaned it back against the head-rest and closed my eyes. That had to work.

"Right. Well, we'll have a drink and maybe we can change that. What do you say?"

I reached down and plugged the plane's cheaper-than-shit earbuds into my ears. With my eyes closed and buds in, I couldn't tell whether Jimmie was talking or sleeping. I liked it that way.

# 6

When I woke up, people were already disembarking the plane. Jimmie was the one to wake me up, giving me a little nudge before rifling through the overhead compartment.

"Eh, mate, we made it," he said when I pulled the earbuds out of my ears.

Glittery streams of sunlight edged in through the window across the aisle, reflecting off a serene surface that I could only imagine to be the ocean. I sure as shit wasn't in Kansas City anymore.

I wiped the crusty edges of my mouth and sat up. Not only were my legs stiff from being jammed into such a tight confined space, a side effect of being six foot four, but my neck was also stiff from the jacked-up way in which I'd slept. Swallowing instantly reminded me about the ninja femme fatale on the flight and brought me back to my current situation.

I had just landed on Paradise Isle for my honeymoon.

Alone.

I groaned as I unfolded myself from my seat and stood up. First thing, my head hit the overhead with a thunk. "Doh," I groaned, ducking. I reached for my head. My hair felt like wet dog fur against my fingers and my head felt like ass, a remnant of my hangover. Yeah, I was feeling good.

The line to disembark went fast as most of the people were already off the plane by the time I was even awake. Jimmie went ahead of me, giving me a backwards glance once and a thumbs-up. "See ya later, mate," he said, slinging his leather jacket over a shoulder.

Damn, a nap had done that man good. I wished I'd woken up as cheerful.

The sweltering ocean air filled the cabin. Like heat pouring from a four-hundred-degree preheated oven, it steamed up the windows and raked my face with its tenacious claws.

Fuck, that heat felt good.

I wanted more of it. I wanted to strip down naked. Tear off the repulsive clothing my cheating fiancée had dressed me in, lay my white ass down on some blisteringly hot sand somewhere, and numb my aches, pains, and feelings with a couple gallons of margaritas.

As I grabbed my suitcase from the overhead compartment, a cute flight attendant stopped to smile at me. "Thank you for flying Delta, sir. Have a great time on Paradise Isle!"

Her chipper, upbeat attitude brought new light to my situation. I was on fucking Paradise Isle. Yes, I felt like something a dog's ass shat out after ingesting dairy products, and yes, I probably looked about as appealing at the current moment, but in general, I was a good-looking guy with nothing else to do but go have some fun. After a shower, a meal, and a few drinks, this trip was going to be fucking epic.

"Thanks, sweetie," I said, feeling a bit of my usual swagger returning.

Disembarking the plane directly onto the tarmac, I had to squint to see anything, the sun was so bright. My virgin Midwestern eyes wouldn't last a second in Paradise without a pair of sunglasses, so I put "stop at the airport gift shop" as number three on my priority list, right behind buying a drink and flirting with anything with breasts.

The other passengers were already being ushered towards the small island terminal, and our luggage was being unloaded by hand onto long wheeled luggage carts. At the bottom of the stairs, an exotic little number with curly brown hair and wearing a pencil skirt kept the traffic moving. Her name tag read Lola.

"Lola," I whispered to myself. Rolling the name around on my tongue, I realized I liked the way it felt in my mouth. I could only imagine her skin would taste as sweet.

I gave her a nod and a smile.

"Thank you for flying Delta, sir. Enjoy your stay on Paradise Isle."

"Thank you, darlin'. Say, do you live on the island?"

"Yes, I do, sir. Something I can help you with?"

Oh man, did I want to tell her exactly what she could help me with. But I resisted. Instead I pulled a business card out of my wallet and handed it to her. "If you ever want to get together, you know, for a drink or something, my cell number's on the back."

She gave me a little giggle and a flutter of her fingers as I blew a kiss at her while continuing along on the tarmac towards the terminal.

I felt like skipping at that point. I couldn't get to my resort fast enough.

Following the general flow of traffic, I got a good look at the island for the first time. Palm trees rustled against a light breeze. The ocean ebbed and flowed, and the temperature was fucking divine.

Inside the airport, Caribbean music played by way of a native steel drum band. I liked music, and I didn't mind dancing. I mean, I wasn't one of those guys that got up at a club and willingly danced all night, but I also wasn't dead inside. Who am I to argue with Gloria Estefan? When the rhythm's gonna get ya, the rhythm's gonna get ya. And fucking straight, that steel drum band had me at hello. My pelvis began to gyrate even before I'd had my first drink.

The line of people from my flight seemed to just somehow know where we were supposed to go, and I followed behind, shaking my hips and randomly tapping my foot like the unrhythmic white guy that I was. The line bottlenecked through a security checkpoint where a couple of airport officials were dubiously checking passports and carry-ons. I wasn't too concerned, because I could see the bar up ahead, and drinks were within reach.

*Goodbye, sobriety.*

*Daddy's almost home.*

Catching a glimpse of a familiar figure, I saw Jimmie peering at me from up ahead. Feeling much more like the easy-going guy I normally was, I gave him a wassup nod. It was funny how some people reacted to heat differently than others. My large frame seemed to drink up the heat, welcoming the stench of my manly charisma. Others, like Jimmie, seemed to immediately turn into sweaty beer cans. He literally looked like a cat trying to bury a shit on a marble floor. I felt bad for the guy. How's a guy supposed to get laid on the beach looking like that?

Jimmie gave me a little nod back. Except it wasn't the kind that I'd given him—you know, the friendly wassup-mate nod. It was more like a side tilt with an eyebrow lift. Like he was trying to tell me something. I glanced in the direction he was nodding and saw Megan Fox staring at both of us.

Oh. Fucking guy's got jokes. I gave him a tight smile and then thought, *Fuck you. You can have a drink on your own, you son of a bitch. I was trying to be nice, and you're gonna rub Megan Fox's esophagus punch in my face?*

The line moved on. I wasn't far away from the front of the line by now, and Jimmie was two people from the front when all of a sudden I see him drop a heel on the foot of big beefy guy who happened to be behind him. He followed it up with an elbow to the gut. My eyes widened. Had I seriously just seen that?

Big beefy guy emitted a grunt, and Jimmie turned around to take the punch in the face that was coming to him.

That was when all hell broke loose.

## 7

THE SECURITY GUARDS ALL LEAPT INTO ACTION AS IF THAT WAS what they'd been waiting for all day. Jimmie, who was trying to hold his own through a squinty eye and a bloodied nose, took the time to glance back at me during the ruckus and give me another nod. Had he been trying to show off for Megan Fox? Was that it? Did he think somehow by getting laid out, he was going to increase *my* chances of getting laid?

*What is this guy's deal?* I wondered, glancing up to take in Megan Fox's reaction. That was when I realized that the rest of the line was being ushered through the checkpoint's fast lane, and Megan Fox was nowhere to be seen.

I grabbed the handle of my wheeled carry-on and, after flashing my passport to a uniformed woman wearing a baton on her hip, cruised my way out of the security checkpoint and straight to the bar.

Goodbye, Jimmie.

Goodbye, Megan Fox.

*Hello*, Margarita.

Rita, as I liked to call her, was a good-looking dame. A tall, thin, refreshing blonde with a kinky lime-green hat cocked at a jaunty angle. She was salty around the edges, and yet sweet in her own cool, calm, and sophisticated way. She was on a permanent vacation, this one. I could tell it by her unassuming demeanor.

Savoring her taste, I relished my place in the world at that single, solitary moment. I let out a relaxing breath.

The island heat.

The cold drink in my hand.

No job to be late for.

No woman to answer to.

No promises made to a God I wasn't sure that I believed in anymore.

I was free.

Little did I know that freedom came at a price. But I'd find that out soon enough.

I tipped my bartender after the second drink and carried the glass with me to the airport gift shop: a kitschy little dive filled with random useless shit like turtles made from puka shells, imitation leather fish hook bracelets, and terra cotta coasters etched with palm trees and starfish. Everything had Paradise Isle emblazoned on it, but I knew damn good and well it had all been made in China. I'd never pay money for most of that touristy crap, but I was thrilled to find one of those spinning racks of sunglasses on the glass counter.

I swirled it around and around at least four times before settling on a pair of knock-off black Ray-Bans. I studied myself in the small square mirror above the rack. Damn. My hair had become a rat's nest somewhere between the cold, shampoo-less shower I'd taken that morning and the hours of planes and airport terminals since. I plucked a black fedora off the rack behind me and popped it onto my head. It rode down low, topping off my glasses and giving me the casual appearance I desired, but also the sense of mystery I knew would draw in the ladies.

I popped it off and dropped it onto the counter along with the glasses and a pair of leather flip-flops to replace the mandals Pamela had bought me (with my money) for the trip. I hadn't wanted the brown Velcro strappy things, but she'd pushed. I'd told her I wasn't an expose-your-feet-kind of guy. The closest I'd ever gotten to revealing my long, hairy-toed size thirteens was going sockless in a boat shoe. My pops had never worn a sandal a day in his life, and that was enough to make me think that real men didn't wear sandals. But love, or perhaps more likely, *lust*, had persisted, and UPS had delivered my first pair of mandals less than a week after I'd sworn I wouldn't wear them.

I had to bend over to unfasten the Velcro. I scooped them off the floor and handed them to the fella behind the counter. "Toss these, will ya?"

I slid some cash over to him and dropped the new shoes to the floor, sliding my feet in like I'd done it all my life. Yes, my toes were still exposed. But there was no Velcro to get my toe hair caught in, and these looked much more appropriate for the locale. Plus, Pamela hadn't picked them out for me. And *that*, my friends, was the three-pointer that won the game.

I slid the sunglasses on, topped the look off with the hat, grabbed my drink, and dragged my bag out of the gift shop. *Now to find a ride outta here.* I was pretty sure my itinerary included transportation. I knew I'd heard Pamela mention it on more than one occasion. Everything was included on this trip. The drinks. The food. The ride. Even some snorkeling and kayaking lessons or some stupid shit like that.

Slamming the remainder of my drink, I left the glass behind on top of someone's luggage and dug through the top front pocket of my suitcase for my papers. There had to be some kind of instructions about where to go from here.

Aside from a hotel confirmation form, there was nothing else. I had to assume the instructions were still lodged inside Pamela's puffy brain, and *that* was still back in Missouri.

The crowd cleared, and I happened to notice a lovely little thing in a powder-blue two-piece dress standing next to a little booth. She didn't have much for tits, but she had killer abs, and she looked like she worked there. That was enough for me.

I rolled my bag over to her. "Excuse me. I'm trying to find my way to the Seacoast Majestic. I was told I could catch a cab somewhere. Can you possibly point me in the right direction?"

Her big almond eyes lit up as she smiled at me. "Oh, welcome, welcome! You can check in for the Seacoast Majestic shuttle right over here." Her words were choppy, as if English wasn't her first language. She pointed to the little booth behind her, which was really only a hole in the wall cordoned off by a counter, filled with island maps. A gangly black man with teeth as white as freshly fallen Missouri snow and a baseball cap on his head sat behind the counter, quietly reading what appeared to be a trashy romance novel.

"Thanks," I said. If she'd been at the hotel, I would have offered to buy her a drink. Small tits didn't bother me.

The man behind the counter gave me directions to find the shuttle bus outside. He said I'd know it was for my resort because the words Seacoast Majestic were painted along the side. I slid him a fiver, and in exchange he slid me a map of the island.

Outside, the heat raked its gritty claws over my skin once again. This time the sun wasn't so bad on my eyes. I had my shades and my hat now, and with the two drinks in my system, I felt calmer, and *much* cooler in the less restrictive flip-flops.

Following the directions I'd been given, I walked around the corner in search of the Seacoast Majestic shuttle bus. I looked right and I looked left, but didn't see a shuttle bus. I wondered if the two margaritas had gone straight to my brain or something and made me suddenly informationally stupid.

So I stood there for a moment, looking like the ignorant tourist that I was while waiting for a shuttle bus to arrive, when a Jeep parked next to a truck with a topper moved out of the way and I saw the words Seacoast Majestic written in black permanent marker on the side of the truck.

Now that I could see it fully, I realized it wasn't really a topper, but more like a corrugated tin roof fashioned over top of an aluminum frame. Somehow they'd bolted four rows of seats onto a flatbed truck in some sort of poor man's trolley. I was fairly confident that this would never pass muster in America. But we weren't in America, and my mother always told me to mind my manners and do as the natives do.

So, by God, I'd found my ride.

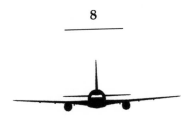

## 8

THE CAB OF THE TRUCK DIDN'T HAVE DOORS, OR WINDOWS FOR that matter, so the driver was able to holler at me unobstructed. "You goin' to the Seacoast Majestic?"

I nodded.

He waved me over in grand fashion. "What's your name?" he asked, looking down at a clipboard that had a Bic pen tied to it with a piece of string.

"Drunk. Danny," I added. You know, on the off chance there happened to be two Drunks on board.

The driver popped the ballpoint of his pen against my name and crossed it off with a flourish. "Hop on in. We've been waiting for you!"

I tugged at the collar of my polo and looked back at the arrangements while the driver took my bag to stow. Right behind the cab, a stairway had been welded onto the truck. I climbed aboard and immediately noticed the old man and woman I'd cut in front of at the airport were sharing a ride with me, as were a handful of other passengers that had been on our plane out of Atlanta. The shuttle was filled to capacity, and I had to stuff myself in between two old women wearing matching t-shirts that read Grannies Gone Wild and carrying wicker purses. As the shuttle took off, I felt like a sore thumb sticking out between the two miniature old women, but the nice breeze quickly took my mind off it.

The driver hollered back through the open-air truck lots of times throughout the long, winding trip, acclimating us to the island. He pointed out touristy points of interest and asked us all to tell where we'd come from and introduce ourselves to the group. I learned that the old woman on my right was Gladys Rosenbaum from Newark and the old lady on my left was Ginger Schmidt from Sandusky. They were old high school chums that didn't mind that I'd split them up because I was a *handsome young man*, and they were both widowed. The old couple from the airport, Al and Evelyn Becker, hailed from a small town in Nebraska. And aside from the honeymooning couple, Kenny and April Jaworsky from Chicago, who were in their midtwenties, I was the youngest guy there by about thirty years.

It took us a solid forty-five minutes of driving on the wrong side of the road to get from the airport to the other side of the island, where our resort was located. We'd passed a multitude of crappy houses and cars, and I wondered when Paradise Isle would start looking like, well, Paradise. That didn't happen until we turned up a long stretch of road that led us to our resort.

The Seacoast Majestic Resort.

It was a lush retreat tucked away in a breadth of palm trees and other colorful native vegetation. The driver gave a honk and a wave as we drove through the open security gate and passed what I could only assume was the employee parking lot and a pair of iguanas mating on the other side of the road.

I'd already seen at least a dozen lizards on the ride in, but this was the first pair that I'd seen mating. Most of the oldies in the truck got a good laugh out of it, and I think I saw every finger point at least once. Those poor old lizards. Wasn't it bad enough that they could never use enough lotion? And now they were getting mocked for doing what was probably the only positive thing they had in their lives.

The thought of mating pulled me right back into the here and now. I was seconds away from a resort full of tail, a hotel room, and unlimited drinks. I could hardly wait. I rubbed my hands together like a hungry man being served a T-bone platter, and Gladys looked up at me.

"You getting excited?" she asked, her Jersey screech on point.

"You bet."

"What are you gonna do first? Go snorkeling?"

Snorkeling? I wanted to laugh. That was a term one of my college buddies had used to mean going under a woman's skirt. I waggled my eyebrows behind my shades and my hat. "If I'm lucky."

The truck rounded a bend, and to my surprise, a nice hotel sprang up behind the palms, and just like that, off in the distance, I could actually see the ocean again.

*Sweet.*

We parked beneath the porte cochere. The driver hopped out as if his seat had ejected him upon braking and began to unload our luggage while a uniformed man waiting in front of the hotel came around to start helping all of the oldies off the bus.

"Welcome to the Seacoast Majestic, sir," he said to me after everyone else had gotten off. "You can leave your luggage with me while you go check in if you'd like."

I glanced over at the mound of suitcases he'd collected from the trusting seniors. As a cop, something about that just didn't sit right with me. "Mmm, it's okay. I didn't bring much, just a small bag. I think I can handle rolling it inside with me."

He bowed at me like I was some kind of celebrity while the driver rolled my carry-on over to me. "As you wish."

As I wish?

Fuck.

The guy didn't even want to *know* what I wished.

But at that precise moment, *I* wasn't even sure if I knew what I wished. If a genie suddenly appeared before me, would I wish that Pamela had never slept with her ex in my bed? Would I wish that the wedding had gone off without a hitch, which in turn would have allowed me to *actually be* here on my honeymoon with my wife and not just an itchy palm? I wasn't sure exactly what I'd wish for in this moment. I hadn't taken the time to think about it yet. So instead of belaboring the point, I did what was expected of me. I padded the driver's hand with a ten spot and rolled into the lobby of the Seacoast Majestic.

The lobby was better than I'd hoped. Two stories of balconied hotel rooms opened to a vaulted ceiling. The walls were navy and white, all nautical like. Everything looked like it was freshly painted and not like I'd stepped into a time warp like some hotels I'd stayed in. The furnishings were upscale. There were nicely cushioned wicker chairs and vases on tables and shit. There was a gift shop directly across from the hotel check-in desk and a fancy-looking clothing store next door.

"How may I help you, sir?" asked the woman at the desk as Kenny and April Jaworsky sauntered off with new matching neon bracelets and hotel maps.

"Checking in. Drunk, Danny," I said.

"I have a reservation for a Pamela Drunk. Is this it, sir?"

I wiped my palm against my greasy forehead. "Yeah, that's it," I muttered.

"Is your wife here, sir? I've got her wristband if you'd like to go grab her."

*Just. Fucking. Perfect.*

"She's not coming," I said. "Long story. Where's the bar?"

The woman in front of me was probably in her midforties. Cuban or Puerto Rican, perhaps. Her hair was pulled back from her face rather sharply, but she had a cherubic face that dimpled when she smiled, softening her features. "Aww, I'm sorry to hear that," she said, her head tilting slightly to the left. She plucked a trifold brochure from a little stand and opened it up, circling something on the right side. "We have singles putt-putt on Thursday nights, and singles dance lessons with Freddy Garcia on Fridays at eight."

"Swell," I said through a clenched jaw as she attached my all-inclusive wristband and room key to my wrist. "The bar?"

"There are several bars, sir. There's one just behind the stairwell there. The main dining room is just behind it. There's also a swim-up bar at the pool, and another bar in the club-house by the restaurant down at the beach." She tore a hotel map off the pad in front of her and pointed out all the different locations of interest. Then she circled my room. It was outside. Like a motel.

I couldn't get to it fast enough. Of course, I stopped at the bar before heading to my room. There was always time for Rita.

## 9

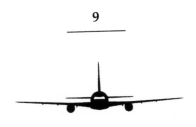

My room wasn't far from the main building. Maybe a half a block at most. The motel rooms curved around the main building, following the coastline, I assumed. The motel buildings were on the left side of the palm-tree-lined cobblestone driveway, and the main resort building on the right. I found lizards everywhere on the walk to my room. They were in the trees, in the mulch, and on the road. I hadn't been prepared for how many lizards I was going to see on this trip. But, I didn't happen to see any more lizards fornicating.

And trust me.

I was looking for them.

There were three levels of motel rooms. Street level, one level above, and one level below the street. My room was on the street level, number 277. I was thankful I didn't have to take any stairs. I opened the door and a hearty blast of air-conditioned air hit me like a pair of iced testicles on a woman —cold and unexpected.

The room was nice. Big. Bright. Tile floor. Enormous bathroom. Huge big-screen TV with a mini bar and a microwave. And there was a balcony with sliding French doors that faced the ocean.

"Fuck me! An ocean view!" I muttered, not entirely surprised that Pamela had spared no expense. My money was like Monopoly money to her—she didn't have to work for it, and she could always get more by passing Go. I opened the balcony door and the quiet, salty air welcomed me with open arms.

"Hey, Drunk, you finally made it," it said. "What are you waiting for? Drinks are down here."

"I'm comin', I'm comin'," I promised aloud, silently praying that I'd be chanting those words in someone's ear before the end of the night.

The view wasn't even a partial ocean view, like where you had to look to your right, squat low and squint to see it. It was quite literally a full-on ocean view. The resort was built up on a hillside, so you could see everything from a bird's-eye vantage. Straight below me was all vegetation. Like an island jungle. But if you looked out further, beyond the jungle, a private beach along a serene cove opened out into the ocean with a few islands dotting the horizon. A boat was anchored in the middle of the cove, and people were swimming, kayaking, wakeboarding, and snorkeling in the sheltered crystalline blue water. The beaches were white and sandy as promised, and I could see the pool and the clubhouse the desk clerk had told me about, only steps away from the shoreline.

I had to admit it.

It was pretty fucking epic.

Strutting back into my room, I left the sliding doors open and sat down on the bed. For the first time since I'd left Missouri, I pulled my phone from my pocket and turned it on, curious if anyone had noticed I was missing yet. While it booted up, I tossed it onto the bed and went to shower. I felt a strong desire to scrub off the disgusting layer of sludge that gripped every crevice of my body and shampoo my hair. Screw it. I might even use conditioner.

Minutes later, I reappeared, dripping wet and with a fluffy

white towel swathed loosely around my hips. I appreciated the puddle of water I left in my wake, as that meant I didn't have a woman chasing behind me, nagging me to dry off properly. It was anarchy at its finest.

I sat down, and my thick hair dripped water onto the foot of the bed, soaking the duvet. Phone in hand, I began to check my messages.

*So* many calls from my mother. I was thankful the woman hadn't gotten into texting. It was much easier to ignore voice-mail messages. Unfortunately for me, Pamela *was* a texter. *And* a chatty one at that.

I scrolled through the messages, scanning them for the fuck I didn't have and therefore couldn't give.

"Danny, please…"

"It didn't mean anything…"

"Where are you?"

"I'm worried about you…"

"I'm going to call your mother…"

"Your mother says she doesn't know where you are…"

"Now she's worried too…"

"Danny, please…"

I swiped left and hit the red Delete button.

Then I blocked her number.

But as I sat there, staring at the suitcase Pamela had lovingly packed for me, I found myself upset about the time she'd made me waste. About all those promises we'd made. About the dreams we'd shared. And I found myself growing angrier and angrier by the second.

*Fuck her.*

*And fuck her perfect tits.*

*And fuck that ass that I never got to fuck.*

*Fuck it all.*

I lifted the suitcase she'd packed me off the table and rushed it over to the French doors, nearly breaking my neck when I slipped on my own trail of water on the tile floor. I stood there on the balcony, holding my suitcase over my head, with my towel hanging on by a thread. I hadn't packed a single fucking thing in that suitcase. Every pair of shorts. Every pair of trunks. Every shirt. And every goddamned pair of underwear had been purchased and subsequently packed by Pamela.

Did I want to spend the next two weeks of my honeymoon thinking of Pamela every time I put a shirt on?

Hell no.

Did I want to feel bile welling up in my throat every time I got lucky and another woman put her hands on the underwear that Pamela had dressed me in?

I'd rather piss fiberglass.

So I reared back and heaved that bag out into the great beyond. It was cathartic. And necessary. Not only had a twenty-seven-pound weight been lifted off my shoulders, but also a one-hundred-and-twenty-pound woman had been lifted off my shoulders.

*Goodbye, Pamela.*

I turned around and paced back into the room. My towel fell off, and the second it hit the floor was the moment that I realized that I'd just chucked every shred of clothing I owned in Paradise out over the balcony.

*Fuck.*

# 10

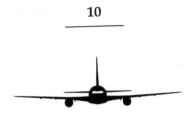

I LEFT MY HOTEL ROOM WEARING THE UNDERWEAR AND SHORTS that I'd worn on the plane, but I decided to forgo the polo shirt. Not only was that also a product of the P word, I decided it didn't match my new hat. I'd have to go to the resort clothing store at some point, but right now I was itching to get down to the beach.

With my wallet and passport shoved into my back pocket and my phone in my front pocket, I realized there was nothing else I owned in the room, except my small ditty bag in the bathroom. The feeling was actually pretty fucking liberating. Like I had nowhere else to be but where I was.

Amen to that.

I had a general sense of where the clubhouse and beach were, but in order to actually get down there, I had to follow the signs posted on the motel's exterior walls. The signs led to a staircase that, I kid you not, was about twenty klicks down the side of the hill. I wondered how all the oldies did that many stairs. Wouldn't they have heart attacks on the way? Now I was curious if I'd find resuscitation stations in little glass-protected cubes that said "Break with Cane in Case of Emergency."

So I took off down those stairs, wishing I at least had a drink or a woman to keep me company on the trek. Having neither, I paid a lot of attention to the jungle I was winding my way through. There were lots of enormous ferns, yucca plants, and cacti beneath the palm trees. I only knew what a yucca was because it was one of the few house plants that my mother seemed incapable of killing while I was growing up. What really got me, though, were the number of chickens, lizards, and cats lounging about on the stairs. Something about seeing chickens chilling with cats and oversized iguanas in the trees really spoke to not being in America anymore.

By the time my feet hit sand, the sun had almost found its way to the far end of the ocean. Ready to call it another day, it streaked the horizon a hazy shade of orange and ushered in a calm navy-blue sky. The temperature was a balmy seventy-nine degrees. Perfection in my eyes.

Straight ahead of me was the lit pool, complete with swim-up bar as promised, a grotto waterfall, and an assortment of hot tubs and kiddie pools. Beyond the pool was the clubhouse, with its long covered front porch. Both the pool and bar area were lit with overhead strings of white globe lights, and the bar had glowing neon under-the-counter lights. I felt like the party was finally about to get started.

The beach was to my right. Rows of lounge chairs lined the sand, and further down the beach, a cabana overflowing with paddleboards, wakeboards, and kayaks, which I assumed were available to be checked out, sat quietly waiting for morning to come once again. The only thing that seemed to be missing was the women.

I set my course for the swim-up bar, which was also a bar for those just lounging poolside. A stocky man of some sort of Hispanic descent shook a cocktail shaker, his hips moving in rhythm with his shakes. Two shakes over one shoulder, hip hip, then two shakes over the opposite shoulder, hip hip. If there was a sweeter sound in the world, I wasn't sure what it was.

I sat down at the end of the bar next to a married couple, but no sooner had I sat than they stood and wandered off with their drinks. I looked to my right, and who was sitting at the end of the bar? None other than Al Becker from Nebraska.

Nebraska and Missouri really aren't that far apart from each other. In fact, one corner of Missouri even gets so friendly as to play just-the-tip with Nebraska, so I felt like Al and I could share some commonalities. I slid over, leaving a chair between us, and waited for the bartender to take my drink order.

When he looked up at me, I pointed at him. "Margarita. On the rocks."

"Lime? Strawberry? Raspberry?" he asked, already pulling out a glass and filling it with ice.

"Lime. Extra salt, *por favor*." I turned, glancing at Al, and scanned the beach looking for Mrs. Al. "Where are all the women?"

Al swiveled his chair to look up at me. Seated on a barstool, he really didn't seem that much shorter than I was, but his feet dangled inches above the ground while mine were flatfooted on the concrete. "Eh?" he said, cupping his ear.

I leaned in a little closer. "The women," I shouted. "Where are they?"

His mouth formed a little O as it had done in the plane terminal. "She's taking a nap. Jet lag." His voice was hoarse, like he had an overabundance of phlegm in the back of his throat.

I nodded, glad to know that Mrs. Al was catching up on her Zs. "Where are the rest of the women?" I shouted over the low rumbling of music on the bar's speakers.

"Eh?" More ear cupping.

I glanced up at the bartender, pleading with my eyes for him to help me out. "It's early," was his response.

I shook my head at Al.

"Where you from?" he asked.

"Missouri," I said.

More ear cupping.

"Missouri," I shouted.

He nodded. "What part?"

"Kansas City." I made sure my mouth was closer to his ear this time.

"The Royals had a good year last year."

I nodded while I sipped the drink the bartender handed me. "You're from Nebraska, right?"

Al nodded.

"What did you do there?"

"Eh?"

"For a job. Work," I shouted. Hell, was I going to have to break out Pictionary? How did his wife do this all day?

"I owned an implement dealership. Case IH."

"No John Deere?"

"Fuck John Deere."

*Right on, man.*

"This your first time here?"

The guy behind the bar laughed.

"Nah, this is my second time." Al took a sip of his drink. "This year. We've got friends here. But we're gonna live here full-time now."

Shit, that would be nice. "Full-time? At this resort?"

Al nodded.

"You hit the lotto?"

He shook his head. "I did alright over the years." Then he thought about it for a second and decided I must look safe enough to tell his secret to. "Plus I bought Bitcoin at a quarter. Cashed out at just under twenty in December."

"Dollars?"

"Thousand."

I blinked. "Total?"

"Each."

"Fuck."

He nodded.

"So you're doing alright, then?" I said, finding it difficult to swallow my drink now.

"Warren Buffet said there's no future in cryptocurrency. See what he knows," chuckled Al. "He's from Omaha, you know. Warren. I sold a 185 Lo-Boy to his sister Bertie once. She's a cutie, that one."

I shook my head. This sounded too far-fetched to believe. "Right, so you and Mrs. Al are just going to live out your days in a hotel room here on the island?"

He hooked a thumb over his shoulders. "They've got some resort cottages down the road. We've got a kitchen and a living room. The whole shebang."

"You walk all that way?" I asked, thinking of the dozen miles of stairs I'd walked to get from my room to the beach.

"Walk?" he repeated with a half-smile, exposing his weathered old teeth.

I nodded.

He glanced up at the bartender, who was drying a glass with a bar rag. They both smiled like they were sharing a joke on me. I looked from the bartender to Al and then from Al to the bartender again.

"There's a golf cart over there that picks you up and drops you off anywhere on the resort property. There's a new one every fifteen minutes until nine o'clock. Then it's every half hour," explained the bartender.

"No one uses the stairs?" I asked, feeling like an idiot.

He lifted a shoulder. "You did."

Right.

"What's your name?" I said to the bartender, extending a hand.

"Manny." He shook my hand.

"Manny, I'm Drunk."

"What's your name?" asked Al, holding out his own hand. Apparently he hadn't caught it on the ride to the resort when I'd caught his name.

I shook his hand. "It's Drunk."

"Eh? Drunk?" He said it like he'd heard me wrong. I was sure he did that a lot.

"*Drunk!*"

Al looked at Manny.

Manny stopped working and put both palms on the counter. "Your name's Drunk?"

I nodded.

"That your first name or your last name?" said Al, still in disbelief.

"Last."

"Huh." He smirked. "I never met a Drunk before."

I laughed. "Really? I've met plenty."

# 11

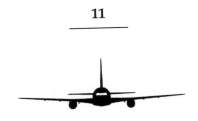

SEVERAL DRINKS, SEVERAL STORIES, AND NO WOMEN LATER, AL agreed to show me where the resort golf cart picked people up and dropped them off down at the beach. It was time for him to check on his wife, and time for me to put something in my stomach.

I'd learned quite a lot about Al over drinks. Al's parents had immigrated to the US from Germany before he was born. He was a staunch Democrat in a sea of Republicans. He knew the stock market and mutual funds like the back of his hand, and he considered Warren Buffett to be a well-regarded friend even though they'd never actually met. He and Mrs. Al had had six children, one of whom had turned out to be a homosexual, and the other five had given him a combined total of twelve grandchildren, two of whom were adopted, and he had a litter of great-grandchildren that he said were too many to count. He drove a Buick back in the States, but he'd given it to his oldest great-grandson before moving to the island. Al's mouth dribbled alcohol when he spoke, and by the looks of his stained shirt, I surmised he dribbled food when he ate too. He still thought his wife was hot, but that didn't mean he didn't take occasional glimpses of other women, because "That's how God intended it."

I rubbed my stomach. "I sure hope they're still serving dinner," I said loudly. I'd spent enough time with Al to know to speak loudly or we'd play the "What?" game until I lost my marbles.

"They're not gonna let you in without a shirt on," he promised. "You have to have a shirt."

"I'll pick one up at the clothing store in the lobby." My stomach growled like crazy. I clapped a hand over it and groaned. Drinking all evening on an empty stomach had probably not been the wisest idea. I'd been waiting for the chicks to show up, but they never had.

He pointed at my stomach. "Your stomach bothering you or something?"

I shrugged. "I got pretty wasted last night. Woke up with a massive hangover. Been drinking on an empty stomach since."

"You take probiotics?"

"Probiotics?" I repeated with a smile. There was an old guy for you. Once upon a time in a man's life, the hot topics of conversation revolved around hot women and fast cars. In the golden years, those things were replaced by discussions of medication lists, medical conditions, and which restaurants had the earliest buffet line. "No. I don't take probiotics."

He pointed at me sternly. "You should. They're good for hangovers."

With one foot resting on the front seat headrest and the other foot casually dangling out the side of the cart, I sipped the last of my drink. "Oh yeah?"

"Yeah. Plus they'll make your balls bigger."

Lime margarita spewed out of my mouth. I looked over at Al with a smile. "Shut up. You're fucking pulling my chain, right?"

He smiled at me. "No, I'm not pulling your chain. Look it

up. Probiotics increase your testosterone and give you bigger balls."

"Sorry, Al, but if my balls get any bigger I'm gonna have to buy all new pants."

The approaching sound of sirens wailing behind us drowned out our easy laughter. The cart pulled off to the side of the road as an island cop wailed by, its lights flashing. Following close behind was an ambulance.

"What the hell...?" I said, following both vehicles with my eyes.

"Oh man. Looks like something happened. I sure hope it's not Evie." He began a mad pat-down of his pockets in search of his phone. "I better give her a call."

"Do you know what happened?" I asked the driver, who had been chuckling along with us only seconds ago.

"I have no idea."

Al fumbled with his small flip phone.

I sat up straight. "Well, can you step on it? Al's got a wife up there somewhere."

The golf cart pulled up to the porte cochere, where several resort workers were gathered outside, staring at the mess of lights further down the block.

"What's going on?" asked the driver.

The resort employee, a tall black, gap-toothed man with short dreads and broad shoulders, pointed towards the lobby. "They found a dead body in one of the rooms down there. Brains splattered all over the place. Ozzy was the one to find the body. He said he'd never seen anything like it." The employee held a fisted hand up to his mouth, like he was going to throw up just thinking about it.

The cop in me, which had slept on the entire flight to Paradise Isle, was now wide awake. I looked over at Al, who had managed to get his wife on the phone. "She okay?"

He nodded, holding a finger in the air. "Stay in the house

and lock the door. Something happened over here. I'll be there in a little while." There was a pause. "Don't worry, I'll be fine. Just stay put." He hung up the phone.

I looked at the driver. "Can you get us any closer?"

The driver stepped on the gas. "I'll get you as close as they'll let us go."

Seconds later, we were stopped by a crowd gathered in the darkness around the outer perimeter of a police cordon. Lights had been brought in to illuminate the scene. Island law enforcement and medical personnel were coming and going from a motel room on the main floor. I made a face. The area looked familiar. I scratched my head for a second. What was my room number? What was my room number?

"Two seventy-seven," I said aloud as the number hit me. My eyes scanned the doors that I could readily see. Two seventy-three. Two seventy-four. A crowd in front of the next couple doors. "Is that two seventy-seven?" I asked the driver.

He nodded. "Two seventy-seven, yes."

"Shit! That's my room! What the hell?" I launched myself out of the golf cart and rushed through the crowd, ducking under the tape.

"Drunk," shouted Al. "Don't do that!"

I waved at him as I yelled back. "No worries." After all, I was a cop. I knew what I was doing. Sort of.

"Drunk!" I could hear him still shouting after me, but I was already approaching a uniformed officer who looked like he was running the show.

Another officer stopped me before I could get to the man in charge. "You! Behind the tape," he ordered.

I pointed at the open door. "But that's my room!" The alcohol in my system gave my eyes a crazed, glassy stare that in retrospect was probably a bit suspect.

His head tilted approximately ten degrees to the left. "*Your* room?"

I nodded.

He held a flattened palm out as he backed up to mumble something to his superior. The superior looked up at me. His cold black eyes were stony and his expression hard. Before he could reach me, Al was next to me.

"Drunk. This isn't a good idea. Police around here aren't real fond of Americans."

"I got this Al, don't worry."

The superior officer strolled over to me. He was a stocky man, maybe stood all of five feet eight inches tall, with skin that matched his black uniform. "This is your room?" His voice was so deep, commanding and articulate that I swear he grew two inches.

I nodded. "Yeah, what's going on?"

The superior narrowed his eyes at me. "What is your name?"

"Daniel Drunk," I said, extending a hand. I would hold off mentioning to him that I was a cop. I was well aware that other countries' police departments weren't entirely fond of American cops. Having Al reiterate to me that these guys didn't like Americans, whether they were cops or not, was enough for me to bite my tongue.

The man's serious face seemed to grow more serious if that were possible. "Drunk, you say?"

My hand hung in the air. "Yes. And you are?"

"Sergeant Gibson." He snuffed at my hand. "You are American?"

"Yeah, I just flew in a few hours ago. What's going on in my room?" For the most part, I was known as being a pretty easy-going guy. In fact, there wasn't much that ruffled my feathers, but seeing my room swarming with island cops and realizing that there might be a dead body inside had me feeling jumpy.

"Gunshots were reported in your room. Resort security discovered a body inside."

I shook my head to clear any alcohol induced cobwebs.

"That's impossible. I was literally in there just a couple of hours ago and there was no one in there then."

"A couple of hours ago?" he repeated as if he were already suspicious of me.

"Yeah. I flew in, took a shower in my room, and then headed down to the bar. I've been hanging out with Al and the bartender ever since." I wanted to be clear about my whereabouts. I didn't want anyone thinking that I was responsible for the dead body in my room. "You're welcome to double-check with Manny, the bartender. I'm sure he'll corroborate."

"I was with him as well, Sergeant," chimed in Al.

"And you are?"

"This is Al Becker. He's a little hard of hearing," I answered for Al. I didn't want the hassle of the sergeant having to play the "What?" game with Al. "He's staying here at the resort too. We met down at the bar. I've been sitting with him for the last couple of hours. There's got to be some security cameras at this resort," I added, glancing up and around at the motel's soffits for any signs of surveillance equipment.

"We will take care of that," he assured me.

"Who heard the gunshots?" I asked. "Have they been interviewed? Maybe they saw something."

"I'm told a maid was heading home for the night when she heard the shots. She reported the event to resort security. I'm told that she witnessed two men fleeing the scene."

Relief flooded over me. Surely at the very least, she'd be able to tell the officers that it hadn't been me she'd seen. "Great, has she been interviewed?"

"Mr. Drunk, I understand you are anxious to get some answers, but my agency will handle this investigation. Right now, I'd like you to come take a look in your room. See if anything's missing. Possibly ID the body."

My brows lifted in surprise. "ID the body? Sergeant, I'm sure I can't help you with that. I don't know anyone on the island. This is my first time here. And I flew in alone."

That's when it hit me.

My eyes widened as her name trickled out of my mouth. "Pamela."

Had she flown in to try and fix things? Had someone broken into our room? Had she been attacked before being killed by an intruder? Despite my feelings about her, I couldn't help but still care if she were alive or dead. My heart hammered inside my chest. I sucked in my breath and rushed to the open door of my motel room, pushing aside law enforcement agents and medical personnel that stood in my way.

A body lay on the floor covered with a tarp. Blood pooled on the tile floor the same way water had pooled there at the foot of the bed earlier, and blood spatter stained the white duvet crimson red.

My heart sank.

*Oh my God, Pam!*

An officer kept me from entering by clenching my arm at the elbow, shoving a hand into my chest, and pushing me back. "You can't be in here," he said gruffly.

I struggled to get past. "But that's my fiancée!"

One of the police photographers who had been kneeling next to the body spun his head and shoulders my way, and that was when I noticed the arm sticking out from under the tarp. The fingers were thick and fat and the arm was hairy.

*Not Pamela.*

I stopped struggling against the officer as an immediate sense of relief washed over me. Though the panic and fear had gone, I was left with the bottom end of an adrenaline spike that made my legs feel shaky and weak. My brain kicked in then. *No time for weakness, Drunk,* I told myself. I held myself up against the doorjamb and forced my cop training to take over. I noticed that, aside from the fat fingers and hairy arms, the only other discernible feature about the arm was that it had a silver-and-black watch on the wrist. Rolex.

I stared at that watch. I recognized it almost immediately.

My intoxicated and adrenaline-filled brain clicked through the pictures in my mind. Where had I seen that watch? It was as if the combination numbers dialed into place and the lock clicked open. *Jimmie!*

## 12

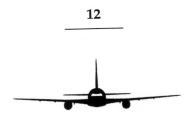

My eyes widened. I stumbled as I instinctively took a step backwards. I'd created quite a scene when I thought it was Pamela. But now that I knew it wasn't her, I felt like I'd just raised my own red flag in this country of people who apparently didn't care for American tourists.

"You know that man?" asked Sergeant Gibson.

I shook my head and tried my best to put space between me and my room. "I thought it was my ex-fiancée."

"Your ex-fiancée? She is on the island?"

"No. This was supposed to be our honeymoon, but we broke up and I came alone. I thought for a second that maybe she'd followed me here and gotten attacked inside my room or something."

"How do you know that it is not her under that tarp, Mr. Drunk?"

I looked at the sergeant like he was insane. "Because it's a man under that tarp!"

"And how exactly do you know that?"

"I saw an arm sticking out! It had hairy knuckles and a men's watch. I just about married a cheating slut, Sergeant, but she was a cheating slut with hairless knuckles." I was working hard to calm myself down. If I showed my agitation with the situation, it was only going to make me look guiltier than I already did.

"Mr. Drunk, I am going to need you to take a look at the body with me and see if you recognize the man in your room."

I shook my head. "But I don't know the guy! I don't know anyone on the island, I told you."

Sergeant Gibson shrugged while beckoning me to follow him. "Indulge me."

I let out a heavy breath. I didn't want to get within fifty feet of that body. I didn't want my shoes to touch a single drop of Jimmie's blood, lest they try and pin the crime on me in some way. So I shook my head. "I'll look at a photograph, or I'll look at him down at your morgue, but I can assure you, I am *not* going back into that room."

Sergeant Gibson didn't look happy, but he turned stiffly and strode towards the motel room without a word.

I walked back over to Al, who was talking on the phone again. I assumed it was his wife.

"Go check on her," I said.

He shook his head and hung up the phone. "She was just checking on me. She's fine. You know who's in there?"

I shook my head. "I thought it was my ex." I hadn't told Al about my honeymoon or about Pamela when we'd visited down at the bar. Mostly I'd just let him do the talking, and he hadn't seemed to notice that I was being tight-lipped. "I thought maybe she followed me here."

"Oh," he said, his eyes widening. "I take it it's not her?"

I shook my head again.

Sergeant Gibson emerged from the room again with a Polaroid in hand. He handed it to me, but I just looked at it from his hand. I didn't want my prints on anything associated with the crime scene. Even the Polaroid photograph.

I fought back a grimace, careful not to let recognition color the expression on my face. It was Jimmie alright. With a small hole right between his eyes. He'd been shot at close range, that much was clear. "Nope. Don't know him."

"No idea what he was doing in your motel room?"

"Not a clue."

"Interesting."

"Why is it interesting?"

"Why would this man be in your room if you didn't know him?"

I shrugged. "I could give you a list of reasons. Maybe he was looking for cash or drugs to steal. Maybe he wanted a passport. Maybe he was drunk and thought it was his room. Who knows why criminals do the things they do, Sergeant?"

"Which is exactly why you should come with me and check out the room," he said. "I'm afraid all of your possessions have been stolen, Mr. Drunk."

"Stolen?"

He nodded. "The killer must have run off with your entire suitcase. Your room is nearly empty."

"I didn't come with much." I realized how ridiculous I sounded. Flying all the way to a beach resort without luggage? The man was going to think it was a setup.

"Surely you had a suitcase..."

I shook my head. "It's a long story."

"Maybe you'll have to enlighten me?"

I let out a heavy sigh. "My ex packed the suitcase, okay? I was just trying to get away from her as fast as I could."

Sergeant Gibson's face was stone-cold. The best poker face I'd ever seen. The man would rake it in big-time with the guys. "You know what *else* is interesting to me, Mr. Drunk?"

I lifted my hat and ran a hand through my sweat-soaked hair. "What else is interesting to you Sergeant Gibson?"

"It is interesting to me that you claim not to know the dead man in your room, and yet we found one of your business cards in his pocket, *Officer* Drunk."

The words *Officer Drunk* hung in the air like the nauseating stench of a skunk's spray. I felt the oxygen leaving my lungs as Al looked up at me. The business card. I'd just been kicked in the esophagus when I'd handed that over to an annoying seat-mate whom I'd just wanted to shut up. I hadn't been at my peak brain function when I'd done that. And I surely hadn't been in my peak brain function when I'd decided to lie to the island police.

*Fuck.*

*Fuckity fuck fuck fucked, in fact.*

I needed to talk to that witness. I needed to look at the security tapes. I needed to ensure that the crime scene was being handled appropriately. DNA samples needed collected. Bloody footprints. Bullet retrieval. Anything. I needed to handle the investigation!

But this wasn't my investigation, and it wasn't my jurisdiction. Hell, this wasn't even my country!

"Officer Drunk?"

I shrugged. "I don't know the guy. But it's my motel room. It's very likely he found one of my business cards in my room and pocketed it."

"Why would he do that, Officer Drunk?"

I threw my hands out on either side of myself. I was out of answers. "You got me."

"Officer Drunk, I'd like you to come down to the station and answer a few questions for me."

My mouth opened, but no sound came out.

"Sergeant," piped up Al, clapping me on the arm. "Drunk here is, well... drunk. He's intoxicated. We've been down at the bar for several hours drinking. He's hardly eaten anything all day. He spent the entire day on an airplane and is exhausted. He doesn't know anything about the dead man in his room, but he'll be happy to come down to your police station tomorrow or the next day, when he's had a minute to come to terms with what's happened and clean himself up.

Maybe by then, you'll have had an opportunity to interview the witnesses and check your surveillance systems."

I looked down at Al, my mouth agape. I could kiss the man. Right there on his bald, liver-spotted scalp.

Sergeant Gibson looked at me intently. "You are not to leave the island until we have spoken."

"Sure thing, Sarge," I said, giving him a little salute. "I'll come visit you soon. I promise."

## 13

AL ACCOMPANIED ME BACK TO THE RESORT'S LOBBY TO BUY MYSELF a shirt. In fact, I bought several new things in Angelita's Bay Boutique, the resort's clothing store. A fifty-dollar package of Calvin Klein men's underwear, because they didn't sell Jockeys or Fruit of the Looms, a pair of swim trunks, a new pair of shorts, and two tank tops. Then I popped into the gift shop to see what they had in the way of toothbrushes and toothpaste and the like, as all my gear was in my motel room, and my motel room was being swarmed by island officials.

When I was done, Al looked up at me. "What now? You don't have a room to stay in."

I shrugged. "I'm sure the resort will find me something."

"Eh?" He cupped his ear towards me.

"I'm sure they'll find me a new room," I hollered.

Al nodded, his mouth set in a straight line. "They better. I'll see to it. Come on. I know the owner." He curled two fingers, beckoning me to follow.

As I tugged one of my new tank tops on over my hat, Al shuffled slowly towards the front desk, where we waited in line while a late arrival checked in. When that man had gone, it was our turn. Al took the lead.

A thick woman behind the counter whose clothes stretched tightly across her chest, adjusted her glasses. "Good evening, Mr. Becker, how may I help you?"

"Yes, Anita, I'd like to speak to Artie Balladares, please."

"Mr. Balladares? Sir, is there anything I can help you with?" She said it loudly. I could tell she was used to talking to Al.

"I appreciate the offer, but no, I'd like to speak to Artie, please. Tell him Al Becker wants to speak to him."

"Yes, Mr. Becker."

The woman disappeared through a door. Seconds later, she came out with a scrawny kid of no more than twenty-two or twenty-three following her. He had disheveled brown hair and baby-smooth skin, making me wonder if he was even old enough for his first shave yet.

"Oh for Pete's sake," groaned Al the second he caught sight of the kid.

"You know that kid?"

"That's Ozzy Messina. This kid's a joke."

"Who is he?"

Before Al could respond, Ozzy stood in front of us. He wore a rumpled grey pinstriped suit that looked to be his father's, about two sizes too big, with a pair of oversized sunglasses hanging out of the front pocket. "Mr. Becker, what can I do for you tonight?"

"I want to speak to Artie Balladares."

"Mr. Balladares is dealing with an emergency situation at the moment and is unavailable. What can I do for you?"

Al looked at me curiously.

"Artie's not available right now," I said loudly.

Al pointed at me. "This is my friend. His name is Daniel Drunk and his room is not up to resort standards. I'd like him to get a new room. An upgrade."

Ozzy looked at me then, tugging on the lapel of his oversized suit. "I'm sorry that your room isn't up to resort standards, Mister…"

"Drunk."

His eyes widened, and a slow smile poured across his baby face. "Your last name is Drunk? How cool is that?"

"Mildly cool, I guess," I said with an unamused half-grimace.

"Are you from the US?"

I nodded.

That seemed to relax him. The responsible adult facade he'd been trying to portray disappeared, and his shoulders visibly relaxed. "What's the problem? Is it the cleaning? I can get someone over there…"

"It's not the cleaning," interrupted Al. "It's the dead body on the floor that's the problem."

Ozzy stopped smiling. "You're room two seventy-seven?"

I nodded.

His body stiffened. "Oh my God. There's a dead body in your room!"

"I hear you were the one that found him?" I asked.

"Yeah, I, uh—" He held a hand up to his mouth, like just speaking about it was conjuring up nauseating images in his head.

"Are you security?"

Al backhanded my arm and then pointed at the kid. "Ozzy's the *head* of security."

*Oh for fuck's sake.* This kid was the *head* of resort security? I wanted to palm my forehead, but I resisted. I was going to have to take matters into my own hands. "So, Ozzy. Can I call you Ozzy?"

Ozzy's mouth gaped a little and he nodded. "Yeah, sure. Call me Ozzy. I mean, that's what the guys call me. Mr. Balladares says I should have guests call me Mr. Messina, but ya know, that's… Mr. Messina's my dad. So, uh, yeah, Ozzy's fine."

I glanced over at Al.

He rolled his eyes.

"Riiight," I drawled. "So, it was the maid that contacted you about the shooting?"

Al hitched his thumb backwards at me. "Drunk's a cop in the States."

Ozzy's eyes widened. "Shut up. That's so cool."

"Yeah," I agreed, already annoyed by the kid. "So you talked to the maid. What's her name?"

"Oh, um, yeah. Her name's Cami, er, Camila. Camila Vergado, she goes by Cami around here."

"So, can you tell me exactly what Ms. Vergado told you?"

Ozzy looked around. The two women working the desk were intently pretending not to be eavesdropping on the conversation. He cleared his throat and leaned forward. "Would you like to step into my office?"

"Of course."

Al and I waited as Ozzy made his way back through the resort offices to let us through a doorway just beyond the front desk. The offices weren't as nicely painted as the lobby. The rugs were worn and the paint scarred in places.

"Right this way." Ozzy opened a door at the end of a hallway. It was little more than a shoebox tucked into the end of the hallway as an afterthought. The pale blue walls were bare. Not a single diploma or certificate from a training program. No pictures of a girlfriend. No personal effects at all. Not even a framed photo of a dog on the desk. A computer desk was shoved up against the far wall, and another desk was in the middle of the office, with an armless rolling chair separating the two. Ozzy gestured to the two wooden chairs parked in front of his desk. The desk was littered with file folders and pieces of paper. "Please have a seat, gentlemen."

Ozzy sat behind his desk, pulling his tie in the way that he'd seen other grown men do in the past, I was sure. I could tell he felt important bringing us back to his office. Like he'd proven something about his capabilities just by having four walls and a door he could call his own.

I didn't waste any time. "So, tell me what you know, Ozzy."

Ozzy's head bobbed. "Right. Well, Cami came to see me. It was probably about an hour ago. She said she was heading home for the night when she heard gunshots. Only seconds later, she saw two men take off on foot."

I pulled a business card from the little holder on Ozzy's desk and caught a glimmer of a smile cross his face, until I turned the card over and began to jot down notes on the back of it. "Did she see what the men looked like?"

He held a hand up over his head. "Umm, she said they were tall. You know, like this, and, uh, kinda big." He held a hand out on either side of himself. "You know, like wide and stuff."

I looked at Ozzy. "Wide and stuff?"

He lifted his brows. "Oh, you want technical terms. Right? Umm, large build."

"Was she able to tell race or ethnicity?"

He shrugged. "I didn't ask her."

"How about distinguishing features?"

He pursed his lips before answering. "Yeah, I didn't ask about that either."

"You didn't ask?" I wanted to reach across the table and swat Ozzy Messina's unpubertized face. "Where is Ms. Vergado right now? I'd like to speak with her."

"She said she had to go home."

"Go home? And you let her? You didn't think to make her wait to talk to the authorities?"

Ozzy swallowed hard. His eyes flicked back and forth between Al's and mine. "You think I should have asked her to wait? I just didn't think that was right. The poor woman was traumatized. I mean, I was traumatized too, just by looking at that dead b..." He sucked his lips between his teeth and then held a hand up to cover his mouth. He held a finger up and nodded, as if to say *hold on, I've got it under control.* "Anyway, she didn't say much else. She just told me she heard shots, she saw two big guys take off in a run, and that was it. I'm sure the island cops will get more out of her when they talk to her."

I could tell Ozzy would prove useless. The kid didn't know his ass from a hole in the sand. I looked at Al. "It's getting late, Al. Let's just get me a room and call it a night."

Al and I stood up.

Ozzy stood up too. "Oh, I can take care of that. I'll get you a new room made up right away, and I'll send someone to your room to get your luggage."

I grunted. I didn't like the idea that I was going to have to wait to get a new room made up. I was exhausted and just wanted to buy a Snickers bar and a Dr. Pepper in the gift shop and call it a night. "I don't have any luggage."

Ozzy looked surprised. "You don't have any luggage? What about your clothes, sir?"

"It's Drunk, not sir, and this is all I need for clothes." I lifted the handled boutique bag.

"Right. Well, then, I'll just see about getting you another room. Follow me."

Al touched Ozzy's arm before he could lead us out of the office. "I want to talk to Artie Balladares about Drunk's room."

"Mr. Balladares is dealing with the events in room two seventy-seven."

Al lowered his chin. "I don't care. Get him over here. Now."

# 14

We met Artie in his office. It was on the main floor, just behind the front desk. His office was much nicer and more orderly than Ozzy's. It was at least twice as big, with an executive's desk stained in a cherry finish and polished to a shine. He had photos of his family on the walls and in frames on the desk. The office had been meticulously decorated to match the theme of the lobby. A faux ship's wheel hung on the wall next to a grand portrait of seagulls flying over a ship named the *Seacoast Majestic*. In the painting, the ship was being tossed by a big frothy wave, and the dark charcoals, greys, and navy blues suggested it was riding out a storm.

Artie Balladares was a large man. So large that large might be a bit of a misnomer. Elephants were large. *Whales* were large. Artie Balladares was immense. If the Big and Tall section at JCPenney's had a daddy, that was where Artie Balladares shopped for his clothing. He wore a white Panama Jack safari hat with a black band, and beneath it, his pudgy red face sweated profusely. A handkerchief wasn't enough to blot the man's sweat. He had to use a bar towel instead, which unintentionally made the room smell like the men's locker room at the gym.

Despite the fact that Artie's office was twice as large as Ozzy's, squeezing Artie, myself, Ozzy, and Al into the room suddenly made me feel claustrophobic. Like Artie was hogging all the air for himself. Of course, the stench of four men's body odors didn't help either.

"Hi, Artie," said Al, like he wasn't having any issues with *his* air supply.

"Welcome back, Al. Glad to have you here for keeps." He spoke loudly, like either he'd been around Al before or his size made his voice naturally come out more forcefully. He looked at me. "Who's this?"

"This is Drunk. He's from the States. We flew in together."

Artie held out a hand. "Drunk?"

I nodded and shook his sweat-stained hand. He squeezed my hand hard, and our fingers squished together like a pair of mating octopuses.

"Nice to meet you. I'm told you're our guest in room two seventy-seven?"

"Yeah. I only got here a few hours ago. I went down to have drinks with Al, and while I was gone, all of that happened. I assure you, Mr. Balladares, whatever happened in that room was one hundred percent not my doing."

"Drunk's a cop in the States," said Al.

"Oh, a law enforcement agent. Nice." He smiled. "And I believe you. It was probably a robbery gone bad. Unfortunately, we've got some crime issues here on the island. No worries. We'll get you a new room. Won't we, Ozzy?"

Ozzy's mouth gaped. "I was going to get him a new room, but he asked to—"

"I want him to have the vacant cottage down by me," said Al. "Vic's old place."

"You want him to have Vic's old place?" said Artie, his eyes wide. "That's quite an upgrade."

"He's a friend," said Al. "And he's been through a lot. His

fiancée dumped him. He's supposed to be on his honeymoon, and there's a dead body in his room. Cut the guy a break?"

Hearing my life in a nutshell, I suddenly felt the low rumblings of the pity party parade marching down my street. I felt like I should be carrying the flag, or at the very least marching along with a baton.

"Oh, uh, rough break about the fiancée," said Artie.

"I can assure you, it's better this way."

"Right." He glanced at Al.

"Oh, come on, Artie. I'll pay the difference if I have to," said Al.

Artie mopped up more of his sweat as he considered Al's request. Finally he let out a heavy breath in a wheeze. "Oh, I'll take care of it. It's fine. Ozzy, make up Vic's old place for Drunk, will you please? The whole thing. On the house. Hit his card with a refund." He shook his head and wagged a finger. "The things I do for you, Al."

Al leaned across the desk and patted Artie's meaty arm. "You're doing the right thing Artie."

"It'll take a bit to get it ready," said Ozzy. "Thirty minutes or so."

Al smiled. "Not a problem. Evie's already got supper on the table back at the cottage. Ring my room when it's ready, will ya?"

# 15

---

I woke up the next afternoon on Al's sofa. Despite the murderous events that had unfolded the night before, the combination of exhaustion, alcohol, and Mrs. Al's cooking had lulled me into a food coma. So when the front desk had called to tell me that my new room was ready and I'd not felt like moving, Al had thrown a blanket on me and said, "Evie and I are going to bed. You can sleep here tonight, kid."

*Kid.*

I was a thirty-five-year-old man with a full beard after two days of non-shaving. I hadn't been called *kid* since my first year in the academy, and that was only because the training officer had a chip on his shoulder.

But I appreciated the offer and didn't have enough energy to pass it up. So I'd pulled the blanket up over my head and was out in less time than it took to count the number of chin pubes on Ozzy Messina's face.

Now it was morning, and from beneath the blanket, I heard voices. Without opening my eyes, I uncurled my long body, sticking a bare leg out of the blanket and over the arm of the Becker's three-person sofa. I followed it up with two arms out

79

over my head and gave a good solid stretch. The sofa had been comfy as I'd drifted off to sleep, but by about two a.m., every part of my body had ached for more room, and I'd struggled to find a good way to lay.

"Maybe if you poke him," said a little voice.

I envisioned Mrs. Al standing over me with a yardstick. My eyes flashed open beneath the blanket. Slowly I pulled it down just below my nose, wincing as the day's rays hit my sensitive eyes.

"Good morning!" said Al brightly. "See, no poking required!"

"G'mornin'," I mumbled as the early warning signs of a headache nibbled at the insides of my brain.

"How about a cup of coffee?" asked Mrs. Al, gesturing towards the kitchen with a rolled-up newspaper.

"Mmm," I groaned. "Not much of a coffee drinker."

Al turned and looked at his wife curiously.

"He's not much of a coffee drinker!" she hollered into his good ear.

Al looked appalled. "Not much of a coffee drinker? You got hair on your balls, don'tcha?"

Mrs. Al swatted her husband with the newspaper. "Al!"

I cracked a smile. This was why I already appreciated Al. Any man who could insult me with a crack about my balls before breakfast was high on my friend's list. Al was steadily climbing the charts. "Wouldn't you like to see," I said with a crooked smile. Then I glanced up at Al's wife. "Oh, excuse me ma'am."

"Oh, don't excuse her," said Al with an emphatic frown. "And don't let the pretty face fool ya. Evie's no shrinking violet."

"Yeah, okay." I put both bare feet on the rug in Al's living room and sat up, making sure to let the blanket cover the morning tent I'd sprung. Mrs. Al might not be a shrinking violet, but I was certain my mother'd kick my ass if I surprised an old woman like that after she'd done me a solid and let me sleep on her sofa. "I just never acquired a taste for coffee. You don't happen to have a Dr. Pepper lying around, do you?"

"We haven't been shopping since we got to the island," said Mrs. Al. "Shopping is on my list for today, though. I'll pick some up for you."

I waved a hand at her. "Oh, you don't have to do that."

"What's he want?" Al asked his wife.

"Dr. Pepper!" she hollered at him.

Al wrinkled his nose. "Is he a specialist or something?"

"He wants a soda, Al."

"Oh. They have soda in the dining hall."

I scratched the back of my head and yawned. "What time is it?"

Mrs. Al looked at her watch. "Almost noon."

"Noon? Damn!" I said, scrambling to my feet, careful to keep the blanket swathed around my waist. "I better leave you two alone and get checked into my room."

"Artie sent someone down with the key this morning. I'll walk you over there whenever you're ready," said Al.

I grabbed my tank top from the coffee table and tugged it on over my head, ensuring it covered the zipper on my shorts before dropping the blanket on their sofa. "I'm ready. Just let me grab the rest of my stuff." I slid my feet into my flip-flops and hooked a finger into the handle of the bag of clothes I'd bought the night before. "Ready."

That got a laugh out of Mrs. Al. "I hope your trip to Paradise gets better, Drunk." She thought about it for a second. "That's quite a name. I can't imagine your mother calling you Drunk."

I laughed. "No. Mom calls me Terrence."

"Terrence? I thought your name was Daniel. Why does she call you Terrence?"

"Because my pops is Daniel Senior. She calls him Dan, or

Danny. She calls me by my middle name. Most of the kids in elementary school did too."

She lifted her chin. "Ah, that makes sense. Mind if I call you Terrence?"

I smiled. "No, not at all. It'll make me feel like I'm at home."

She patted my arm. "Good, I'm glad you could stay with us last night, Terrence. Maybe you'll join Al and me for dinner again sometime."

"Consider it a date," I said. I leaned over and gave Mrs. Al a side squeeze around the shoulders. "Thanks for dinner last night. Having a home-cooked meal was exactly what the doctor ordered to get my head on straight."

"Alright, sweetheart, I'm going to show Drunk his new place. I'll be back." Al kissed his wife's cheek while I put on my new hat and shades.

Seconds later, the two of us stood outside on his deck. It was the first time I'd seen the area in the light. The night before had been a blur, and I'd only blindly followed Al to his cottage, so I had no idea what to expect.

Standing outside now, in the daytime, I was shocked at what I discovered. Al's cottage faced out to the ocean with only a white sandy beach separating his place from the water's edge. The undisturbed ocean view made my jaw drop. The salty ocean air. The peaceful sound of the water lapping at the shore. The gulls squawking and the sound of the breeze rustling the palms overhead played like a nature soundtrack. I stood staring, taking it all in, for what felt like minutes. "Holy shit, this is amazing!"

He gave a gentle backhand to my arm. "Right? Now you get it!"

My brain was still in awe as I mumbled, "Yeah, I get it alright."

"Eh?"

"Now I get it!" I hollered.

Damn. I didn't just get it. *I was jealous.*

To live out the rest of your years like this? Al had it made in the shade. Literally. I looked up to see a grove of coconut trees overhead. The fronds swayed in the gentle ocean breeze, shading his deck.

"Come on," he beckoned. "Your place is down this way."

## 16

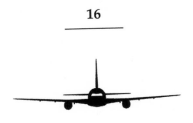

AL LED ME AROUND THE BACK OF HIS COTTAGE, WHICH I discovered was actually a duplex.

"Glenn Anderson and his wife, Fern, live on the other side. They're from Atlanta. Glenn moved here full-time about a year ago. He's a retired orthopedic surgeon. Evie and Fern are good friends. She's the one that put the idea in Evie's head to move here permanently. Glenn's alright, but all he talks about is his food allergies. He's even allergic to dairy, and yet the man eats more cheese than anyone I've ever met before. Drives me nuts."

"What's it to you if the man eats cheese?" I said loudly.

Al stopped walking and looked up at me. "You ever meet anyone allergic to dairy or that's lactose intolerant?"

I shrugged. I mean, it was possible, but no one readily came to mind.

He pointed at his stomach. "Their gut. It doesn't know what to do with cheese. So it sits in there and ferments and ferments, and by the time it comes out, it's the worst-smelling byproduct you could ever imagine. Toxic chemicals. Literally. It'll knock you out. The man's like a walking stink bomb."

I suppressed a grin. "You're saying you don't like Glenn Anderson because his farts smell bad?"

"I mean, I'm eighty-seven years old, so I don't have a lot of room to talk, but yeah, it's a bothersome quality for a friend to have." He shrugged and started walking again.

On the other side of Al and Glenn's cottage, a sky-blue Toyota Land Cruiser filled the dirt parking stall.

"Well, this is a beaut," I said, patting the back of the vintage vehicle.

"This is Gary Wheelan's. It's a '78 FJ40. Gary bought it at an auction about fifteen years ago and spent almost ten years restoring it to mint condition. It's his baby. He spent a bundle to have it shipped over here when he moved to the island full-time."

"Wow," I said, nodding in appreciation.

Al kept walking and gestured to the cottage next to the Toyota. "Of course, this is Gary's place. He's a pal of mine. He's single. His wife passed a few months before he bought the Land Cruiser. Now he's got one of those yippy dogs."

"Yippy dogs?" I asked, looking at Al with my head tipped sideways.

Al nodded and held his hands out in front of him about two feet apart to explain the size of the dog. "Yeah, you know, one of those little dogs that yip—a little ankle biter. Pain in the ass is what it is. Gary's a nice guy, but he's a little uptight, sort of like his dog. You know? He's former military. Got out early, though, then went on to do security."

We passed a couple golf carts and two more duplexes. Al was able to name the residents of several of them and tell me a little about them. A couple of the rooms didn't have full-time residents and were still being rented by the week.

The duplexes were all alike. They'd all been stuccoed and painted Pepto-Bismol pink with white shutters and trim and white flower boxes brimming with colorful flowers beneath the windows. The front of each duplex shared a deck that faced the ocean. The back faced the cobblestone road that led back to the resort. Each duplex had a side door that opened to a picnic table and a parking space for a golf cart or a vehicle. Al explained that most of the people in the cottages either rented or owned private golf carts. Hardly anyone owned a car as the resort provided complimentary shuttle service into town to shop or go to the airport. Al said he and his wife were planning to buy a golf cart now that they were permanent residents.

"But why spend all the money to live in a resort? Why not just a rent a condo or something?"

He lifted a shoulder. "Eh, Evie and I have friends here. We've talked about maybe buying our own place on the island someday down the road, but I like the idea of being able to eat at the restaurant whenever I want. There's something to be said for a good buffet. The cooks here are top-notch. And if I can afford it, why not?"

Why not, indeed.

Finally, he stopped walking and pointed. "This one was Vic Hoffman's. Vic's a retired lawyer from New York. Glenn told me that he went back to the States two days ago because his granddaughter had her first baby. He'll be back next month."

He handed me the key to Vic's place.

"Vic's not going to mind me staying here?"

Al waved a hand. "Eh, Vic's a cheapskate. He refuses to pay for his cottage while he's gone, so he knows it's gonna get rented out and there'll be someone else sleeping in his bed while he's gone. He's used to it. One time his wife found the vase on her end table stuffed full of women's underwear. I guess some guy had a bachelor party at their place while they were gone. He knows the risks."

I climbed the two steps to my side door. Unlocking it, I walked into a furnished living room almost identical to Al's. The five-piece floral rattan living room set looked like something that had come off a Golden Girls' garage sale. Straight across from me was a flat-screen television set. Forty inch at best. And to my left was the small cottage kitchen that housed full-sized appliances, a two-person kitchen table, and a slider to the deck and my ocean view. Beyond the living room was a bedroom on the left and a bathroom on the right. Everything was neat and tidy. Of course, it wasn't as new and sleek as my motel room had been, but there was more room and it was definitely homier and more comfortable. I was pleased.

"Great place, Al. Why would Artie do this for me?"

Al looked at me curiously, then cupped a hand behind his ear.

"Why would Artie do this for me?" I hollered.

"He's not doing it for you, Drunk. He's doing it for me."

"I got that. But it seems sort of like Artie Balladares owes you one. What's the story?"

Al grinned. "Artie is the *new* owner of the Seacoast Majestic. He hasn't owned the place for long. But I've known Artie for years, long before he ever bought the resort. See, he used to own an International Harvester dealership in Bridgeton, New Jersey. And as owners, you know, from time to time we would get these all-expenses-paid incentive trips from the dealers." Al lifted his brows. "Oh man, they've sent Evie and me all over the place. To New York City, to Las Vegas, to Cancun, and of course, to Paradise Isle."

I grinned at Al. "Sweet! Sounds like I went into the wrong business. The only place the station has ever taken us was to Q39 for our Christmas party. I mean, don't get me wrong, it's the best barbecue in Kansas City, but it certainly was no Cancun."

Al chuckled. "Yeah, we had a pretty good deal going. Well, on one of those trips, I met Artie. And he and I became pretty good friends. We kept in touch, and we'd see each other on trips every year. Our wives got along really well, so we always double dated for dinners and went on excursions together. And we liked the island so much that even after we'd sold our respective implement dealerships, we continued to make annual trips down to visit each other and the island. By then, our wives had become dear friends. Though Artie lost Jennie in 2013, we still all enjoyed visiting each other."

"So that's why he was so willing to help you out? Because the two of you were such good friends?"

Al smiled and shook his head softly. "Well, that's part of it. But you know, I'd told you that I cashed out my Bitcoin back in December, when it was at its peak. Originally I'd invested in 2011. It was a project I'd started with my oldest great-grandson to teach him about the importance of saving and compound interest. He told me about this new thing he'd learned about in these chat rooms, cryptocurrency. He tried to tell me it was the wave of the future. And I had some loose change floating around in my pocket, so I decided what the heck, I'd put a few hundred bucks into it. They were only a quarter at the time. I mean, I had the money to lose. Shortly thereafter, in June, a single Bitcoin was up to thirty dollars! Well, that was right around the time we were to fly out to the island to meet Artie and Jennie. I told him all about my investment and how it had already grown, but I also explained cryptocurrency's weakness, which in my mind was its severe volatility. Up, down, up, down—the stuff could be all over the place, but I could see how it might make a decent investment if held over time. Artie researched it. Gave it a while. Watched the ups and downs and did some reading and ended up making his own investment when it got back down into the five-dollar range."

"Ahhh." I nodded. "I think I know where this is going."

Al's head bobbed. "Yes. Over the years, Artie kept investing. Now, see, I just did my initial investment and let it sit. I kind of forgot about it, in fact. Every once in a while, my grandson would fill me in on the price, but Artie, he was always trying to time it just right. In the end, he did quite well for himself. He cashed out in November when it hit twelve thousand dollars a coin. He didn't think it was going to get much higher, but I held out a little longer and ended up cashing out at just shy of twenty thousand a coin only a month later."

My jaw dropped. "A month later? I bet he was kicking himself that he didn't wait!"

Al shrugged. "That's the breaks, you know. And Artie knew it. But he'd invested more than I had, so he walked away an incredibly wealthy man, and he'd been wealthy to begin with! Artie already knew what he wanted. After Jennie died, he'd set his sights on someday moving to the island. But cashing out in November was the final catalyst. The resort had been for sale for a while, and so he decided that was what he wanted to do for the rest of his life. It would be his legacy. It was a cash sale, so it happened fast. By Christmas, he was the proud owner of a Caribbean resort."

I shook my head. The story was amazing. I realized in that moment that I needed to get my shit together and put money away so I could have my own legacy someday. "So impressive."

Al nodded. "Thank you. It is rather impressive," he said with a chuckle.

"So Artie feels like he owes you for helping him get the resort?"

"In a way. He feels like I was the one that pushed him to invest in cryptocurrency."

"Well, I sure appreciate you scoring the room for me," I said, taking the opportunity to shake my new friend's hand.

He scratched the back of his neck. "Well, you know. I'd rather have *you* here than some pain-in-the-ass guy who's gonna throw some wild bachelor party and disturb the peace around here."

The truth was out. Al liked me. I quirked a grin. "Thanks, Al. I like you too."

## 17

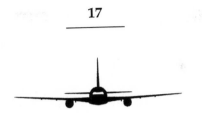

I DAWDLED AWAY THE AFTERNOON BY UNPACKING MY NEW clothes and trying not to give Jimmie's dead body too much thought. I was, after all, innocent, on vacation, and, in truth, not an overly ambitious cop. I was more of an *I'll let you slide on that speeding ticket* kind of cop. Especially if there was a pretty woman behind the wheel.

I'd actually only been on the force for about two years. When I'd made the commitment at age thirty-two to clean up my life, stop drinking, and find a wife, I'd also decided I needed direction. Up until then, partying and chasing women had taken top priority. So when my pal Mikey had suggested that I join the police academy, I'd thought that sounded like a cool thing to do. Of course, not being a big fan of studying, I'd barely graduated from the academy, and then once I'd joined the force, I'd only made it off probation by the skin of my teeth and likely at the urging of Mikey, who was much higher up the ranks than I could ever hope to be.

I refolded my three new pairs of Calvin Kleins and put them in the top bureau drawer, tucked my swim trunks in next to them, and put my new shorts and my remaining tank top in the middle drawer. I wondered if this was the kind of shit that Al did all day.

When that was done, I walked up to the resort to partake in their lunch buffet. According to the A-frame chalkboard by the entrance, the theme was Taste of Italy. Preparing for a night of drinking margaritas at the bar, I decided it would be best to carb up. I even did something that I didn't usually do, and I loaded up on water. I'm sure that there are idiots in the world that don't realize a human body needs water to survive, but I'm also sure that there are even more idiots in the world that assume there's enough water in the food that they eat and the soda that they drink to get by without actually having to *drink* water.

*I* am one of those idiots.

For the most part, I believe in the four main food groups: carbonated and caffeinated beverages; alcoholic beverages; meat and potatoes; and chocolate. I was partial to Snickers bars, but I wasn't a snobby chocoholic. I ate whatever was available and I never complained about it. Unless it was a Mounds bar. I mean, who the fuck thought it was a good idea to put coconut in a candy bar? Find 'em for me, will ya?

Anyway, I decided to load up on water because about a week before my nuptials were scheduled to take place, my mother told me about an article she'd read about a man dying of dehydration on a tropical island because he drank only mixed drinks for a week straight and never got out of the sun. She'd made me promise to hydrate, and since I still hadn't told anyone where I was, I figured I probably shouldn't die before sending someone a text message.

Now, Taste of Italy was an interesting concept. Pasta was vaguely foreign to me. Aside from an occasional spaghetti feed or something that Chef Boyardee cooked up for me, I considered myself pasta-sheltered. Who knew there were so many different kinds of noodles and sauces? I had to say, I was pretty impressed with the spread. I was even more impressed with the dessert table. There were six different chocolate options. Chocolate cake, chocolate cheesecake, chocolate mousse in little edible chocolate muffin liners, chocolate pudding, brownies, and a chocolate soufflé. And what kind of man would I be if I didn't sample them all?

On my way out, while cradling my food baby, I discovered the resort gym. The equipment was all new and shiny. Everything looked immaculate and hardly used. Which didn't seem odd at all. Almost everyone I'd seen thus far was either elderly or honeymooning. Who wanted to be pumping iron on their honeymoon when there were so many other, *more enjoyable*, recreational ways to keep fit?

I'm not gonna lie.

The thought of those other *more enjoyable* honeymooning activities made me almost instantly horny. So my mind promptly drifted from working out to finding a woman on the beach to take back to my place. That was the only motivation I needed to make a beeline back to my cottage. Within forty-five minutes, I'd shit, showered, and shaved and found myself poolside and ready for action.

"Another margarita, Drunk?" asked Manny.

A solitary woman sat at the bar. She was the first anywhere near my age bracket that I'd seen alone on the island since I'd been there. I cocked my head towards her. "I'll have what she's having."

She looked over at me and smiled. She was an attractive woman. A little older than I usually went for, maybe early fifties, but Little Drunk wasn't particular. The truth was, I'd had a lot of good experiences with older women. The woman had long blonde hair, gold dangly earrings and stacked gold bangle bracelets. She wore a red sarong tied around her hips and a red string bikini top. For an older woman, her medium-sized breasts were incredibly pert, making me wonder if they were real.

I shot an easy smile back her way. One of my best Drunk

flirting mechanisms, I was told. "What is that, anyway? Please tell me there's no coconut water in it."

She shook her head. Her blonde hair rustled over her bare shoulders in the breeze. "No, no coconut water. It's a Cool and Deadly."

I slid down the bar a little closer to her, careful to leave at least a chair between us. "A Cool and Deadly? Intriguing. What's in it?"

She looked up at Manny, speechless, and splayed her hands out. "You know, I'm not really sure what he puts in here."

"Two different kinds of rum, pineapple juice, orange juice, triple sec, and grenadine. My specialty."

"Sounds amazing."

She slid her drink down the bar. "Would you like to try it?"

I held a hand up. "No, thank you. Manny's making mine. But you like it?"

She pulled the drink back towards herself and took a long pull from the straw. "It's delicious. It's the only drink I've had since coming to the island."

"Oh? When did you get here?"

"Two days ago. I'm just here until Wednesday. You?"

"Thanks, Manny," I said, taking the drink he slid my way. "I got in last night. I'm here for two weeks."

"Two weeks!" Her green eyes widened. "That's a nice long trip."

I nodded. I was about to try something new. My first attempt at a pity pickup. I had a buddy who used the routine often and claimed it worked like a charm, but I'd never been so desperate before as to actually stoop to trying it.

But what can I say?

Desperate times called for desperate measures.

"Yeah." I hung my head slightly. "It's supposed to be my honeymoon."

Her upper torso turned about a quarter of the way towards me. "Supposed to be?"

"Yeah, I haven't told anyone this yet," I began, giving a glance up at Manny, who I knew was listening, "but I caught my fiancée in bed with another man the night before our wedding."

The woman sucked in her breath, her ringless hand covering her mouth. "You're kidding me!"

I shook my head. "Nope. I wish I was."

"What did you do?!"

"I hopped on the first plane to Paradise!"

"I mean, what did you do about your fiancée?"

"Oh, her?" I waved a hand dismissively. "I left her back in the States."

"Oh, you poor thing!"

I nodded, ashamed that I'd had to use my pathetic sob story to hit on a woman, but the way Little Drunk ached, I felt like a man with only hours to live, and the clock was ticking.

"So you're here all alone?"

I shrugged. I didn't want to look *too* pathetic. "Well, at least I've got Manny."

We both looked up at Manny then. He smiled. That was when I noticed the two missing teeth on the left side of his mouth.

"I'm Cynthia, by the way," she said, extending a hand to me.

I took it and kissed the top of it lightly. "It's nice to meet you, Cynthia. I'm Drunk."

She pulled her hand away giggling. "Drunk? Have you been down here all day?"

"No, this is my first drink today, actually. *My name* is Drunk."

That was worthy of a full torso turn and a partial barstool swivel. "Drunk? Your *name* is Drunk?"

I sipped my drink. "Mm-hmm. This is really good, by the way, thanks for the recommendation."

She ignored my thanks. "I've never met anyone by the name of Drunk before. That's pretty cute."

I winked at her. "You're pretty cute."

I heard Manny coughing then.

"Yeah, she is pretty cute. She's also taken," said a deep voice behind me.

I grimaced and let out a sigh. *Dammit.*

"Greg, this is Drunk. Drunk, this is my boyfriend Greg."

I gave a half turn and nodded at the bulldozer of a boyfriend. Women should really come with warning labels— you know, taken, taken by a large man, taken by a large man with fists the size of bowling balls. "Nice to meet you, Greg."

"Drunk caught his fiancée cheating on him the night before his wedding," Cynthia revealed to Greg. "He came on his honeymoon alone."

"Is that so?"

"Mm-hmm." I nodded, my smile tight and my eyes swung down towards the concrete.

Surprisingly, Greg slapped me on the back. "I'm sorry to hear that buddy. Lemme buy you a drink. Manny, give this man another one of whatever it is he's having," he said before flashing his all-inclusive bracelet Manny's way. "Cynthia, let's go."

Cynthia grinned at me sympathetically before walking away. "Bye, Drunk."

Manny slid another drink forward. "Here you go, Mr. Drunk."

Swiveling back around to face the bar, I leaned over my drink. Only my eyes my looked up at the bartender. "It's Drunk, Manny. Just Drunk."

**18**

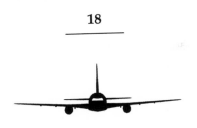

"WHERE ARE ALL THE WOMEN, MANNY?" I GROANED THREE hours and six drinks later. I was pacing myself. One drink every half hour on the dot. No need to get sloppy drunk before a good-looking single woman showed up.

"Drunk, the women that come here are on their honeymoons or are married. We don't get a lot of single women."

"Well, why don't they put that shit on the brochures? 'Don't come here if you're looking for a good time.'"

Manny laughed and mopped the bar top with a white towel. Since I'd been there, I'd met a variety of people, all of them either old or taken. I was starting to think I'd have been better off staying in Missouri. I'd have been laid by at least two different women by now if I'd stayed in Missouri. "The single women are at the clubs, man."

I stopped drinking and looked up at him. Had he been holding out on me? "Where are these clubs you speak of?"

"In town," he explained. "Of course, those aren't always the safest places for tourists to visit."

Fuck it.

I knew how to handle myself.

I sucked the last of my drink through my straw and slid it forward to Manny. I was going to go find the ladies even if it killed me. I pulled out my wallet. That kind of information deserved a tip.

"I'll have whatever he's having," said a smooth voice next to me.

My body tensed up for a split second. My head turned forty-five degrees towards the sound of the voice. I couldn't believe my eyes when I saw her. It was Megan Fox, the woman who'd throat-punched me on the plane. My eyes widened.

That was when she turned to me. "Hello." Her voice was melodic and smooth, and every bit as beautiful as she was.

I swallowed hard. I was sure my throat felt sore again. Without a word, I slid a tip Manny's way and then hopped off my seat. "Thanks for the advice, Manny."

"Running off so soon?" The woman's voice rode in on the ocean air behind me.

I gave a half turn to look at her out of the corner of my eye.

She wore a skintight black sleeveless dress that ended just below the swell of her perfectly round ass. Her arms were cut. Her physique lean. How could I walk away so quickly from that? Even though every instinct in my brain told me to ditch the ruthless bitch, Little Drunk begged me to give her an opportunity to apologize and make amends.

I pointed towards the golf cart. "I don't want to miss my ride."

"In a hurry to get somewhere?"

I glanced backwards at the ocean. The water glittered like diamonds beneath a low-lying sun that had just begun to think of retirement. It *was* early. I shrugged a single shoulder. "I think I'd rather hang out with someone who doesn't throw right jabs at my neck."

She curled forward, against the bar suggestively. "I'm sorry," she purred, plumping out her bottom lip. "You creeped me out. Hasn't anyone ever told you women don't like to be sexually assaulted in airplane lavatories?"

Dammit if that didn't make me smile. "No. See, no one's ever told me that before. How was I supposed to know?"

She tipped her head to the side. Her silky dark hair was pulled back in a low ponytail with only her blunt-cut bangs and a few wispy strands framing her face. "Well, now you know." Her red lips curved into a smile.

"Yeah, now I know," I agreed. Maybe if she'd slapped me in the face or kneed me in the groin, I would have considered staying, but she'd punched me in the *throat*. I walked away. Little Drunk couldn't believe what I was doing. But Big Drunk was in control, and Big Drunk knew a sociopath when he saw one.

I'd gotten around the pool and past the hot tub when she caught up to me, two drinks in hand.

"At least let me make it up to you," she begged. "Come on."

I stopped walking and turned around.

She stood with her high-heeled legs spread shoulder width apart and her hip cocked to one side. She had her black handbag clamped tightly under one arm and held a drink out towards me with the other hand. A peace offering. She tipped her head seductively. As if that was going to work?

"Please? I'm really sorry about the plane."

I didn't budge. "If I'm such a creeper, why do you want to have a drink with me so badly?"

She glanced around the almost-empty pool area. "Lack of competition?" she offered with a grimace and a shrug.

She had a point. But I didn't move. She still made me nervous, and my throat still hurt just looking at her.

She shook the glass in my direction. The ice clinked enticingly. "Oh, come on. Just one drink. Then you can go do whatever exciting thing you were going to go do."

I let out a sigh. Little did she know I didn't have any exciting thing to do except to go haphazardly looking for a hot woman on the island. And by golly, there happened to be a hot woman on the island standing right in front of me, offering me an alcoholic beverage. I reached my hand out. She could bring the drink to me. I wasn't about to go walking into another throat punch. And believe me, I'd be on high alert. This time, I'd know to duck.

She swallowed back whatever morsel of pride she had and came to me with the drink. "Here. Can we go sit down now?"

"One drink?"

"One drink."

The walk back to Manny's bar was the most awkward walk I'd ever taken with a woman. I didn't know if I should hate her, want her, or fear her. Little Drunk, of course, had a vote in the matter, and I struggled to keep him from expressing his opinion.

Manny looked at the two of us curiously when we showed back up again, but he didn't say anything.

"So. I'm Natasha. And you are?" she asked, extending her tanned hand.

"I'm Drunk. Natasha what?"

"Prince. What do you mean you're Drunk?"

"It's my name."

"Your name is Drunk?"

"That's what it says on my driver's license." I wasn't playing it cute with this one. I was still a little salty.

"Wow. That's a new one. Where you from, Drunk?"

"Kansas City. You?"

"Denver. Are you alone in Paradise?"

I lifted a shoulder. "Why do you wanna know?"

"Geez, you want some help getting that chip off your shoulder?" She turned and took a long drink from her glass.

"You punched me in the throat. Do you have any idea how much it hurts to get punched in the throat? People get killed from getting punched in the throat. It's very dangerous."

"Are you serious?" she asked, finally pulling off the kid gloves. "You're not willing to take any responsibility for that?"

"I mean…"

"You said you were cleared to go down my landing strip and then you asked me if I wanted to join the mile-high club with you!"

Behind the counter, Manny let out a chortle.

I glanced up at him and shot him a look that clearly read *shut it.*

The smile washed away, and he gave us his back to take an order from a customer on the swim-up bar side.

"Yeah, well, you looked hot. I was paying you a compliment. Why don't chicks get that?"

"You couldn't just say, hey, you're hot?"

I lifted a shoulder. "I mean, I could have. You just looked a bit spicier than that. I thought I had to lead harder than usual."

"Alright, well, I had to punch harder than usual. So call it even, will ya?"

"I have *balls*, you know. You could have kneed me in them. Or even slapped my face. But, no, you went for the jugular. You're kind of scary, to be honest."

"Ohh, poor Drunk's scared of little old Natasha?" she said in a mocking baby voice.

Goddamn, the woman was sexy. I could only imagine the kind of voices she could make in bed. "Yeah, I am, as a matter of fact."

"You need me to make it up to you?"

*Of course I do!*

I put on my best pitiful face. Big eyes. Plumped-out bottom lip. "Make it up to me? Maybe. What'd you have in mind?"

She stood up and put a hand on my shoulder. Tracing her finger along the line of my shoulders, she walked around to my other side. I turned the barstool to face her, just waiting for her offer to take me back to her room and make my boo-boo all better. Instead, she stood there, legs spread shoulder width apart, hands on her hips, and eyes closed.

I tipped my head curiously. "What are you doing?"

"Hit me."

"What?"

"Hit me. In the throat. If it'll make you feel better, hit me."

"I'm not going to hit you."

"No. I'm tired of you holding that one little thing over my head. Go on. Hit me! Let's make it even."

"Fine!" I got up off the barstool and walked over to her. She still had her eyes closed and her hands on her hips. Her red lips were plumped together in a sexy pout. Even in her heels, I towered over the woman by at least five inches. I scooted my body up as close as I could get it without touching her and leaned over and planted my lips on hers.

Natasha's eyes popped open. She tried to pretend her little game hadn't worked as she'd planned, but I knew the truth. It had worked *exactly* as she'd planned, which was why she didn't push me away. She hadn't wanted a throat punch any more than I wanted blue balls. She'd wanted me to lay one on her.

So lay one on her I did.

It was a hard kiss.

Needy and intrusive.

One born out of a hell of a lot of sexual frustration and anger. Whether the anger I felt was directed towards her, towards Pamela, towards Pamela's ex, or towards the guys that had left Jimmie's dead body in my room, I wasn't exactly sure. But my mouth melded against hers, and our tongues wrestled until I felt her body melt into mine. That was the moment I pulled away. *Always leave them wanting more, fellas.*

I wiped my mouth with the back of my hand and strode back over to the bar, where I drained my Cool and Deadly without even a backwards glance at what I'd done to the woman.

It took her a minute to regain her composure and rejoin me at the bar. She drained her drink and pushed the empty glass across the counter. "Another drink, Manny."

I looked at her. "Make that two, Manny."

## 19

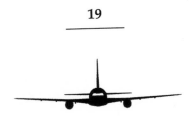

"HOW'D YOU MANAGE TO SCORE ONE OF THESE CUTE COTTAGES?" A giggle bubbled out of Natasha's mouth as the golf cart carried us down the road to my new pad.

I finished the drink I'd taken from the bar and handed it to the golf cart driver. "Take this, will ya, pal?" I was too intoxicated to notice if I'd offended him by making him my personal valet. I scooted closer to Natasha and draped an arm over her shoulder. With my free hand, I traced a finger along the exposed heart-shaped outline of her cleavage while nuzzling her ear. "Wouldn't you like to know," I whispered, inhaling the spicy scent of her perfume.

"Yes, I would," she murmured before I clamped my lips down on hers once again. Her mouth was cold from the iced beverages we'd spend the last few hours consuming, and she tasted like rum. I savored her flavor. It was as refreshing and sweet as the beverage itself had been.

The driver stopped. "Cottage eleven, sir."

I barely heard his clipped accent while devouring Natasha. She had to push on my chest, parting our mouths with a sloppy smacking noise. "We're here, Drunk."

I looked up at the pink cottage. "So we are." I pulled out a couple dollar bills I had in my pocket and cupping them in my hand, I patted the driver on his shoulder with them.

"Thank you, sir."

I followed Natasha out of the golf cart. "My pleasure."

I threw my arm around her again as the driver tore off into the darkness. "What, you're not even going to wait for us to get inside safely?" I said to the dust he'd kicked up.

Natasha giggled before tugging me towards my cottage. "You have your key?"

I dug inside my pocket and produced the key Al had given me earlier in the day. "Voilà," I said, holding it up as if I'd just produced a quarter from behind her ear. "Magic."

It was dark outside my cottage. The streetlights were several paces away, and I hadn't thought to turn my security light on before leaving. The moon was obscured by the coconut trees overhead, but I could see it in the distance reflecting off the ocean. I held Natasha around the waist with one arm while I blindly searched for the keyhole with my key.

"You want me to do that for you, Slugger?" she asked with a sly grin on my fourth or fifth attempt at finding the hole.

I shut her up with my mouth.

When we came up for air, I tried again. This time I found the keyhole, and I pushed our way inside and flipped on the light. Both of our eyes needed a minute to adjust, but once they had, she looked at my fine furnishings and grinned. "Beachy."

"I call it Golden Girls chic," I said with a crooked smile before flipping my hat, shades, and key onto the end table. "Care for a little music?"

She nodded. "What do you have?"

I flipped on the little portable radio that I'd found in the kitchen earlier in the day and turned the dial until I found a crackly station playing a line of smooth jazz. I held my hand out to her. She took it, and I pulled her in for a little slow dance on my kitchen's tile floor.

With her head resting on my chest, I did my best imitation of a sober man on a dance floor, turning the two of us around in time to the music. It was sexy and easy, and I felt Little Drunk telling me enough with the foreplay already, time for the main event.

I took her hand then and spun her around. Natasha giggled and played along. She held on to me with one hand while her other hand gripped her handbag, but she spiraled out as if she'd taken lessons.

And then a new song started up and the tempo changed.

This music was faster, more islandy.

She let go of my hand and began to freestyle. Her hips gyrated to the music. Her hands started at her sides and ran up the length of her body slowly. I couldn't tear my eyes off of her. She was magnificent and sexy. Perfect in every sense of the word. She slowly began her mating dance around me, and when I tried to follow her with my eyes, she ticked a finger at me. "Uh-uh-uh," she chastised seductively.

Holy shit, I wanted her.

Little Drunk pressed hard against my trousers.

And then I felt something press hard against the back of my skull.

"Turn around, Drunk. Slowly."

"What?" I said, wondering if this was all part of her act of seduction.

"Don't try anything funny. I have no problem pulling the trigger."

My brows furrowed together as I frowned. She couldn't be serious?

With slumped shoulders, I turned around to find myself nose to muzzle with a small black handgun. "What the fuck, Natasha?" I breathed as my hands instinctively went palms up next to my shoulders.

"Where is it, Drunk?" Her face was somber, and any hint of

her intoxication had vanished completely. Mine still clouded my brain. The room felt like it was spinning.

"What the actual fuck?" I repeated. First a throat punch and now a gun in my face? This chick was fifty shades of fucked up. I should have known better!

She stood unwaveringly with both hands on the grip. "Don't make me blow your fucking head off, Drunk. Where is it?"

"Where's what?"

"Don't gimme that bullshit. I know you have it. Hand it over and we're good."

My mind reeled. The only thing I *had* was an erection and now even that was gone. "Look, lady, what kind of psycho bitch are you? I don't have jack shit."

"You're full of it, Drunk. I know you have it. I saw you with Jimmie on the plane. You two were working together."

"Jimmie!" I barked. "I don't know Jimmie! I met him on the plane, you fucking nutjob."

"Bullshit. I saw the signal he gave you at the security checkpoint."

My mind flashed back to the airport and Jimmie giving me that odd head nod. My frown deepened. "That fucker was whack. I don't know what his problem was. He punched a guy to impress you or some shit like that. I don't know what that was about."

"I'm not in a mood to be fucked with, Drunk. I know you're in this with Jimmie. Now hand it over," she said, holding a flattened palm out. "I'm losing my patience."

I eyed the gun. She only had one hand on it now, and I knew a defensive move or two. Unfortunately, I was half-blitzed and was having trouble standing upright on two feet, let alone trying to pull off some crazy move I hadn't tried in years. I straightened my shoulders and pulled myself up to my full height. I wanted to look and sound as intimidating as I could. I lowered my voice an octave. "Listen, I have no idea what you're talking about. I didn't know Jimmie before I got on the flight."

"Fine, then you two met up on the plane and worked out an arrangement to get through security. Whatever. I don't care how you did it, I just want it back."

I shook my head at her and threw my hands out on either side of myself. I was getting annoyed. "I don't know how many different ways I can tell you this, lady, but I don't know what the fuck you're talking about. Jimmie slept the entire trip to the island. Then I went back to the bathroom and got assaulted by your skinny psycho ass. I came back, the guy was awake and wanted to chat. We said like five words to each other, and I fell asleep for the rest of the flight. That was it." I looked at her suspiciously then. "Wait. Are you the person that killed Jimmie?"

She rolled her eyes. "No, I didn't fucking kill Jimmie."

"But you know he's dead?"

"Yeah, I know he's dead."

"Then who killed him?"

She pursed her lips and tipped her head to the side. "As if you don't know?"

"No, I don't fucking know! That's what I'm trying to tell you!" I sighed and strode out of the kitchen towards the living room and plopped down on the sofa. I wished I'd brought a spare drink back with me.

"Hey!" she hollered. "Where the hell do you think you're going?"

As I put my feet up on the rattan coffee table, I leaned back and drew a line in the air back and forth between her and me. "I'm over this whole little seductive thing you've got going on here. The femme fatale game might've been hot for the first ten to fifteen seconds, but now it's overdone. I'm gonna check the scores."

"You think this is a game, Drunk? Do you think I'm playing with you?"

"Honestly, I don't know what the fuck you're doing, lady. I don't know anything about Jimmie. I don't know anything about whatever it is that you're looking for. I came here because I busted my fiancée having sex with her ex-boyfriend in my apartment, on my bed, the night before my wedding. This is my honeymoon, Natasha, and I flew in alone. And I didn't think it could get any worse, but then you assaulted me on the plane, a dead body showed up in my motel room, and now you wanna blow my brains out. So you know what? Go the fuck ahead and pull the trigger. I'm out of fucks to give, alright? Get it? No more fucks will be given tonight, or any other night for that matter." And if I had to tell another soul that my fiancée had cheated on me, I might have to blow my own brains out.

I ignored Natasha while she stood in the kitchen. I knew she was likely debating what to believe or what tack to take next. I didn't care. I blindly surfed through the channels, looking for something to watch and hoping I'd happen upon a porn channel. I preferred dying with a good image fixed in my head.

Finally she strode over to me, the handgun hanging by her side. "You seriously have no connection to Jimmie?"

I refused to look up from the television. "That's what I said, sweetheart."

"Then why was he killed in your room?"

"Your guess is as good as mine."

She sighed, and for the first time, she didn't seem as in control as she wanted me to believe she was. "Well, you have to know *something*."

With one arm slung over the back of the sofa, I turned to look at her. "Listen. Jimmie made conversation with me on the plane. He asked where I was staying, and when I told him the Seacoast Majestic, he said that was where he was staying too. He asked me if I wanted to meet up for a drink later. Stupidly, and because I'd just been assaulted in the bathroom, I said sure, and I gave him my card with my cell number. I checked into my room and went down for a drink, and when I came back a few hours later, Jimmie was dead on my floor. Alright? That's it. That's the extent of the information I know."

"And he didn't give you anything?"

"Other than a migraine? No, he didn't."

"And you didn't find anything that didn't belong to you in your suitcase?"

"I didn't bring a suitcase."

She looked at me with pursed lips. "Who doesn't bring a suitcase on vacation?"

"I don't, alright. My ex packed my clothes for the trip, and I didn't want to be reminded of her, alright? So I left it behind."

She stared at me.

I pointed to the garbage can in the kitchen. "You can look in the garbage. You'll find a shopping bag from the resort clothing store and a receipt in it for a package of underwear and some clothes. Check my room if you don't believe me. The new clothes and the ones I wore on the way here are the only things you're going to find."

I watched her consider my words. Did she trust me, or did she not? She let out a groan and then stomped into the bedroom. I could hear her searching through my meager belongings. She was back in the living room seconds later. "Fine. I believe you, Drunk. Your ass is clueless."

"Fuck you very much." I rolled my head on my shoulders. "So, now that we've got that out of the way, are you going to tell me what the hell is going on?"

She gave a little puff of air out her nose and then aimed the gun at me again. "No, as a matter of fact, I'm not. I'm leaving. And if you tell anyone about this visit tonight, I'll find you and finish the job I came here to do. Got it?"

I looked down at Little Drunk. "Promises, promises."

## 20

WEDNESDAY, FEBRUARY 21, 2018

THE NEXT MORNING, THE SUN BEAMED IN THROUGH MY WINDOW, heating my skull until I thought it was in danger of exploding. I pinched an eye open and focused on the alarm clock on the nightstand.

*Fuck. 7:17.*

I hadn't gone to sleep until a little after two. I'd been too paranoid to sleep. My tropical getaway had turned into the vacation from hell, and in my intoxicated state, every little sound had me on edge.

I rolled over onto my back, and Little Drunk and I stared up at the ceiling together. The image of Natasha Prince conning me at the bar rolled back through my mind. I should have gone with my gut instinct, and I should have listened to my mother. "Don't bring home strays." How many times had she told me that?

*Fuck.*

When would I ever learn?

I thought about Natasha's demands. She wanted something. Something that she obviously thought Jimmie had given me. *Wanted what?* I wondered. I figured the people that had

ZANE MITCHELL

killed Jimmie in my room had been looking for the same thing that Natasha was looking for. Had they found it?

Natasha said that she'd seen the nod Jimmie had given me in the airport, and that was what had led her to believe that we were together. That nod *had* seemed odd to me too. Of course, how was I to have known that Jimmie was going to wind up dead on my motel room floor hours later? If I'd known that, I might have put more thought into his actions on the plane and in the terminal. But hindsight doesn't pay the rent, now does it?

Bits of our conversation echoed dully in my head.

*"And you didn't find anything that didn't belong to you in your suitcase?"*

*"I didn't bring a suitcase."*

Hey, whoever said I didn't have acting chops must not have seen my high school production of *Our Town*. I played Joe Crowell, Jr., and I sold the hell outta that paperboy.

I suddenly wondered if somehow Jimmie had managed to stash something in my bag. Maybe when I'd followed Natasha to the lavatory. The thought actually made sense.

I sat up in bed. I thought maybe I'd think better if I were vertical. The pulsing in my head told me it was a bad idea. Gripping my skull between my hands, I fought the headache and continued thinking.

Jimmie had been asleep when I'd gotten out of my seat, and he had been awake when I'd come back. He'd made sure to find out where I was staying. He'd gotten my cell number. He'd created a diversion at the airport. And then he'd found my room. The pieces were all coming together.

Despite my headache, I thunked my hands on either side of my head. What an idiot I'd been. How had none of these things registered in my brain as they were happening?

Shaking my head, I crawled out of bed and headed for the shower. I was going to need to get that suitcase back. I could only hope it was still exactly where I'd put it.

## 21

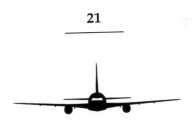

SHOWERED AND DRESSED IN MY LAST NEW TANK TOP, SHORTS, HAT, sunglasses, and flip-flops, I stood at the top of the stairs to the beach and peered over the railing and through the expanse of jungle that separated the resort from the ocean. Roosters pecked at the dirt, and a white-and-orange cat wandered about, weaving a figure eight between my legs.

A young couple with two small children came from the resort, carrying sand buckets and a duck-shaped inner tube. "Good morning," chirped a pear-shaped woman with a toddler on her hip.

"Morning," I grunted. I'd yet to have my morning Dr. Pepper or my morning constitutional, and I was anxious to have both. Especially since the latter relied on the former. I planned to stop into the resort gift shop after retrieving whatever item Jimmie had put inside my suitcase and pick up the soda. And after a night of boozing, I could safely assume I'd also be in the market for some new bathroom reading materials. I thought maybe I'd pick up an island newspaper and see if Jimmie's death had made island news.

I watched the young couple as they helped their small children navigate the long, winding stairs to the pool. I wanted to make sure they were far enough away before making my move. I didn't need anyone reporting to resort security that there was a strange man roaming the jungle. Especially since there was a sign posted on the other side of the railing that clearly read, "Guests Not Allowed Past This Point."

When the family was at a safe distance, I put a hand on the wooden post and scissored over the top rail, thus beginning my hunt for my suitcase.

Weaving and ducking through the thick island flora was a challenge. Never before had I seen trees like those I was now climbing through. Dense thickets plagued every step. In many places, roots stuck up out of the ground and caught my flip-flops. Strange snakelike seed pods lay in clumps on the forest floor, scaring the living shit out of me as every step made me think I was stepping in a snake den and had my heart in my throat.

Not only was the trek a challenge, but I also had to keep a close eye on the motel windows that faced the jungle. Many of them had curtains drawn, but there were a few that were open, though I had yet to see anyone. I was also counting them. Before I'd started, I'd counted how many rooms were between my original motel room and the stairs to the beach, and now I was trying to count the windows in reverse.

I struggled through the jungle for what felt like an hour before I came to what should have been the window beneath my motel room. I looked up at the balconies above me. They all looked alike, so aside from counting the windows, I had no way of knowing for sure if I was in the right spot. At least the curtains in the window on the ground floor were drawn. I was safe to start looking. I turned and faced the ocean with my hands on my hips. I could barely see glimpses of blue through the dense jungle.

"Where are you?" I mumbled into the forest, my shaded eyes scanning the forest floor. Only the vague sound of bird chirps and ocean waves answered me.

I pictured myself standing on my balcony, bag over my head, and wondered how far I would have been able to toss it. I pictured it landing several yards in front of me, so I began my search there. A half an hour after not readily finding the bag, I wondered if it had already been found. Had someone in the room on the ground floor seen it and gone exploring themselves to see what goodies lay inside? Or had these weird podlike snakes merely camouflaged it?

I removed my glasses and rubbed my temples. I'd been looking forever, and I was now filthy. My legs and feet were scratched up, and my new tank top had a tear in it. Why I'd thought it was a good idea to shower and dress *before* tromping through a tropical jungle was beyond me. I guess I'd thought hunting for my suitcase would be like a trek through the Black Hills or something. I'd pictured myself on solid ground with a nice little hiking path straight to my bag.

Just about to give up, I came to a realization. What if my bag had never actually made it to the ground? What if it had been caught up in the trees? I took my hat off and looked up into the forest webbing. Was it up there somewhere? I wandered around for another ten minutes, staring up at the trees.

Finally, I went back to my starting point, beneath the window I was sure was several rooms below mine and looked out at the trees. Vinelike branches hung about, cradling clumps of pod-snakes and other vines. And there it was. Slightly to my right, six yards ahead of me, cradled by a vine and covered with pod-snakes.

"Hot damn," I said, a smile finally covering my face. I'd found it!

I paced over to it and realized retrieving it wasn't going to be as easy as I'd thought. It was too far over my head for me to touch. I jumped, but because of the exposed roots of the trees, and the ridiculous shoes I wore, I quickly discovered that jumping was futile. I'd have to scale the tree and climb over.

*Fuck.*

Worst. Vacation. Ever.

Fucking understatement of the year.

I wallowed in self-pity for about ten seconds and then forced myself to suck it up. In my youth I'd been a Boy Scout. I'd climbed plenty of trees to feel comfortable doing it, and in a tiny twist of luck, I realized that these viney trees were actually easier to climb than regular trees because there were lots of hand- and footholds. So, climbing the nearest tree, I managed to get to the height I needed, and then I had to hang like a monkey on a vine. The word "monkey bars" didn't seem so silly now. One hand over the other, I scooted closer to my bag and worked to shake it loose.

"Ooh ooh, ahh ahh ahh," I belted out as I hung, using my weight to pull on the vines to loosen up their hold on my bag. Yes, making monkey noises was childish and immature, but not once have I claimed maturity. And in that moment, I needed the release to buoy my spirits.

My legs kicked as I hung—trying to keep the momentum going. I bounced and bounced and watched my bag bounce with me. At times I thought it should have fallen, but it didn't, and by now my arms and shoulders burned. Finally, I gave one more solid bounce, and a vine let go of its grasp, sending the bag tumbling to the ground.

"Wooo-hoo!" I wailed excitedly before leaping off the vine to the ground.

And then I promptly heard a scream. I glanced up and over my shoulder to see a woman with enormous jugs, clad only in a pair of panties in the first-floor window screaming. My eyes widened as my pulse thundered in my ears.

*Fuck.*

"Ahhhh!" she wailed, wrapping an arm over her shoulder and another over a hip.

I wanted to rush up to the window and assure her that I wasn't a Peeping Tom and that as scantily clad as she was, I'd seen it all before, but I didn't think she was in a mood to listen. So instead, I grabbed my suitcase and headed in the opposite direction of the way I'd come. I prayed there would be a break in the motel somewhere close and that it would get me closer to my cottage, where I could lie low in case she decided to call security.

The trek back to my room wasn't any easier than it had been getting there. In fact, it was actually more difficult because I had a suitcase in tow, and I felt like I was being chased. The upside was, it ended up being half the distance. I half-expected there to be highly armed security guards waiting for me when I emerged from the jungle, and I wasn't disappointed not to find them. In fact, no one waited for me at the exit. No angry husband or boyfriend. No maids. And no guests heading to the beach. There wasn't even a railing to climb over. Just a nondescript opening in the wall that led back to the cobblestone road.

I took pause to dust myself off and examine the red scratches and welts on my feet and ankles before extending the handle on my suitcase. Then I headed for my cottage, further down the road. That walk was more pleasant. And not feeling the pinch of security guards breathing down my neck, I half considered turning around and going back to the resort for my Dr. Pepper, but I didn't want to bump into Natasha Prince after having told her that I'd not brought a suitcase with me on my vacation. With that thought in mind, I was careful as I headed back, clinging to every shadow I could and making sure to stay as well hidden as possible despite the bright light of daytime.

Soon enough, the long run of motel rooms ended and the cottages began. I passed the first couple, then Al and Evelyn's. They were cottage number three, and Glenn Anderson was number four. Gary Wheelan was number five, and I passed duplexes six through nine before I noticed a truck parked between my cottage and the cottage next to mine. We shared a parking area and a pair of picnic tables. I was sure the truck hadn't been there when I'd left. I harkened back to Al's words. *"Hardly anyone has a car."*

The thought made my muscles tense up, and I suddenly wished I had a firearm tucked into my suitcase. I slunk ahead, stowed my suitcase behind a grove of trees and snuck around the beach side of duplexes nine and ten, until I could see the front end of the truck. It was parked on my half of the parking space. I had a sneaking suspicion it wasn't ten's truck. I swallowed hard and wished I'd thought to bring my cell phone. Not that I knew exactly how to call 911 on the British-owned island.

So I hunkered down behind the neighbor's cottage and waited. I made mental note of the truck. It was a black Chevy Silverado with a roll bar and a run of fog lights across the top —no license plates on the front. I debated sneaking around to the back to check for a back plate, when the door to my cottage burst open and two men carrying guns emerged.

## 22

I WATCHED THEM AS THEY TUCKED THEIR GUNS INTO THE BACK OF their jeans and covered them with their shirts. They were big guys. One white. One black. The white guy wore cowboy boots and a cowboy hat, and the black guy had an eye patch, a bald head, and a tattoo on the back of his neck. Neither one of them looked particularly friendly. I felt fairly confident they hadn't shown up to take me to lunch.

The white guy got into the driver's seat and, without so much as a backwards glance, tore into reverse and sped away, his tires spinning up a cloud of dust in my parking spot. I waited in my hiding spot for a few minutes, just to make sure no one else was going to pop out of my cottage wondering where their buddies had gone, before I slid across the grass to my cottage and peered inside the windows.

They'd broken the door's window so they could reach around to unlock it, and they'd trashed the place, that much I could see. I couldn't see anyone else inside, so I figured it was safe to go in. I went to the side door, gave one more look before opening the door, and called out from the doorjamb, "Hello!" Unarmed, I decided I'd rather deal with an intruder outdoors than in. Only silence greeted me.

I stepped over the pile of glass in the living room and looked around. The sofa cushions had been pulled off. The kitchen drawers had all been pulled out and emptied. Vic's wife's vase lay shattered on the floor. "Ooh, tsk tsk tsk," I chastised, shaking my head. "Mrs. Vic isn't going to like that."

I went to my room next, where I found the same thing. Drawers pulled out and emptied. I fingered the bedsheets they'd torn off the bed. "Oh thanks, the maid will appreciate the help," I said.

And then I heard a noise coming from the kitchen. I followed it. It was coming from beneath the counter in the kitchen. I squatted down and removed the toe kick from one of the cabinets. I stuck my hand inside and pulled out my phone and my passport. Right where I'd hidden them the night before, when I'd worried that Natasha Prince might come back while I slept.

I looked down at my phone. There was no Caller ID, just a number I didn't recognize. "Hello?"

"Officer Drunk?" said a deep voice on the other end. I recognized it right away.

"Sergeant Gibson! How's it going? Hey, listen, why don't you just call me Drunk?" I didn't like my cop status being tossed around so freely. I preferred to keep that on the DL until we'd gotten everything straightened out.

"Office Drunk, would you mind meeting me at my office? I've got some things I'd like to talk to you about."

I looked around my destroyed cottage. "I've got some things I'd like to talk to you about as well."

"Good. Then I'll see you soon."

"Yes, as..." The line went dead. I looked at the phone and muttered to myself, finishing my sentence. "As soon as I can find a ride and get myself some caffeine." I sighed and jammed the phone into my pocket.

Looking around, I felt sick to my stomach as the realization sunk in that those two island hillbillies had been here to kill me. I let my head fall back on my shoulders for a moment. My mouth hung open. "Ugh!" I grunted. "Fuck!"

There was a knock at my door. "Drunk? You alright?"

My heart lurched at the sound, but I was thankful to recognize Al's voice. I padded over to the door and peered at him through the shattered glass. "Yeah, I'm alright." I opened the door.

Al came inside and took one look around. His bushy white brows lifted, wrinkling his forehead more than usual. One gnarled hand went to his gaping mouth. "Drunk! You throw a party?"

I put a hand on my hip and stared at him. "No I didn't throw a party, Al. I think the guys who killed Jimmie came looking for me." I said it loud, so I wouldn't have to repeat myself.

"How do you know it was the guys who killed Jimmie?"

"I don't, but you have to assume. Otherwise it's quite the coincidence, wouldn't you think?"

He looked up at me. "Eh?"

"I don't know! I just assume." I was feeling frustrated.

Al's head bobbed up and down as his watery eyes took in the damage they'd done to the room. Then he winced. "They broke Shirley's vase! Oh, she's not going to like that."

"No, she's not," I agreed. "Hey, Al. I need to get into town. The cops wanna speak with me. You know how to get me there?"

"Sure," said Al. "Want me to go with you?"

I lifted a shoulder. Having someone who was more familiar with the island customs and people than I was wouldn't be a bad thing. "If you have the time?"

"Are you kidding? I'm a retired old man on an island. Time is all I've got. Let me just go tell Evie where I'm going."

I nodded. "Hey, you mind if I stow something over at your place?"

"No, of course not." He beckoned me as he stepped carefully over the glass in my doorway. "Come on. And don't worry about this mess. We'll get the desk girls to tell Ozzie what happened and get a better door put on this place and have them clean up this mess. No big deal."

"Thanks, Al."

"No problem, no problem." He shook his head as he started towards his place. "There are some guys that have all the luck, you know? And then there are the other guys, Drunk. Sucks to be the other guys."

I nodded. "Yeah, it does, Al. Yeah, it does."

# 23

After storing my suitcase at Al and Evelyn's place, I walked with Al up to the resort. I bought a Snickers bar and a Dr. Pepper for breakfast while he scored us a newspaper and a ride into town. The tourist shuttle had already left for the day, so we got to ride in one of the resort's cars instead. It was a four-door white Ford Taurus with the resort's logo pressed onto the doors.

Riding in the backseat, I fiddled with my cell phone, scrolling through all my missed calls and missed texts.

None from Pamela, thank God. The thought of her messages being undelivered and her figuring out she'd been blocked brought a smirk to my face.

"What's so funny?" asked Al in the seat next to me as he browsed through the newspaper.

I lifted a shoulder and pointed at my phone. "I blocked my ex. The thought of her being mad about that brings joy to my heart."

"She dump you, did she?"

"No, she cheated on me," I said loudly so I wouldn't have to repeat myself.

I caught the driver glancing at me in his rearview mirror.

"What'd she do that for?"

"Hell if I know."

He gave me a sideways glance. "There's always a reason people cheat. Either they're unhappy, or they're not getting something at home that they want so they go out looking for it somewhere else."

I looked at Al sharply. "She wasn't getting banged. That's what she wanted that she wasn't getting."

"She wasn't getting banged? You and her weren't..." He wiggled his fingers at me.

"No. We were saving it for our wedding night."

He stared at me while rolling that around in his mind. Then he gave a momentary glance down at my lap. "Ahh. Is the old escalator in need of repair?"

I rolled my eyes. "My escalator is working just fine, thank you. My escalator goes to the top floor and beyond! Hell, my escalator blows the roof off buildings, alright?"

Al closed his newspaper. "You're not trying to tell me you're a virgin, are you? I mean, you aren't exactly a spring chicken anymore."

I puffed air out my mouth. "Fuck no, I'm not a virgin. And neither was she."

"Then why weren't you... ya know, doin' the old in 'n' out?"

"It was a thing I was trying. You know. A thing. To save myself. For marriage. She was supposed to be doing the thing too. Apparently I was trying harder than she was."

He frowned and his brows lifted. "Well, that was a stupid thing. I mean, who does that in this day and age?"

"Thanks, Al. I appreciate that."

He opened his paper again. "No problem."

Sighing, I turned my attention back to my phone and scrolled through the texts and missed calls. I had messages from some of my buddies on the force checking on me. About eight dozen missed calls from my mother. Zero missed calls from Pops. And several missed calls from numbers I didn't recognize. Either it was Pamela calling from a friend's phone or it was work stuff. I didn't know, but I had a minute and I decided I better use it to call my mother before she freaked out and did something stupid like filing a missing person's report.

She picked up on the second ring.

"Hey, Ma."

I heard her suck in her breath on the other end. "Terrence? Is that you?"

I rolled my eyes. "Who else calls you Ma from my phone number?"

"Danny, it's Terrence!" she screeched into my ear. "Terrence, where are you? Your father and I have been worried sick."

I glanced out the window at the palm trees and the blue-and-white puffy sky as it rolled by. It was the middle of February. It was probably twenty-five degrees back home. There had been snow on the ground when I'd boarded the plane. "I'm in my apartment."

"Don't lie to your mother," she snapped. "I know you're not at your apartment. You're out of the country, aren't you?"

"Well, if you know where I am, then why did you ask?"

"I didn't think it was my place."

"Obviously you didn't think that, Ma. Otherwise you would have just let me lie to you."

"I taught you not to lie to your parents. Now, where are you? On that island?"

"You tell me. You seem to know so much."

"Don't get smart with me, Daniel Terrence Drunk."

My head rolled forward on my neck. "Ma, listen. I'm fine, alright? Don't worry about me. I just need time to clear my head."

"Well, when are you coming back?"

"In about a week and a half."

"You shouldn't be alone right now. Pam's really sorry for what happened, Terrence."

"Mom. Tell me you haven't been speaking to Pam."

"She keeps calling!"

"Hang up on her!"

"But she's like my daughter-in-law. I can't hang up on my daughter-in-law."

"She's not your daughter-in-law, Ma. She's a heartless bitch that you used to know."

"Terrence," hissed my mother. "Language!"

"Sorry, Ma. Listen, I can't talk. I'm headed into town to do some souvenir shopping. You want something?"

"Ooh, get me one of those hula dancers that sway when they're on your dashboard. I've always wanted one of those."

"I'll see if I can find one. No more talking to Pamela, alright?"

"What do I do if she calls, then?"

"Hang up. Promise?"

My mother was quiet. And then finally, in a meeker voice, she said, "Oh, fine. I'll try."

"Thanks. Tell Pops I said hey. He'd like it here. All the booze you can drink."

She sucked in her breath. "Terrence! You're not drinking again, are you?"

"Ma, you're cutting out. I can't hear you. Ma?" I hit the End button, and the car fell silent.

Al shook his head while reading the newspaper. "Tsk tsk tsk."

"What?" I huffed.

"Lying to your mother."

"As if you've never lied to your mother?"

"My mother's dead."

"Yeah, well, I'm sure you lied to her once or twice while she was alive."

Al didn't say anything, just continued reading his newspaper.

"What's so interesting in that goddamned newspaper?"

He pointed at it. "Merck shares are up."

"So?"

He made a face and lifted a shoulder. "Eh, they hit a rough patch the last half of the year. I'm glad to see they're finally hitting their stride again."

I groaned and let my head fall back against my headrest. I heard Al turn the page in the newspaper.

"Ooh, looky looky," he sang.

I opened one eye.

"There's an article in here about the shooting at the Seacoast Majestic."

My head popped up. "What's it say?"

"Says a man with no identification was found in an American tourist's motel room at the Seacoast Majestic. Authorities are searching for witnesses and have yet to notify the family. As of now there are no leads."

"Fucking great," I grunted, letting my head fall back against the seat again. "Just fucking great."

## 24

STANDING OUTSIDE THE CAR IN FRONT OF THE PARADISE ISLE Royal Police Force, I passed Akoni, the driver, a twenty. "We won't be long. Can you wait here for us?" I looked up at the large white building that looked more like a seedy Florida hotel than an island police station. The arched doorways and clay roof tiles were vaguely reminiscent of the apartment building that Jack Tripper lived in on *Three's Company.* Only the cruisers parked out front gave away the fact that it was actually a police station.

"Yes, sir," he agreed. He pointed to the parking lot across the street. "I'll be over there."

I nodded and Al and I entered the building. I glanced up at the man working the front desk. He was young, likely in his early twenties with a round, dimpled face and onyx eyes that didn't quite look in the same direction. His name tag read Jefferson.

"Excuse me, I have an appointment with Sergeant Gibson."

"Are you Officer Drunk?"

I looked at Al and grimaced. "Just Drunk is fine."

"He's waiting for you. I can take you back there." The man looked at Al and pointed towards three rows of chairs in a small room off to the side. It was half-full of scantily clad women, scruffy-looking men, and other nefarious characters. "Sir, you can have a seat there."

I pointed at him. "He's with me."

"Yes, sir, I see that, but Sergeant Gibson didn't ask to speak with anyone else. Just you. If we need your friend, we'll know right where to find him."

Al hobbled towards the shoddy waiting area. "It's alright, Drunk. I'll be fine. You just go do your thing."

"You're sure?"

"We don't really have a choice, now do we?"

I sighed. "Alright. I'll try and make it fast."

He nodded and shooed me away.

I followed Officer Jefferson through the busy office full of cubicles and uniformed men and women to a windowed room. He knocked on the door and then poked his head in. "Sergeant Gibson? Officer Drunk is here to see you."

"Send him in."

I rolled my eyes.

"You can go in now."

"Thanks."

"Officer Drunk," said Sergeant Gibson, giving me the stiffest of head nods. The man's expression hadn't changed since the last time I'd seen him. He was still stone-cold somber, and even though I was taller than him and outweighed him by at least fifty pounds, he was more than slightly intimidating. "Thank you for coming in today."

"Sergeant Gibson." I nodded back, reflexively deepening my voice. "Not a problem."

"Have a seat." He gestured to the chair in front of his desk. "So, Officer Drunk. How is your vacation to the island thus far?"

Crossing my leg over a knee, I quirked a smile. "Eh, I've had better."

"Yes. Not quite the vacation you had intended," he said in his stilted accent and only a hint of a smile.

"No. Not quite."

"So tell me a little bit about your reason for visiting Paradise Isle, if you don't mind? You said something about it being your honeymoon?"

I pursed my lips and uncrossed my legs, pushing myself up higher in my seat. "Yes. It was supposed to be."

"Do you care to expand on that?"

"Not much else to say. I was engaged, and the night before my wedding, I found my fiancée in bed with her ex-boyfriend. And instead of staying at home to wallow in self-pity, I went on the honeymoon without her."

"Very upsetting, I am sure."

"I'm alright."

"So, when did you say you flew to the island?"

"The day before yesterday. I'd literally only been on the island maybe a handful of hours before the man was discovered dead in my room."

"Interesting, isn't it, Officer Drunk? You fly to my island, and a man is killed less than a few hours later."

I winced. I didn't care for his tone. "I flew in with a plane full of other people too, Sergeant Gibson. What does that have to do with anything?"

"That plane full of people didn't just happen to find a dead man in their room hours later, did they, Officer Drunk?"

"Listen, I don't know what you want me to say. If you've checked with any of the witnesses, they'll tell you. I was at the bar while the guy was killed. Have you talked to Cami Vergado yet? She'll tell you it wasn't me she saw coming out of the room."

"Cami Vergado?"

I nodded. "Yeah, Camila Vergado. The maid who heard the shots and saw the guys fleeing my room. She'll tell you it wasn't me."

"How do you know the witness's name?"

I made a face. "Because I *asked*." I felt like adding, *duh*.

"Now I know that I've asked you this before, Officer Drunk, but can you tell me exactly how you knew the man in your room?"

My breath caught in my throat. I'd mentally prepared myself for this answer. I'd already told Sergeant Gibson that I didn't know the man. And if I retracted that answer, I was going to look even more guilty. But the truth of the matter was I *didn't* know the man in my room. I'd sat next to him on the plane—*period*. He'd told me his name and where he was from, but I had no way of knowing if that was all the truth. He could have easily been lying to me. "Like I told you that night, Sergeant. I didn't know that man."

Sergeant Gibson scratched his chin and leaned back in his chair. "His name was Jimmie Wallace. He was an Australian man."

My stomach immediately did a flip-flop. So he'd been telling the truth. "Okay?"

"And he happened to have an airline ticket in his pocket."

In that moment, I wanted to close my eyes and put my head between my knees. "Did he?"

Sergeant Gibson lifted his almost invisible eyebrows. "He did. As a matter of fact, we did a little bit of digging, and you'll never guess what we discovered."

I swallowed hard. "That he was a famous rugby player?"

Sergeant Gibson's brows lowered as he leaned forward. "No. That he was your seatmate from the United States to Paradise Isle. Can you believe that?"

I put on my best confused look. "My seatmate? Sergeant, I didn't get a chance to get to know my seatmate. He was sleeping for the first half of the trip, and I slept for the second half of the trip. I couldn't even tell you what the man looked like."

"You didn't get to know him, and yet somehow he showed

up in your hotel room just a few hours later? You expect me to believe that?"

I lifted my hands up on either side of myself. "Maybe he followed me! Maybe he was planning to rob me. I don't know!"

Sergeant Gibson leaned back in his seat again. "I find it very interesting that he had your business card and personal cell phone number in his pocket. Don't you?"

"Again—I carried a few business cards in my ditty bag. He had to have pocketed one when he was in my room, trying to rob me."

"Uh-huh. Officer Drunk, would you please relay the exact events that happened once your plane landed on my island?"

I sighed and retraced my every move for him. I knew he was just waiting for me to change my story in some way or add a new detail or mess up in some way, but when you're telling the truth, there's no chance of that happening. The only thing I wasn't being forthcoming about was that I had spoken a few words to Jimmie on the plane. That was it, but that didn't mean I'd *killed* the man.

When I was done giving him the play-by-play, I leaned forward in my seat a little. "Now, listen. I came here to talk to you as well. Artie Balladares got me a new room over at the Seacoast Majestic, and right before I left to come here, two big guys in a black Chevy Silverado with a roll bar broke into my new place."

He cocked his head to the side. "Is that right?" His tone spoke to his disbelief.

"Yes, that's right." I felt my face heating up. I pointed at his notepad. "Don't you think you should maybe jot this down? It's gotta be related."

"Why do you think these people are so interested in the rooms that you are staying in Officer Drunk?"

"Please. It's just Drunk. I'm not an officer on your island, so I'd just prefer to be called Drunk."

Sergeant Gibson leaned back in his chair and steepled his fingers. "I'm glad to hear you say that you realize you are not an officer on my island, Mr. Drunk. I would not want you to take the law into your own hands. My men and I will handle this investigation."

"Yes, I understand that, but I'm going to do whatever I have to do to ensure that I don't killed before returning to the States."

"*If you're allowed* to return to the States, Mr. Drunk."

# 25

My eyes widened. "What's that supposed to mean? I didn't kill anyone. Why wouldn't I be allowed to return home?"

"Because I may need to ask you more questions."

"I'm here, aren't I? Ask away. What else do you want to know?" I pointed at his notepad again. "How about taking down descriptions of the guys that broke the window in my cottage? I saw them, you know. They tore the place apart looking for something. I also had a woman pull a gun on me last night."

"Is that right?"

"Yes, that's right!"

"Why are you getting so anxious, Mr. Drunk?"

"Because it seems like you aren't taking me seriously."

Sergeant Gibson's tone remained steady. "Of course I am taking you seriously."

"And yet you're not even remotely curious about any of these other people?"

Sergeant Gibson looked down at his desk. "Mr. Drunk, did anyone else *see* this woman pull a gun on you?"

I frowned. "No, it was in my room. We were alone. But the bartender saw us together at the bar."

"Oh, I see. So you were drinking with a woman at the bar and then you returned to your room with her, and she pulled a gun on you?"

I cradled my head in my hands. *Fuck*. Why did it feel like he was twisting my words? I sat up straighter again. "No. You don't understand. She wanted something from me."

"I'll bet she did. And did you give it to her, Mr. Drunk?"

"No! I didn't! I didn't have what she wanted."

"And that's why she pulled the gun on you?"

"Ugh!"

"Why so testy, Mr. Drunk?"

I needed to reset the score and take a minute. I looked up at him. "Can I have a glass of water or something? I'm feeling kind of parched."

He stared at me but then pushed a button on his desk. "Officer Cruz, can you make yourself useful and bring in a bottle of water for Mr. Drunk?"

A crackly voice clipped through the speaker. "Yes, sir."

We stared at each other then, in a silent challenge of sorts. Finally, the door opened and in walked a young female officer. She had her long, straight black hair pulled into a sleek ponytail. She was average height and had an athletic build, with high cheekbones and a long, narrow nose. Her dark chocolate eyes glanced down at me as she dropped the bottle of water on Sergeant Gibson's desk. "Here you go, sir."

The second I saw her, I instinctively rose to my feet. My head tipped sideways as I drank in her beauty.

He nodded at her stiffly. "That will be all, Officer Cruz."

I smiled at her as I took the water off the desk and unscrewed the cap. She was an uplifting vision. "Thank you, Officer Cruz. I really appreciate it."

Sergeant Gibson frowned. "No thanks necessary. She wasn't busy. Were you, Officer Cruz?"

Her small smile disappeared almost immediately. She

didn't say anything else before walking out and shutting the door behind her.

Taking a swig, I cast a half glance over my shoulder. Something about seeing her had done something for me. Centered my gravity or restored the wind to my sails. Oddly, I no longer felt alone on an island, so to speak.

I looked at Sergeant Gibson, this time with a straightened spine. "Look, Sergeant Gibson. I didn't kill that guy Jimmie. I know you'd like to pin it on the American cop tourist and wrap the whole case up with a nice red, white, and blue bow, but that's not what happened. So, you're actually going to have to do some detective work and find Cami Vergado and the woman that pulled a gun on me last night, and the two guys in the Chevy Silverado that broke into my room today. I'm willing to bet they're the same guys that killed your victim. Alright? Now, I don't know anything else that would help you. But I'm sure if you poked around, you'd quickly discover that I'm telling the truth and you'd find your guys. Now. If you don't have any other questions for me, I'm going to go. This is supposed to be my vacation, but I've had a lousy week. I'd like to go bury my ass in the sand somewhere and take advantage of the all-inclusive resort I spent a lot of money on. So, if you'll excuse me..." I stood up then.

"I was not finished with the interview, Mr. Drunk," he said authoritatively, yet without moving.

"You have no evidence to tie me to your victim, except that he broke into my room and lifted one of my business cards and sat next to me on an airplane. Otherwise, you'd have me incarcerated by now. So I'd say this interview is over, Sergeant Gibson. Call me when you've done your job and have some real evidence to go on."

I stormed out of his office then and down the hallway to the front door. I'd had enough of Paradise Isle. It certainly didn't seem like Paradise to me. I was ready to get the hell outta Dodge, and I was thankful that Sergeant Gibson hadn't confiscated my passport.

"Let's go, Al," I grunted from the vestibule.

With his head rolled back on his shoulders, Al snored softly.

I walked over to him and gave him a squeeze on the shoulder. "Let's go."

He jolted awake, his eyes wide. "What?"

"Time to go. These cops here are jerks. I'm over it." Whether I said it loudly for Al's benefit or so that the cop at the counter overheard my complaint, I didn't know. All I knew was that I was frustrated.

Al put a hand on either side of his armchair and pushed himself up slowly. "What happened?"

I pointed to the door. "I'll tell you in the car."

Outside, the sun hit my eyes, causing me to wince. I put my hat and sunglasses back on and scanned the parking lot across the street. I was thankful to see that our ride had actually stuck around as promised. No sooner had I taken a step off the curb than I heard the door open behind me and a female voice call out to me. "Officer Drunk, wait."

I turned around to see Officer Cruz staring back at me.

"Do you have a second?"

I looked at Al. Whether he had heard her or not, he knew a beautiful woman when he saw one. He lifted his brows in surprise. Then he pointed at the car. "I'll, uh, just go wait for you in the car."

"Thanks, Al." I looked at the woman. Her brows were knitted together pensively. "Officer Cruz, right?"

"Yes," she said before casting a backwards glance over her shoulder. "I only have a moment. I just wanted to let you know that you need to be really careful. Okay?"

"Be careful?"

"Law enforcement on the island doesn't take very kindly to Americans. I don't understand it, but it's the way it is."

"I've noticed." I'd also noticed how perfectly imperfect the band of freckles across the bridge of her nose was, and how sincere her big brown eyes were when they looked at me.

She nodded. "The word around the office is that you're a police officer back in the States?"

"Yeah, well, unfortunately that doesn't help me down here."

"I know. If anything, it's made things worse," she admitted. "Sergeant Gibson's not going to be very helpful in getting you out of the predicament you're in."

"I didn't expect him to be." I lifted a brow and ran a hand across the back of my neck. "Maybe you'll be helpful?"

Her head dipped sideways, and a stray piece of hair slid out of her ponytail. "I'm at the bottom of the totem pole here, Officer Drunk."

"Please, just Drunk. Being a cop down here just makes things worse."

"Drunk," she agreed with a half-smile. "I wish I could do something to help you out, I just don't know what I can do. I only thought I should warn you. The cops here aren't going to have your back."

I shook my head. "I don't understand. Why would you wanna help me?"

"I'm from the States. I was born there, in Florida. And then my family moved to the island when I was in grade school. Those guys in there know where I'm from, and they hold it against me. The fact that I'm a female doesn't do me any favors either. That's why I'm on the bottom of the totem pole, even though I've been working here longer than some of them. It'll never change. And I just don't like the way tourists get treated by the police here. Especially American tourists. I just thought you'd like to know you've got an advocate on your side."

"You think I'm innocent?"

She shrugged. "I'd like to think you're innocent. You're a cop."

"There are lots of dirty cops out there, though. Being a cop doesn't make me innocent."

A soft smile crossed her face. "I don't know. Maybe I just sensed something different in you. You seemed like one of the good guys."

I pulled off my sunglasses and smiled at her. "I am one of the good guys."

"We'll see, won't we."

"Yeah." I looked back at the car, where Al was waiting for me. "Hey, look. I gotta go. Mind if I call you if I run into any snags?"

"No, I'll help how I can."

I gave her a smile before starting across the street. Then I glanced back at her. "What's your first name, Officer Cruz?"

"It's Francesca. Francesca Cruz."

"Francesca. Fitting."

"Fitting? What does that mean?"

"A beautiful name for a beautiful woman." I lifted my hat to her and gave her a winning smile before I got in the backseat of the car. "We'll talk soon, Officer Cruz."

## 26

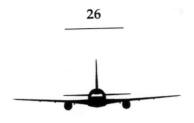

"Well, how'd it go?"

I felt Al's eyes boring into me as we drove away. "Not so great. They don't like American tourists. Especially ones that are cops."

"I told you that, didn't I?"

"Yeah, you told me that. They're gonna try and pin this on me. I can feel it."

Al grimaced. "I won't let 'em. You were with me the whole night."

"You know, the only way I'm gonna be cleared of this is if I do my own investigation. I don't think Sergeant Gibson could give a rat's ass about finding out what Cami Vergado saw that night. I bet he hasn't even asked Ozzy Messina for copies of the security tapes yet. He doesn't want to prove that it wasn't me."

Al's head bobbed. "Alright, then, so you're gonna have to prove it yourself. You're a cop. You know what to do."

I shrugged and looked out the window. "I'm a patrol officer. I pull people over and give them speeding tickets and make 'em walk the line if I smell booze. I'm not a detective. I've never even tried to pretend that I *wanted* to be a detective."

"A cop's a cop, Drunk."

I sighed. "That's not true."

"You graduated from the police academy, didn't you? You've been getting a paycheck, haven't you?"

I shrugged. "You just don't get it, Al. I only became a cop because there came a point in my life where I needed to stop fucking around and get a real job. So I went to the academy. At thirty-two years old, I was the oldest motherfucker in my class. All the other fresh-faced cop wannabes there knew they wanted to be a cop since they'd been in diapers. I was only there because my buddy Mikey was a cop and he suggested it. I thought a badge, a gun, and some flashy lights didn't sound all bad. Plus, cops seemed to have a sense of purpose, and according to my folks, that was something that was sorely lacking in my life."

Al stared at me after my little speech before shaking his head. "I'm not entirely sure I heard everything you just mumbled. Why don't people enunciate their words anymore? It's a lost art, really." He waved a hand. "You think you're a terrible cop? What's that got to do with the price of eggs in China? I mean, seriously! Who gives a hoot if you were the worst damn cop in the whole continental United States? If you're accused of a murder, you defend yourself. You got hair on your balls don'tcha?"

I flinched. "You really wanna get a look at my balls, don't you, Al?"

He threw up his arms. "For crying out loud, it's a saying, you moron. You're a man, ain't ya?" He didn't wait for an answer. "Then be a man! Solve your own damn problems. These cops aren't gonna coddle you, Drunk. They're not gonna hold your hand. So what if your girl screwed around on you? So what if you're on vacation? You think these cops care that you got two weeks off work and want to spend it trying to get laid? They don't give a shit. You gotta man up and do what you have to do to clear your name."

I sighed. Maybe Al was right. I'd been so busy licking my wounds and focusing on getting laid that I hadn't been on the offense. I'd been playing defense, and *barely*. I was like a linebacker with a gimp. How's a guy gonna sack a quarterback if he's too busy covering his head so he doesn't get hurt by the guy in front of him? If I was going to untangle myself from the situation I was in, I needed to think and act like the cop that I was.

"Yeah, alright. I catch what you're throwing, Al. I'll get it together."

"Good."

We drove in silence for a while. Finally, Al looked at me again. "So, where we gonna start?"

"We?" I asked before taking the last flat swig of my Dr. Pepper.

"Yeah, *we*. Cops don't work alone, do they? Don't they have partners? All the good ones do anyway. Starsky and Hutch. Tango and Cash. Crockett and Tubbs. Cagney and Lacey."

I nearly spat out my soda. "Cagney and Lacey? You know they're women, right?"

Al held up a finger in front of his crazy smile. "Right, but they were partners."

"Listen, Al. I like you, but I can't be dragging an old-timer around this island while hunting for bad guys. They have guns, you know. You could wind up shot. And then what's Evelyn supposed to do?"

He waved a hand. "Eh, she's got Fern. She doesn't need me."

"Al, be serious. If I'm seriously going to find out who killed Jimmie, things could take a real bad turn if I'm not careful. I can't risk you getting hurt."

He thumped his chest with the pads of his fingers. "You wouldn't be taking the risk. I'd be taking the risk."

"Whatever, Al. I don't know about partnering up. I tell you

what—you get your wife's permission, and I'll think about letting you tag along."

"Tag along? You think I want to go with you just to *tag along*?"

I curled my lip. "Well, what else would you call it?"

"I call it lending you my years of wisdom and experience."

"I call it babysitting, Al."

Al threw up his hands in disgust. "Fine, then don't take me if you think you'd be babysitting."

"Oh, now you're just being petty."

"Petty! You little asshole. You think just because I'm a few years older than you, I need babysitting? Just because my ears don't turn up loud anymore and it takes me longer to pee than it used to doesn't mean my brain isn't working just like it did when I was your age."

"I never said your brain wasn't working."

"Alright, then. What's your problem?"

"Well, for starters, you said it. Your ears don't turn up loud anymore. I have to yell at you for you to hear me. I can't be yelling at you when we're hiding from the bad guys."

"Fine. I'll put my hearing aids in. I hate the goddamned things, but if that's your issue, I'll do it."

"And what if we get chased by guys with guns? You're not especially spry anymore."

"You think I can't take a fall? Guys my age fall all the time. It's what we're known for."

"Right, well, it's the getting back up that's the problem, now isn't it?"

"Why do you think I need a partner? I fall, and you give me a hand to get back up."

"Well, what's in it for me?"

"You don't know anybody on this island, but I got connections! I gotcha that sweet cottage, didn't I? See, I know people!"

I shook my head. "I just don't understand why you'd want to help me, Al. What's in it for you?"

Al's face took on a wistful look then as he looked at me sideways. "You think it's fun to be retired?"

"Yeah! I do, as a matter of fact."

"Well, I'll tell you the truth. It's fun for about a month."

"Only a month?"

Al waved a crooked finger at me. "At first you sit around in the mornings. You know, because you can. You don't have to rush off anywhere or do anything. But after you've worked your whole life, sitting gets old real fast." He held out an arm and tapped a gnarled finger against his skin.

"I've got German blood flowing through these veins. Germans can't just sit around. So you start doing the things you've neglected. You organize the garage and clean the gutters. You sharpen the blades on your lawn mower. You paint the shed. You trim the privets in the yard—you know, do the whole honey-do list.

"And then one day, you're done with that. And so you try and find a hobby. Finding a hobby when you're my age isn't like finding a hobby at your age. I'm not gonna learn to play golf at this age. Yeah, I enjoy fishing, but I don't wanna spend the rest of my life cleaning fish. You know? So then what happens is, you get bored.

"And so when your wife says, 'Let's move to an island in the Caribbeans,' you go, 'Alright, dear. Whatever you want.' Because you can't think of any reason why you *shouldn't* move to an island in the Caribbeans.

"So now you're here. You can only play cards so often. You can only drink so much coffee or so many whiskey sours or soak up so much sun. You need other things to keep your mind young. So, I figure, helping you figure out who's trying to kill you might give me something to do for a week or two. And if it gets me killed in the process, eh, I've lived my life. I'm at peace."

I stared at Al. I'd never looked at a retired person and thought, *Poor you, you don't have to go to work anymore.* I always assumed they were looking at me, thinking, *Poor you, you schmuck, you still have to go to work for the next thirty years.* I sighed, tired of arguing. "Fine, Al. You can be my partner. Alright?"

"Alright."

We sat quietly for a minute. I pictured Mrs. Al swatting me in the back of the head with a newspaper for letting her husband go with me to hunt bad guys. "But I'm not taking you anywhere until Mrs. Al gives her approval and you put in your hearing aids. Got it?"

He looked up at me and nodded. "Yeah, I got it."

"Alright, so do we have a deal?" I held a hand out to him.

He took it, giving it a solid squeeze, and then smiled at me like a man who'd just traded his life savings in for a Ferrari. "Deal."

## 27

BACK AT THE RESORT, AL AND I STOPPED AT THE FRONT COUNTER. The woman who had checked me in two days prior was working again today.

"Good morning, Mariposa," began Al. "We want to speak with Cami Vergado."

The woman smiled. "Good morning, Mr. Becker. I'm sorry, but Cami isn't here right now."

I leaned forward on the counter and gave the woman a winning smile. Part of good detective work was establishing rapport. Al seemed proficient in that arena already. If I was going to get anywhere with the staff at the resort, I knew I needed to do the same. "When's the next time that she works?"

Mariposa's dark eyes swiveled from me to Al. He gave her a little wink, causing her to smile. "She was supposed to work today."

"She didn't show up?" asked Al.

Mariposa shook her head.

"Is that unusual for her?" I asked. "Not to show up for work?"

The woman shrugged. "I couldn't say. Can I have someone else help you with something, sir?"

I grimaced. "No, I just really need to speak with Cami. Did she come in yesterday?"

"No, sir. I don't believe she did."

"Mariposa, may we please speak with Ozzy Messina?" asked Al.

"Mr. Messina is out to lunch right now. Would you like me to have him call you when he gets back to the resort?"

Al nodded and then, with a glance at me, he pointed at Mariposa. "Give her your number, Drunk."

I wrote it down and handed it to her. "Thank you, Mariposa, we really appreciate your help."

I thought I saw a glimmer of a smile, but I couldn't be sure that I'd softened her up. I made a mental to note to keep working on it.

Al scratched the white patch of hair behind his ear. "Now what?"

"Now you're going to go have a talk with your wife and put your hearing aids in. I'm going to go back to my room. I need to make a call."

---

WHILE WE'D BEEN GONE, someone had covered my cottage's broken windowpane with a piece of plywood. The broken glass had been swept up, but the rest of the apartment was still trashed. Apparently maid service hadn't made it that far down the block yet.

I spent a few minutes tidying up. I put all the cushions back on my sofa and righted a lamp that had been tipped over, straightening the shade. I put the kitchen drawers back on their sliders and dumped an armful of silverware and other random kitchen paraphernalia into the sink. I even found a broom in a small closet and swept up the remnants of Vic's wife's vase, dropping the shattered blue-and-white pieces into the garbage can.

Then I sat down on the sofa and put my feet up on the coffee table. I pulled my phone out of my pocket and dialed. The person on the other end picked up on the third ring.

"Schwarzkopf here."

"Mikey, buddy, it's T-Bone."

"T-Bone! Where the hell are you? You got a lot of people worried about you."

"Worried about me? Why the fuck are people worried about me?"

"Because you haven't returned anyone's calls. I went by the hotel on Monday, but you'd split already. I've been by your place three times since then, but you're never there. Your girl is freaking the hell out. She won't stop calling the station."

"She's not my girl anymore, Mikey. We're over."

"Tell that to her. She thinks there's hope, buddy."

"Puh," I breathed. "Trust me. There's no hope for that one anymore. I'm already over it."

"So where you at, then?"

"I went on the trip. You know, the honeymoon. I used the tickets we had."

Mikey laughed on the other end. I could picture him leaning back in his squeaky detective's chair and putting his feet up on his desk. "Get outta here! You went without her?"

"You think I'd bring her with me?" I shook my head. "No, man. I was hoping there'd be some chicks out here, but this place is all geriatrics and honeymooners."

"No kidding?"

"It's kinda crazy. Hey, listen. I'm in kind of a predicament down here. I was hoping maybe you could help me out."

I proceeded to give Mikey the lowdown on the girl on the plane, Jimmie, Al, the guys who trashed my room, everything. When he was done laughing at the fact that a female had pulled a gun on me just as I'd thought I was going to score, I gave him her name. "Natasha Prince. She was on my flight out of Atlanta. She knows what's going on here, Mikey. I need to find her."

"Yeah, I'll see what I can dig up."

"Check the seat next to mine too, would ya? Find out what you can about Jimmie. The cops think his last name is Wallace, and he claimed to be from Australia. But you know, see what you can dig up on him, get his priors and whatnot. Alright?"

"Yeah. I'll get right on it. So what's your plan?"

I sighed and pulled my feet off the coffee table. Leaning forward, I let my head fall into my free hand. "I really don't know, Mikey. This detective stuff is what you're good at. Not me."

Mikey's calm, cool voice poured out of the receiver. "Listen, T-Bone. You got this. Alright? You're a smart guy. You've got the brain. You've got the training. You just need to have a little faith in yourself. You know, it was cool when we were younger that everyone thought you were this easy-going, wiseass party guy. But you're a grown-up now. Now *your* shit is on the line. Now's the time to buck up. You know? Handle your business."

Despite the fact that he couldn't see it, I gave him a half-smile. "Yeah, buddy. I know. You sound like a guy I know down here. He's blowing the same bullshit in my ear."

"It's not bullshit, T. If someone's telling you that down there, you listen to him. He sounds like a very wise man."

I chuckled. "Yeah. He's also a wiseass, but I hear ya."

"Alright. Gimme some time on this and I'll get back to you."

"Okay."

"Stay safe, my friend."

"You too, buddy."

I hung up and stared at my phone and wondered what Mikey would do next. I scrolled through my missed calls and recognized the area codes of almost every single call except one. I'd gotten it the night I'd flown in, sometime after I'd gotten off the plane. I quietly wondered if that had been Jimmie, calling me to go get that drink with him.

I stared down at the phone and debated calling the number back. Just to see if anyone answered. And then my phone rang. I nearly climbed out of my own skin.

I didn't recognize the number. My heart pattered faster as I slid the little green phone to the side. "Hello?"

"Drunk? Hey, man, this is Ozzy Messina, up in resort security. I had a message you wanted to talk to me."

"Oh, yeah, Ozzy. Thanks for calling me back. Al and I wanted to chat with you. You free?"

"Sure. I just got back from lunch. I'm available for the rest of the day."

I nodded. "Alright. We'll be up there shortly."

---

I STOPPED over at Al's cottage and knocked on the door. I'd thought Al might want to walk with me up to meet with Ozzy.

Mrs. Al answered the door. She was wearing her World's Best Grandma visor with a matching pink tennis skirt and a white tank top. Even wearing athletic shoes and standing on the top step, she was still about a foot shorter than I was. "Good afternoon, Terrence." Her voice was slightly less friendly than it had been the last time I'd seen her.

"Hey there, Mrs. Becker. I was wondering if Al could come out to play." I said it with a smirk, hoping it would loosen her up a little.

"He's already up at the resort. He said he'd be in the gym, lifting a few weights and working on his balance."

I plumped out my bottom lip. Al was really taking this whole partner thing seriously. "Really?"

"Yes, really. He said to be a detective, you had to be able to chase down the bad guys and that you thought he fell too much."

I swung my eyes away guiltily. "I didn't say I thought *he* fell too much. I just said that old people in general fall too..." I stopped speaking when Mrs. Al gave me the stink eye.

"What's all this about, playing detective with my husband, Terrence?"

I hung my head. I suddenly felt like a schoolkid being reprimanded by the teacher. I lifted my shoulders. "Mm-mmm."

"Was this your idea?"

My eyes widened then. "No! I told Al I didn't think he should be my partner. He was the one that said he wanted to!"

She sighed. "That's what he told me too."

"But I told him he had to get your permission, and he had to wear hearing aids before I'd even consider working with him."

"Yes, well, you got your wish. He put his hearing aids in as soon as he got back from the police station. That was a miracle. He's had those things for years but refuses to wear them. They pick up a lot of background noises and drive him nutty, he says."

"Well, I feel bad for that, but I can't be screaming at him if we're on an important stakeout or something."

"Yes, I understand," she said with a nod. "His hearing can prove to be an inconvenience at times."

"Did he ask your permission? I mean, you didn't have to say yes."

Mrs. Al shook her head. "You've never been married, have you, Terrence?"

"No, ma'am."

"Then you don't know how marriage works. My husband doesn't need my permission to do anything. He's a grown man. He's worked hard all his life to be able to do the things he wants to do. He moved all the way out here because he wanted to do something that I wanted to do. Yes, he needs to tell me what's going on. Good communication is key in a good marriage. But I certainly don't need to give him *permission* to go off playing cops and robbers with his friend."

"It might be dangerous…"

"I understand that," she agreed with a curt nod. "But that's why I'm hoping that I can count on you to keep Al out of any dangerous situations."

"I mean, I can try—"

"Because I just don't know what I'd do without my Al," she continued, cutting me off. "He's my whole world, and the last thing I want is for something bad to happen to him. So, I'm going to need you to keep my Al safe."

I nodded. "Well, yeah. Definitely, I'll do my best to keep him safe."

The little old woman clasped her hands together and smiled up at me. "You will?"

"Of course!"

"I can count on you?"

I gave an emphatic nod. "Absolutely."

She smiled then and took hold of one of my hands, grasping it between both of her cold, rail-thin hands, like a Drunk sandwich. She gave it a shake and patted the top of my hand. "Aww, good boy. Terrence, your mother would be so proud of you."

## 28

I FOUND AL RIGHT WHERE HIS WIFE SAID HE'D BE—IN THE RESORT gym. He was lying on a workout bench with a pair of ten pound barbells in either hand.

"Sixty-six, sixty-seven," he puffed as I walked in.

"Don't you mean, six, seven?" I said with a chuckle. "Heard me coming a mile away, didn't ya?"

He winced and held a hand over either ear. "Well, criminy, Drunk! You don't have to yell anymore! I can hear you now! I put my hearing aids in."

"Loud, are they?"

Al shook his head. "I can hear a pin drop on the mainland now."

"Nice!" I nodded my head.

He winced again. "Shhh. You're going to have to start keeping your voice down now."

I gave him a thumbs-up. "Well, you got the hearing aids in, that's a start. But did you have a chance to talk to the missus?" I was going to pretend that Mrs. Al and I hadn't had the conversation that we'd had. Then he'd know that I was morally and contractually bound by some awkward handshake to keep him away from shoot-outs and the like.

Al's watery blue eyes widened. "I sure did!" he said excitedly. "Just like I knew she would, she said I didn't need her permission and that I was welcome to do whatever butters my biscuit. I'm just not allowed to get my head blown off. I thought that sounded fair, don't you?"

"Yeah, sounds very fair," I said with a nod.

———

"Come on in, Mr. Becker, Officer Drunk," said Ozzy Messina. He wore a wide smile on his face as he ushered us into his office. "What can I do for you today?"

"Well, for starters, you can just call me Drunk."

Ozzy's mouth opened, but no words came out as he nodded. Then he smiled. "Okay. Yup. Drunk. So, Drunk, Al, what can I do for you today?"

"I'm Mr. Becker to you, kid," snapped Al.

Ozzy looked down at his desk and cleared his throat. Then he looked up again. "Got it. So Mr. Becker, Drunk, what can I do for you today, gentlemen?"

"You've obviously heard about the break-in at my cottage?" I removed my hat and glasses and leaned an elbow onto his desk.

Ozzy retracted slightly, as if my encroachment into his territory made him self-conscious. He straightened his tie and tugged it slightly tighter. The wide smile faded. "Oh, yes. I-I don't know what's going on. We've never had this issue before, where we've had two incidents in a week. At least not since I've been here, anyway." Ozzy glanced at Al. "I had one of our maintenance guys cover the window until we can get a new door put in."

"I noticed that. Thank you. The way these guys trashed my room, it leads me to think that they were looking for something."

"Looking for something? Like what?"

"I don't know. That's what I need to find out. I feel like these guys think I have whatever it is they're looking for."

Ozzy's eyes widened. "You think they're after you specifically? But why you?"

I shook my head. "I'm curious, Ozzy. How'd they find out which room I'm in? Are your desk clerks allowed to give out that information to anyone that asks?"

Ozzy's eyes swung down towards the desk. "No, of course not. B-but I have to admit, Drunk. We do our best to preserve our guests' privacy, but sometimes mistakes are made."

"You think it was a simple *mistake* that one of the desk clerks gave out my room number *twice*? If I had been there when those men broke in today, I'd be dead right now, and you'd be dealing with two murders blemishing your resort's reputation. Now, Ozzy. I'm sure Mr. Balladares wouldn't want that, would he?"

Ozzy's eyes widened as his head shook. "No. No, of course not. I'll make sure to reiterate to our staff that they don't give out room numbers."

"Of course it's too late for me now. These guys already know which room I'm in."

Ozzy picked up the handset on his phone. "We can move you, Drunk. I can find you another room, no problem."

I winced. What good was that going to do? Obviously they had a snitch in their midst. Even if he lectured the staff until he was blue in the face, it wouldn't matter if those two thugs had someone on the inside working for the hotel. I pushed his hand down and cradled the receiver. "No. No, it's fine. I can handle myself. I just gotta find these guys before they find me. Listen. I'm going to need a copy of the security footage from the other day."

"Security footage?"

"Yeah, Ozzy. You know the tapes from the security cameras?"

"Oh, well, yeah. Sergeant Gibson already took those."

"But you've got the originals still, right?" asked Al.

"The originals? No, I gave him everything I had."

I rolled my head back on my shoulders. "Hell, Ozzy! Why the fuck would you give him everything?"

Ozzy looked uncomfortable. "He's the police, Drunk. Was I supposed to say no to the police?"

"Well, you can give them a copy, but you don't give them the originals. What if you needed it yourself!"

"I-I'm sorry. There wasn't much information on there anyway. It was dark, and the cameras weren't at good angles. You can barely make out a shape moving." He fidgeted in his seat and then finally leaned forward, loosening the tie he'd just fiddled with tightening. "Look, guys. I'll be honest here. This is my first big security job."

Al's eyes widened dramatically. "You don't say."

"Yeah." Ozzy nodded. "It is. And I really don't have a lot of experience. I'm sort of flying by the seat of my pants here."

I shook my head. "I don't understand, Ozzy. You've got no security experience. How in the world did you manage to get this job?"

Ozzy's eyes flipped back and forth between Al and myself. "Oh. Well, my dad used to work for Artie. When he owned his implement dealership back in the States. I've got computer experience, so when I was in high school, I helped out once in a while. You know, installing new computers and doing updates and stuff. And then I went to college for computers, and when I graduated and needed a job, my dad made some calls. He said that Artie had just bought this resort on an island and he needed someone who was good with computers and stuff. I just didn't realize it was going to be security. I thought it would be all computer stuff. Anyway, Artie said I'd get on-the-job training. And I did, for a while. But then the head security guy had to quit because he had a stroke."

Al nodded. "Yeah, Phil. Great guy. I heard he didn't make it in the end." Al made the sign of the cross. "May he rest in peace."

"Yeah, so he left and then it was just me, so I'm learning as I go here. This place is generally pretty quiet. You know, once in a while I have to send a bouncer down to the bar because someone got too intoxicated and started a fight. But for the most part, nothing exciting happens here."

"It's alright, Ozzy. I understand," I said with a nod. "Okay, so no security tapes. How about the dead guy? The cops said his name was Jimmie Wallace. Was he a guest here?"

"Y-you know his name?" asked Ozzy, his eyes wide with surprise.

"Of course I know his name. You don't?"

"I just didn't know the cops had released it. I thought it was confidential information." He kind of looked sad then. Like if the cops were passing out that information, he suddenly wasn't as important.

"I guess it's not. Was he staying here?"

Ozzy shook his head. "No. I looked him up. He wasn't listed as a guest. Unless he registered under another name or was staying with someone else."

I frowned. So Jimmie had lied to me. Which meant he'd purposely come to the Seacoast Majestic following me.

Al tipped his head sideways. "What about Cami Vergado? Have you spoken to her since that night?"

Ozzy made a face. "Cami hasn't been into work yet."

"But surely you've spoken to her. When she called in," said Al.

He shook his head. "That's the thing, she hasn't called in. She just hasn't shown up."

I ran a hand through my hair. "Has anyone tried calling her?"

Ozzy nodded. "Of course. We've called her several times. She doesn't answer her phone. I've personally left messages. But she's not returning any of my phone calls."

Al looked concerned. He splayed his hands out in front of himself. "Has anyone actually tried going to her house to make sure she's alright?"

Ozzy looked slightly embarrassed then. "Well, no, not that I know of. I mean... I'm sure she's..."

"Can I have her address?" I interrupted. I didn't have time for Ozzy to make excuses for why no one cared about the well-being of an employee who had witnessed two men leaving a murder scene.

"Her address? I mean, I really can't give that to you..."

I'd had it with the kid. And the cops. And the whole damn island. I reached across the desk, grabbed hold of Ozzy's jacket and pulled him closer to me. "Ozzy. Your employees gave my room number to a couple of psychopath men who wanted to kill me. I'm a freaking *cop*. It's my duty to protect, okay? I only want to find Cami Vergado to make sure that she's *safe* from the psychopathic killers, and you're not gonna help me out with that?"

Ozzy's eyes were wide as I held him inches away from my face. "I mean, it's against resort policy, Drunk... I-I could get fired."

I let go of Ozzy's coat and pushed myself back into my seat, trying to regain my cool.

"Ozzy, you're killing us here," said Al. "You gotta give us something."

"I'm sorry, fellas. I really am. I'll talk to Artie about giving you Cami's address. Alright? It's the best I can do."

I let out a frustrated groan and pounded the desk with my fist. "Ugh, this is bullshit, Ozzy. Get Balladares on the phone right now."

Al patted my arm. "It's the best he can do, Drunk. Okay? Relax. Artie'll give him permission to give us Cami's address. Until then, we'll figure something out. Okay? Come on, let's go." He stood up.

I followed suit and the two of us walked to the door. We didn't have time for useless Ozzy Messina. "Yeah, alright. Just call us when you hear from Artie. Got it, Ozzy?"

Ozzy nodded. I caught a slight look of fear in his eyes. "Yeah, you got it, Drunk. I'll call you."

## 29

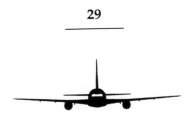

"Drunk, oh man, that was a great good cop, bad cop routine we had goin' on. It was perfect. I mean, you had Ozzy practically pissin' in his shorts back there," said Al, hobbling alongside me as we left the resort lobby.

I stood at the curb, waiting for the next golf cart to pick us up. "I wasn't playing good cop, bad cop, Al. That was just me getting frustrated with the little asshole. And even if it was good cop, bad cop, it didn't work. He didn't give us shit. We're literally working with no clues."

"Relax, Drunk. He's gonna talk to Artie," said Al, climbing into the back of one of the golf carts that would take us back down to the cottages. "Artie'll give us the girl's address. I have faith in him."

I shook my head as I climbed in next to him. I wasn't sure that I had faith in anything except the fact that Ozzy didn't know shit from Shinola. My phone rang then. I pulled it out of my pocket, looked down at the number and smiled with relief. "Mikey! I'm glad you called. Please tell me you've got something good. I'm running out of leads."

"Hey, T. I wish I was calling with more information. I just

called to tell you that there was no one by the name of Natasha Prince on your flight from Atlanta."

I shook my head. "No, no, Mikey. Look again. She was on the flight."

"I believe that she was on your flight, T. But she just didn't book the ticket under the name Natasha Prince. Do you know what her seat number was? Maybe I can look her up that way."

I let out a heavy breath and recounted where I'd seen her sitting, four rows ahead of my seat. "Yeah, I think it was seat 23B."

"Okay, I'll do some more digging."

"Did you find out who was sitting next to me?"

"You were right. His name is Jimmie Wallace. He has an Australian address and passport. There's not much else here to tell, buddy. He was only in the US. for a short amount of time. Just over a week."

"That's all you got on him?"

"Sorry, man. I wish I knew more."

I rolled my head backwards on my shoulders and let out a breath. "Yeah, I wish you knew more too. Just find out what you can about the woman in seat 23B."

"Will do."

"Hey, thanks for your help, Mikey. I appreciate it a lot."

We ended the call, and I looked up at Al. "Nothing to report. Just that Jimmie's last name was indeed Wallace, and he had an Australian passport and address. Same as the cops said. He doesn't know who the girl was yet. We'll find out, though."

"So what's the plan now? Just wait for him to call us back?"

I shook my head. "No. There's something else that we need to do." I tapped the golf cart driver on the shoulder and pointed to Al's cottage. "You can let us off at that one."

The driver pulled over. Al and I got out. "I need to get my suitcase from your place. Mind if I come in?"

"No, of course not. Come on." He led me inside. Mrs. Al was nowhere to be seen.

"Where's your wife?"

He cocked his head towards the opposite wall. "Oh, I suppose it's lunchtime. She's probably up at the resort with Fern."

I pulled my suitcase from the closet I'd stashed it in and rolled it over to Al's coffee table.

"So what's with the bag? I thought you didn't bring any luggage."

"My ex packed the suitcase. I tossed it over the balcony when I got to my room."

"Tossed it over the balcony?" A smile crossed over Al's face. "You're kidding?"

"No, I'm not. But now I have this sneaking suspicion that Jimmie hid something in my bag while we were on the airplane. The fact that I tossed it meant that it wasn't in my room when Jimmie got killed, and it wasn't in my cottage earlier today. I think whatever he hid is what those guys were after."

Al looked surprised. "He told you he hid something?"

I lifted the bag up and laid it on the coffee table. "No, I've replayed the flight and everything in my mind lots of times now, and it's the only thing I can figure out. He gave me some kind of signal in the terminal, right before we got to the security checkpoint, and then he started a fight. Made me wonder if maybe he wasn't trying to pull something, you know?"

Al and I both stared down at the bag. "And you haven't opened it yet?"

"No! I haven't. It took me over an hour to climb through the jungle beneath my balcony this morning, and then right as I was getting back to my cottage, I found those guys breaking in. Then Gibson called, I stashed the bag over here, and we left. This is the first chance I've had to look."

Al clapped his hands together. "See? This is the good stuff.

This is exciting. What do you think he put in there?"

I frowned. "If I had to guess? Drugs."

Al's eyes widened, and he looked at his door as if he was afraid to get caught with drugs in his room. "Really?" he breathed. "You think there's drugs in there?"

"Only one way to find out." I unzipped the bag and opened it. The contents were all jumbled about from the flights, the layovers, the toss over the balcony, the jiggling of the tree vine, and the long walk back to my room.

"This is how you pack?" scoffed Al.

I swatted his arm with the back of my hand. "Oh, shut it. This bag's been through a lot."

Without touching anything, Al's head tipped from side to side like a cat staring at a bug as it walked across the floor. "I don't see any drugs."

With two fingers, I plucked out one of the Hawaiian shirts Pam had bought for me, held it over the bag and gave it a good shake, making sure that there wasn't anything rolled up inside.

"You were gonna throw that shirt away? What's wrong with it?"

"My ex bought it. It's not exactly a Drunk shirt, you know."

Al frowned and widened his eyes, like he didn't get it. "But it's a nice shirt. You're just gonna keep buying new shirts in the clothing store when you have these perfectly good shirts to wear?"

I shrugged. "Maybe. Or maybe I'll make you take me into town and we'll buy some of those cheap t-shirts they were selling in the tents on the corner."

Al folded the Hawaiian shirt and placed it neatly on his sofa. "I'm not going to let you throw that away. It's still got the price tag on it. That cost your fiancée good money."

I rolled my eyes. "Ex-fiancée, and you mean that cost *me* good money. But do whatever. You can have it." I plucked out the next shirt and shook it, and nothing came out.

Little by little, Al and I sifted through the contents of the bag, checking all the pockets, but ultimately coming up empty. "Well, what the hell?" I said by the time we'd emptied the bag and found only the shorts, underwear, and hideous button-down shirts Pam had packed. The only thing I'd found of interest was a pair of running shoes that I'd forgotten I'd packed for myself. For a split second, I was thankful that I'd gone back to get the bag, just so I could have a pair of real shoes again. Despite that discovery, I frowned. I'd been sure that Jimmie had done something to my bag.

Al's eyes scanned the clothes scattered around his living room and then the empty suitcase. "You checked the front pockets?"

I swished my lips to the side. "No. It hadn't occurred to me that whatever Jimmie had put in my bag would be small enough to fit in one of the outside pockets." I flipped the bag shut, unzipped the top pocket, and stuck my hand inside. There was an empty Dr. Pepper bottle and my travel itinerary. "Nothing."

Al pointed to the bottom one. "Try that one."

I held my breath. It was literally the last chance we had. I unzipped it and stuck my hand inside. I felt something! My fingers wrapped around what felt like a plastic bag, and I slowly pulled it out of the suitcase. Holding the bag in the palm of my hand I showed it to Al.

"What is it?" he asked, looking down at it.

"I don't know."

"It's not yours?"

I shook my head. "Definitely not mine."

His wrinkled hand trembled as he covered his gaping mouth. "So he did put something in there. This is exciting."

I strode into the kitchen, where the light coming in from the outside was brighter, unzipped the baggie and poured the contents onto Al's kitchen counter. There were several different items. One looked like a flash drive. Another looked like some type of key fob or remote car starter attached to a lanyard. The third was a small piece of stainless steel slightly larger than a credit card. It was hinged on one side and opened up to expose a series of letters and numbers. I shook my head. "I have no idea what any of this is. You?"

Al touched the assorted items while shaking his head. He was just as clueless as I was. "At least you were right about Jimmie putting something in your bag. This has to be what those guys wanted."

"It has to be," I agreed. "Just wish I knew what this stuff was." I lifted the flash drive. "I mean, I know what this is. It's like one of those storage drives. It's probably got something important on it, but I don't have a computer. And if I did, I'm probably not going to know what I'm looking at. How about you? You got a computer lying around?"

Al shook his head. "No. No computer for me."

I put a hand on my hips. "This really sucks, Al. You know, if we were in the US, I could turn this stuff over to a network of people and they'd, you know, analyze it and tell me what it is. Down here, we're on our own. There's no network of people to rely on."

Al grinned. "Oh, you don't think I have people down here?" He raised a finger into the air. "What did I tell you? I've got people."

I pursed my lips. "*You* have people."

Al did his best to look offended. "Hell yeah, I have people. Lots of people. There's Big Eddie and Ralph the Weasel. Not to worry, I'll hook you up."

I couldn't help but smile. "Big Eddie and Ralph the Weasel? You're consorting with mobsters down here, Al? There something I should know about you?"

"All you need to know about me is that I got this. Okay? Trust me?"

I shrugged. "Fine. Let's go see your people, Al. I trust you."

## 30

POCKETING THE CONTENTS OF THE BAGGIE, AL AND I TOOK A GOLF cart down to the pool. It was hot by now and well past lunch.

"You want a sandwich? I'm starving." Al pointed to a little poolside shack where two young women in white aprons were making sandwiches on request. The snack bar was little more than a picnic-shelter-style roof set atop wooden posts and surrounded by a waist-high counter on four sides with an opening in the back. There were two chest freezers in the center, set end to end, and two under the counter refrigerators. On top of the counters were simple gadgets like an industrial-size panini maker, a microwave, and a commercial deep fryer. The key word there was *casual* dining. "They have the best chicken wraps here."

"Yeah, I'd take a chicken wrap." My stomach had been set on a low, steady rumble ever since leaving Ozzy's office. A chicken wrap sounded divine.

He nodded and knocked on the countertop. Despite the long line of poolgoers looking for a snack, one of the workers gave a half glance up at Al. "Just a min..." Recognition crossed her eyes. "Oh, Mr. Becker. You're back! It's good to see ya. I'm almost done with this one. You want the usual?"

He shot her a wink. "Trinity, good to see you too, dollface." He pointed at me. "This is my friend Drunk. It's his first time on the island. You wanna make him one of your special wraps too?"

"Sure thing. He's gonna fall in love with them just like you did."

"I'm counting on it." Then he pointed towards the clubhouse. "We have a meeting inside. But we'll be back in about ten minutes, alright?"

She nodded. "I'll have 'em ready by the time you're back."

"Thanks, sweetheart."

We walked away, and I looked down at Al in his ribbed white Hanes tank top and green shorts with pink hibiscus flowers that exposed his knobby knees. My whole life, I'd considered myself somewhat of a charmer, but Al seemed to have the market on charm cornered. "Do you know *everyone* on this island?"

"I know everyone who works at the resort and all the regulars that come here," he admitted. Then he shrugged and shot me a wicked smile. "I only know *half* of the people who live on the island."

"Half, that's all?" I grinned, not believing his bullshit for a second.

He led me up the stairs to the wraparound porch of what he called the clubhouse. Inside there was a fancy dining restaurant, a sports bar, a dance hall, and some meeting rooms. We walked through the restaurant all the way to the back and out the French doors to the porch on the other side. Six old men sat around, playing cards and smoking stogies.

"Fellas!" called out Al.

"Albert, how ya doing, buddy?" called one of them. He was an overweight, boisterous man in a motorized four-wheeled scooter, wearing a blue bucket hat with a cord that hung down over his chins.

Al clapped the man on his meaty shoulder. "I'm good. I'm

good. Fellas, I want to introduce my new friend to you. This is Drunk. Drunk, this is..."

"Lemme guess. This is Big Eddie?" I interrupted, extending a hand.

Al's smile disappeared. "No. Big Eddie? No, why would you say that? This is Tony." He pointed across the table to a shriveled-up old man in a short-sleeved white button-down shirt with a pocket protector. His skin was so pasty white that he looked as if he'd spent the last fifty or sixty years holed up in a windowless basement doing people's taxes. "*That's* Big Eddie."

I shook my head. I should have guessed. "Hey, Big Eddie, Tony," I said, nodding at them both.

Then Al pointed at the guy to his right. He was a tall, thin black man with fuzzy white hair and a flat nose. He reminded me a little of Morgan Freeman, but without the speckles on his face. "This is Ralph the Weasel."

"Hey, Ralph," I said, shaking his hand.

Next he pointed at a man wearing a pale pink polo shirt tucked into his belted denim jeans. The man had a potbelly and a receding hairline. "That's Gary Wheelan. He lives down the road from you. He's the one with the Land Cruiser. And that's Bob Hope and Elton John." Al pointed at each of the men in turn as he named them.

I leaned down towards Al and whispered out of the side of my mouth. "Those are their real names?"

Tony chuckled. "Yeah, and I'm Tony Soprano."

I smirked. "Okay, now I *know* you guys are fuckin' with me."

Tony laughed again. "Hehehe. It's nice to meet you, Drunk," he boomed, clapping me on the back. "You wanna play some cards?" He pointed at one of the men. "Deal 'em in, Bob."

Al held up a flattened palm. "Oh, no, no. Trinity's making us lunch out at the snack bar. I just wanted to introduce you. I was also hoping that maybe we could pick Big Eddie's brain for a minute."

Eddie looked up in surprise. "My brain?" His voice was timid, like he didn't get his brain picked often and he wasn't sure if he liked the sound of that.

"Yeah. You're the computer genius around here." He looked at me and then pointed at Eddie again. "Big Eddie here used to work for Dell."

"It's been over ten years," said Eddie. His eyes shifted nervously as he fidgeted with the cards in his hand.

Al waved a hand in the air. "Ah, it's just like riding a bike. You don't forget that stuff."

Eddie shrugged. "It's not exactly like riding a bike, Al. Bike's haven't changed much over the years. Technology changes constantly. But I'll do what I can. What do you need?"

"Show him," prodded Al.

I walked around the table and dropped the baggie of stuff in front of Eddie.

Eddie picked it up and turned it slowly in front of his eyes. "What is this stuff?"

"We're not really sure," I said. I pointed at one of the items. "I think that one's a flash drive or something."

"Well, yeah, I can see that much. What's on it?"

"That's what we were hoping you could tell us. Drunk and I are working on something. Something big, fellas. Now I can't say much just yet, and we need extreme professionalism here. You can't go shooting your mouths off about this, okay?"

Their eyes were all wide as they nodded seriously, like they'd been let in on a secret mission. "What's going on, Al?" asked Tony.

"Well, you heard about the shooting the other day in room two seventy-seven?"

They nodded in unison, but no one said a word.

"That was Drunk's room. Someone snuck those items into his bag on the plane in from Atlanta, and we think the people who killed that man were looking for the things in that bag. So whatever that stuff is, it's big."

Eddie's hands recoiled and the baggie dropped onto the table. "S-someone got killed because of the stuff in this bag?"

"Now don't go getting your knickers in a twist, Eddie. No one knows you've got it, so you'll be just fine. Like I said, just don't go running your mouths, understand?"

Everyone around the table nodded, but Eddie looked hesitant to pick up the bag. "I-I don't know, Al. I don't want any trouble."

"Oh, for pity's sake, Eddie. Grow a pair, will ya? We were all just talking about needing something to spice things up down here. Well, I'm bringing you the spice!"

Eddie pointed at Tony. "Tony a-and Gary were the ones talking about that. I-I'm okay with it being quiet down here."

"Oh, come on, Eddie," begged Tony, wide-eyed. "What's the worst that could happen?"

Eddie's eyes widened as a roll call of the worst things that could happen apparently flashed in front of his eyes. "L-lots of things," he said, pushing his glasses up between his eyes. "These guys could kill me, for starters. Or, you know, torture me to get information."

"They'd have to know where you were to kill you. *And* they'd have to know that you had their stuff," I said. "They don't know either of those things. You're totally safe, Eddie."

"Listen to him, Eddie. Drunk's a cop in the States."

Everyone looked up at me with pride shining in their eyes then.

"Drunk, you're a cop?" asked Tony.

I was forced to nod. I gave them a tight smile. I was going to have to tell Al to quit telling people that. The more people who knew, the more people who would actually expect something out of me.

"I was a security guard at the Mall of America for thirty-two years, Drunk," said Gary from across the table.

"Nice."

Al nodded. "See, Eddie? Gary can stand lookout when you see what's on that flashy doohickey."

Eddie's timid brown eyes flashed up to look at Gary, who gave him a confident nod. "Well, I suppose I can check this stuff out."

"We appreciate that a lot, Eddie," I said, giving him a squeeze on his bony, turned-in shoulders.

Eddie winced.

"Okay, Drunk. We need to keep moving if we're going to make any progress today." He looked at the guys. "You know, Eddie, we could really use that information today if possible. Drunk here doesn't have a lot of time to mess around. He's supposed to fly back to the States next week, but the island cops aren't going to let him if this murder investigation is still hanging over his head."

Eddie sighed and threw down his cards. "There's a computer room in the clubhouse."

Tony zoomed forward on his scooter. "We don't have to finish our card game fellas. Why don't we go check it out now?"

Gary dropped his cards too. "Yeah, what are we waiting for, then? Let's go."

I rubbed my now-fiercely-growling stomach. "Al and I will be in shortly. But first, we have a date with a chicken wrap."

## 31

TWO BASKETS OF CHICKEN WRAPS AND FRIES WERE WAITING FOR US at the snack bar when we returned. The line had gone down significantly, and the two women were taking time to clean and restock their work areas before another big rush hit.

"Busy today," remarked Al while squeezing some ketchup into his basket.

"Nonstop," agreed Trinity. She stopped wiping the counter and looked up at us. "When did ya get back to the island, Mr. Becker?"

"Two days ago," he said, sticking a fry in his mouth.

A warm smile spread across her face as she leaned on the counter. She was a pretty girl, young and curvaceous. Her skin was like smooth chocolate, and her eyes sparkled like twin emeralds. She wore her hair in long braids, gathered and bound at the nape of her neck. "Two days ago an' ya haven't come by to say hello yet?" Her long eyelashes fluttered downwards, pretending to be offended.

"Easy now, I've been busy. I've been running this guy around the island."

She turned her eyes on me then. "And who is this guy again?"

"Drunk," I said, extending a hand. "You've got the most beautiful eyes I've ever seen. They're mesmerizing."

She turned her warm smile on me next. "Well, aren't ya a sweet one," she purred in her pronounced Caribbean accent. Then she gestured towards my basket of food. "Have ya tried the wrap yet?"

I shook my head. I didn't need to be asked twice. I picked up one of the halves and jammed a third of it in my mouth. I tasted bacon and ranch dressing with the chicken. "Mmm," I moaned suggestively, closing my eyes as I swallowed the first bite. Perhaps I'd exaggerated a bit for her benefit, but I was starving and hadn't taken the time to properly savor that first bite. I'd pay more attention to the next bite. "So good," I said with a mouthful.

She smiled from ear to ear. "My specialty."

"I'm going to be down here every day now that I know where the good stuff is."

"I like this guy," she said to Al, hooking her thumb over her shoulder in my direction.

With another mouthful of food, I smiled broadly at Al as if to say, "See? I can charm people too."

Then her smile disappeared, and she tipped her head sideways. "Wait. Your name is Drunk? As in Officer Daniel Drunk?"

My smile was fast to fade. Reflexively, I swallowed. The mostly unchewed bite of food went down hard, causing me to sputter and cough. I looked up with watery eyes. "Where'd you hear that name?"

She plumped out her bottom lip. It was pink and pillowy and ridiculously adorable, and at any other time I might have made a cavalier offer to bite it, but something inside me told me this was no time for jokes. "Some fellas were lookin' for ya earlier," she said with a faint shrug.

"There were people looking for Drunk?" asked Al, astonished.

"Big guys?" I asked.

She nodded. "One white man with a cowboy hat an' boots, an' the other was a black man with an eye patch."

"Have you seen them around here before?"

She shook her head. "First time I've ever seen them. Friends of yours?"

"Not quite, but I did see them breaking into my room earlier."

Her green eyes bulged. "Breaking into your room? You've got to be kidding. Did ya report it to resort security?"

"You mean to Ozzy?" I wanted to laugh. How anyone could call Ozzy Messina resort security, I wasn't sure. I didn't think the guy could keep a bird out of a cat's mouth, let alone keep an entire resort safe. "Yeah, we told Ozzy."

"What did he say?"

I waved a hand. I didn't want to talk about Ozzy. "Listen, what did these guys say to you?"

The bottom lip came back out again, and I realized that was the look Trinity gave when she was trying to think. "Not too much. They said they were looking for a man by the name of Officer Daniel Drunk from the US."

"Did they have a picture or describe what I looked like?"

"If they had a picture, they didn't say. All they seemed to have was a name."

"They say anything else? Like how to contact them if you did see me?"

She shook her head.

"So there's nothing else you remember about the men that might help me to find them?"

"Not really," she said. Then she held out a finger. "They did have an accent. I'd guess Australian, but I don't know how that would really help ya to find them."

I smiled at her. "Lot of Australians on the island, are there?"

She grinned back. "That's true. I guess that could help."

My phone rang in my pocket then. I glanced up at Al. "I'll be right back."

He gave me a knowing nod and stayed at the counter with Trinity while I stepped away to take the call. It was Mikey calling back.

"Hey, buddy, you find out about the woman in 23B?"

"Yeah man. Her name is Nicolette Dominion. She's a US citizen and has a Maryland address. I'm texting you a snapshot of her passport photo right now."

"Maryland? The chick is from *Maryland*?" I don't know what I'd been expecting. Maybe someone from a rougher state, like New Jersey or something. But Maryland?

"Yeah, but, T, listen to this. She's former CIA. She worked in cyber security in D.C. before moving to Maryland for a private job."

"Former CIA, huh? Well, I guess that explains the bitchy attitude and the throat punch." I winced, rubbing my throat.

"Yeah. Listen, you're going to want to approach this chick with extreme caution. This isn't like a playdate with a girl from church, okay? This chick is the real deal."

I lowered my head. Lifting my hat with my free hand, I scratched my forehead with the back of my wrist. "Yeah, okay, Mikey. I appreciate the update."

"Everything okay? You don't sound too good."

I looked back at Trinity. Mikey didn't need to know that two Australian meatheads with guns were now asking around about me. "Nah, everything's fine. I got this under control. Don't worry about me. Thanks for the help."

"Yeah, call me if you need anything else."

I hung up and scrolled to my text messages. I had a message from Mikey already waiting for me. It was a photograph of the airplane psycho's passport. In the short two days since I'd laid eyes on her, I'd known her as Megan Fox, Natasha Prince, and now Nicolette Dominion. I wondered if Nicolette was even her real name or if this was some kind of forged passport. Shaking my head, I returned to Al at the snack bar.

"Who was that?"

"My pal Mikey. He got a name and a passport on that woman who was on our flight." Now I just needed to find out where she was. As long as those items that had been in my suitcase were still with me, I had a sneaking suspicion that she was still on the island. A thought occurred to me. Natasha or Nicolette, whatever her name was, had been down at the bar picking me up the day before. I wondered if maybe Trinity or her friend hadn't seen her.

She was across the snack bar, pouring a bag of frozen fries into a deep fryer basket. I cleared my throat. "Trinity, do you have a second to take a look at this picture?"

She nodded. "I'll be there in just a minute."

I showed Al the picture. "Her name isn't Natasha Prince. It's Nicolette Dominion. Mikey said she's former CIA cyber security."

Al lifted his puffy brows. "You don't say?" He looked at the picture and let out a whistle. "My goodness, Drunk, that's one good-looking woman." He laughed then. "And you thought *she* was coming on to *you*?"

I lowered my brows and sent Al a seething look.

He held up two hands and chuckled. "Okay, okay."

"Do you remember seeing her on the plane? She was wearing a black leather jacket."

He shook his head. "Evie and I barely made the flight, and once we were on board I fell asleep. I don't remember seeing anyone."

After dropping the basket into the deep fryer, Trinity walked over to our side of the counter. "What's up, Drunk?"

With two fingers, I enlarged the photo of Nicolette so all that was visible of her passport was her photograph and turned the phone around. "Have you seen this woman at all?"

Trinity took the phone and held it closer. "Hmm," she said,

swishing her lips to the side. "I actually think I have. She was standing right over there." She pointed to a shaded spot beneath a tree maybe twenty yards away at the foot of the stairs to the clubhouse. "It was right around the time those Australian men were looking for you."

I gaped. "Today? You saw her today?"

Trinity nodded. "Yes. I'm sure it was her. She stood out because she wasn't wearing a bathing suit like everyone else. She was in a tank top, shorts, and hiking boots. No one comes down here in hiking boots." She laughed.

"No, I wouldn't think so," I agreed. "Did you speak to her?"

Trinity shook her head. "No. She didn't come up to the snack bar. She just stayed back. In fact, it kind of seemed like she was checking out those men."

"Did you see where she went?" asked Al.

"The men went that way," she said, pointing towards the long flight of stairs to the motel. "I'm pretty positive she followed them."

I rubbed the full growth on my chin. "Interesting. Very interesting."

## 32

AL AND I FINISHED OUR LUNCH AND THEN HEADED BACK TO THE clubhouse to see what Big Eddie and the guys had figured out, if anything.

"You know what I'm thinking now?" I said to Al as we breezed through the front doors of the clubhouse. I gave a little two-fingered salute to Gladys Rosenbaum and Ginger Schmidt, the two old ladies I'd sat between on the shuttle ride to the resort. Enjoying their lunch a few tables away, they giggled like schoolgirls while fluttering their fingers back at me.

"Drunk, I couldn't begin to guess what goes on in that head of yours."

"I think the only way I'm going to be able to clear my name and prove to Sergeant Gibson that I had nothing to do with Jimmie's death is to either find Cami Vergado or find this woman." I held up her picture on my phone. "Nicolette Dominion is ex-CIA. She knows *exactly* what's going on, and I'd place money on the fact that she knows who killed Jimmie. If I can find her, maybe I can coax her into filling Sergeant Gibson in on what she knows and clearing my name."

"Well, that sounds good and all, but how exactly do you propose we find her?"

"If she's following those two Aussies, then we find them and we find her."

Al nodded. "Logical, but how are we supposed to find them?"

"I have an idea. It's kind of a long shot, and it'll require asking Big Eddie for a second favor."

"Ooh, in that case, I think we'd have better luck knocking on every door on the island to find those fellas than asking for more help from Big Eddie."

I patted Al on the shoulder. "That's what I was afraid of, but that's where you come in. I'm hoping your charm skills are on point today."

Al stopped walking and looked up at me. "My charm skills are always on point."

"Then what are you standing around for?"

Al laughed and led me to the computer room in the back of the clubhouse. It was a dark paneled room with only one window. There were only a handful of computers spread out around the room. All the guys had sat down at their own computer. Gary, Ralph, and Elton each played solitaire while Bob checked his email. Big Eddie was navigating through the computer's file explorer program with Tony sidled up next to him.

"Find out anything?" asked Al.

"Nothing yet. This computer doesn't have the necessary software to open the file that's on this USB. I'm going to need to find it and then download and install it. It'll take a while."

"No problem," I said. "In the meantime, we could use your help with one more thing."

Eddie's eyes widened. He shook his head. "Oh no. This is all I'm willing to do."

"Oh, come on, Eddie. Give the kid a break," said Al. "He's had a rough go of it lately."

Eddie leaned back in his seat and crossed his thin arms over his chest. "I'm not getting killed over this stuff. I'll help you figure out what's on the flash drive, and then you're taking it all back!"

Tony's arms flew out dramatically. "Oh, for Pete's sake, Eddie. You're not going to get killed over this stuff! You need to simmer down!"

Al pulled up the chair next to Eddie and sat down. "Hey, Eddie. You do this for Drunk and me, and I'll see if I can't get Evie to set you up with one of her girlfriends."

Eddie's chin lowered slightly and his shoulders slumped just enough to tell me that he was relaxing. Al had piqued his interest.

"Eddie! You're on the prowl?" I said with a toothy smile. "I know a couple of ladies who are ripe for the picking."

Eddie and Al both looked up at me. "You do?" they said in unison.

I nodded. "Are you kidding me? Absolutely, and there are two of them. You'd get to take your pick."

He swallowed hard. "Two of them?"

Holding up two fingers, I nodded with a big smile.

Eddie adjusted his glasses and cleared his throat. "What would I have to do?"

"I've got a phone number for a cell phone that I believe to be somewhere on this island. I need to find out the exact GPS location of where the phone is right now."

Eddie visibly relaxed. "That's it?"

"That's it."

"Oh, well, that's easy." He leaned forward in his seat. "There are all kinds of programs for doing that." He clicked around on his computer.

"See? I knew I had the right guy for the job."

"I'll just need the person who has the phone to install an app on their end, and then we're good to go."

I winced. "Eddie, I think you're missing the point here. I think I have Jimmie's phone number."

Al looked at me like I was crazy. "You have the dead guy's phone number? How in the world did you get your hands on that?"

"Well, I told you I'd given Jimmie my business card on the plane. Earlier, when I went back to my cottage, I checked my missed calls, and I realized that the only number I didn't recognize at all called me while I was at the bar with you the night Jimmie was killed. It makes sense that it might have been Jimmie trying to meet up."

Al shrugged, as if having Jimmie's number was no big deal. "So what's that going to get us? Jimmie's dead. I hate to break it to you, Drunk, but the guy's not taking any more phone calls where he's at."

"Yeah, well, you're right. It's possible it won't lead to anything. Because either the cops have Jimmie's phone or those two Aussies have Jimmie's phone. But if Jimmie was calling me to retrieve whatever he put in my bag right before he was killed, I'm going to guess those two jugheads weren't far away. I'd venture a guess that *they* took his phone before the cops could."

Eddie furrowed his brow. "I don't care *who* has the phone. In order for us to track it using GPS, we need an app installed on the phone."

Tony let out a belly laugh. "Eddie, you don't get it. Let me break it down for you. Drunk and Al need to track the phone without the bad guys knowing."

Eddie gave Tony, Al, and me one of those looks that said, "I can explain it to you, but I can't understand it for you." "Yeah, well, without their consent, we can't just hack their location."

"You *can't* or you *won't*?" asked Tony.

Eddie shrugged. "Both, I guess. I mean, without consent, I'd have to figure out how to bypass the security function.

Even if I could, that's illegal, and I mean, two women are nice and all, but I'm not willing to go to jail just for a date."

I rolled my head back on my shoulders and groaned. "Oh, come on, Eddie. We'd be putting away a couple of criminals with your help! How could that possibly be wrong?"

"You tell me if it's wrong. You're the cop," said Eddie with one raised eyebrow.

"Fine," I said through clenched teeth.

We all sat around thinking about other ways to figure out the GPS location of the phone. Finally an idea hit me. "Hey, Eddie. Let me see if I understand this correctly. Whoever has Jimmie's phone just has to install something in order for us to track it?"

"Exactly," said Eddie, punctuating it with a bob of his head.

"How do you do that? Like, send them a link or something?"

He lifted a shoulder. "I mean, yeah, you could send them a link, or they could go to the app store and download it to their smartphone that way. That's how most people would do it."

"Well, obviously that second option isn't happening. But these are a couple of meatheads. They're not going to know what's going on. What if we sent them a tempting message with the link embedded in it somehow?"

"I don't know how that would be any different. They'd still have to click the link in the message."

"Does it download automatically, or do they have to read a bunch of legal mumbo jumbo and then give permission?"

Eddie made a face. "I think I could find the right software that would mean all they have to do is click the link and the software will run on its own. Clicking the link in essence would be the permission needed to install. You know how you get those suspicious emails, and everyone says not to click on any of the links? The reason is because clicking the link allows those dangerous files to download to your phone or computer. Essentially this would be the same thing."

"Nice. So if I sent these two fellas a link to the hottest girls on the island and they click on the link, you could remotely install the app on Jimmie's phone without them knowing?"

Al smiled and nodded. He could finally see where I was going with my line of questioning. "See, now you're thinking like a detective! I knew you had it in you!"

I was getting excited too.

"Yeah, I could set it up like that. All I need is the phone number. And I'll send the link from an anonymous number so they can't trace it back to the resort or you or me."

I wanted to kiss Eddie's wrinkly old face. "Eddie, you're the man. You get me that GPS location, and you just got yourself a date with two of the hottest women on the island."

## 33

"Ginger, Gladys, how was lunch?" I found the girls beachside several hours later. They were sipping colorful cocktails garnished with cherries and pineapple wedges and fanning themselves beneath a red umbrella stuck in the sand.

"Drunk, good to see you," said Gladys with a big smile. "You get to go do any snorkeling on the island yet?"

I hung my head. *I wish.* "No, darn it. It's been a long couple of days, to be honest. I haven't had time to do much of anything."

"Aww, poor Drunk," sighed Ginger. She adjusted her glasses so she could get a better look at my abs.

"You girls look awful lonesome sitting way over here just the two of you," I said. "Have you met anyone on the island yet?"

"Well, we met the bartender, Manny. He's such a nice man."

"Very nice," echoed Gladys.

"You know, I've met a couple of fellas myself since I've been on the island. A couple of *single* gentlemen, in fact. They said they'd been looking for a couple of dames to take out to dinner and asked me if I knew anyone. I said I happen to know a couple of cuties from the shuttle ride that might be interested in having dinner."

Ginger shook her head, her puffy white curls shaking with her, "Oh no, we already have dinner plans. Reservations for two at that little Japanese restaurant in the lobby."

"Not a problem. Lunch tomorrow, then?"

Gladys sucked in her breath and pretended to be offended. "Drunk, you're not trying to set us up on dates, now are you?"

"As a matter of fact I am, Gladys. I think it's just what the two of you need. A little romance for your island vacation. You'll be telling stories about this trip for years! What do you say?"

"Well," breathed Ginger. "I don't know. Gladys and I watch *Dateline*. Have you heard all the horror stories of people being conned while on vacation...?"

"Or worse. Murdered!" Gladys nodded, her green eyes wide.

"Conned! Murdered! What kind of friends do you think I keep? No, no, no," I said, waving a hand and sitting down on the side of Gladys's beach chair. "These are a couple of the best gentlemen you will ever find. One of them, his name is Eddie —well, they call him *Big* Eddie"—I elbowed Gladys—"and it's not because of his height, lemme tell you, eh, eh?" I grinned.

Gladys couldn't restrain her giggle.

"He used to work for Dell. And then we've got Gary. He used to be a security guard at the Mall of America." I was throwing Gary in as a bonus to sweeten the pot. Eddie didn't think he could handle two women, and Gary was the only other one who was interested in dating. Bob, Elton, and Ralph had wives, and Tony said he wanted to lose a few pounds before picking up chicks. I promised to work out with him in the gym once or twice before heading back to the States. "See? So how can you go wrong with a security guard and a guy who worked for Dell?"

"Drunk, I don't know..." sighed Ginger, looking over at her friend.

"I tell you what. Do you two remember Al and Evelyn, that married couple that rode in with us from the airport?"

Recognition filled Ginger's face. "Oh, yes. We bumped into Evelyn and a friend of hers having lunch yesterday up in the dining room." She pointed at her head and looked at Gladys. "Remember, Gladys? Evelyn was the one wearing the pink visor on the airport shuttle."

Gladys bobbed her head. "Oh yes, I remember her."

"They seemed like nice people, didn't they?" I asked, feeling more and more like an "as-seen-on-TV" salesman. *But wait, there's more! If you act now, I'll throw in the nice old couple from the airport shuttle...*

"Yes, they seemed like a lovely couple," agreed Ginger.

"They're from Nebraska. Al owned an implement dealership there. Nicest people you'll ever meet. These fellas I'm talking about happen to be a couple of his buddies. I'll bet I could convince Al and his wife to go along, you know, make it a triple date. Just so you feel safe and all. You have my personal guarantee that Big Eddie and Gary are going to be on their best behavior."

They looked at each other, both of them smiling from ear to ear, but each of them afraid to speak first.

"Oh, come on," I prodded. "You only live once. Whaddaya say, ladies?"

"Well, if Evelyn and her husband are going to be there, I guess I don't see the harm. Do you, Gladys? I mean, we have to eat."

Gladys shook her head. "I don't see the harm. We won't be leaving the resort property, will we?"

"Oh, no, no, no! You'll stay here," I said. "You can either dine in the clubhouse or at the buffet. Whichever you prefer. Tomorrow for lunch. Are we all in?"

Gladys nodded. "We're in. Aren't you sweet, making love matches. Is this what you do for a living?"

I laughed. "Hardly! I can't seem to find a nice girl to save my life." *Or a psycho, throat-punching one for that matter.*

## 34

"Drunk, you can't be serious. But how can I go with you if I'm stuck on Big Eddie's date?" complained Al the next afternoon in his cottage.

"Listen, we gotta do what we can to keep Big Eddie happy. We still don't know what those things are that Jimmie stashed in my bag." I pulled out the suitcase I'd left in Al's closet and set it on his coffee table once again.

Al raised his eyebrows as his hands splayed out in front of him. "But he got that app installed on Jimmie's phone."

I nodded slowly as I unzipped my bag. "Yes, exactly. And we made him a deal. We get the GPS location and he gets a date."

"We didn't promise him Evie and I would go on a date with him!"

"No, I understand that wasn't part of the *original* deal, but the women didn't want to go out with a couple of strangers. Apparently they've met Evelyn and they felt like if she and her husband went along, it would be safe." I didn't want to add that if Al was tied up for the afternoon, there was zero chance of him getting shot on a daredevil mission to find Nicolette Dominion and the Aussie brigade.

Al hung his head. "But, Drunk, you can't go looking for these guys alone. Something really bad could happen! Why can't you just wait for me?"

"It's just better this way, Al. If something bad is going to happen to me, it's better if you're here and not there. Then I've got someone to alert Sergeant Gibson when I go missing." I sighed as I dug through the suitcase, looking for my running sneakers. "Listen, Al, I know you wanted to do this with me, but I really think it's best if you stay here and keep Eddie happy. Maybe after your lunch date, the two of you will be able to put a little more time into figuring out what those things are, and you can call me with the intel. Okay?"

Al grimaced. "I don't like this one little bit, Drunk. Partners don't leave each high and dry like this. That woman pulled a gun on you, and you *saw* those two men with guns. And here you are bringing a pretty face and some abs to a gun show. I don't see how this is gonna end well."

I sat down on Al's sofa and slid my feet into my sneakers. I lifted one foot onto the edge of the coffee table and tied the laces while looking at Al. "I don't have a choice, buddy. I don't have a gun. I'm just going to have to rely on my wit to get by."

Al curled his lip. "Forgive me if I'm not a believer." He shook his head. "Maybe Gary can help us out with a gun. I'll give him a call."

I looked at my watch. "You better hurry. I'm supposed to be up at the resort to catch my ride in ten, and you're supposed to be on your double date soon too."

Al took out his cell phone and then stepped outside to dial Gary while I turned my phone to silent. I couldn't very well have someone calling while I was on a stakeout. As I adjusted the volume, a call came in. I didn't recognize the number, but I recognized the area code. It was from back home.

"Hello?"

"*Danny?* Oh my God, I'm so glad I finally got ahold of you! I've been so worried!"

My mouth went dry and the blood drained from my face. "Pam?"

"Yeah, sweetie. It's me."

My head dropped forward into my hand. "Why in the hell are you calling me, Pam? I don't wanna talk to you."

"Where are you, Danny? I've been calling your parents a—"

"Stop calling my folks, Pam. I mean it."

"I'm sorry. I only called them because Mikey won't tell me anything."

"Shit, Pam. Quit fucking calling Mikey."

"But you didn't tell me where you went. I've been—"

"I don't have to tell you where I went. That's what happens when you break up."

"B-but you don't want to *break up* for good, do you, Danny? You just need some time to cool off, right?"

I could hear the pleading in her voice. I'd heard it before. And to her credit, there had been a point when Pam pleading with me for something, anything, meant I'd give in. I'd have done anything she wanted, whether it was making a fool of myself on a dance floor, or going to church and then out to brunch with her and her mother, or taking her to see the dumbest chick flick on the planet.

But not now.

Now I felt my wall going up.

I wasn't falling for it, and I had a job to do. I lifted my head. "Pam. Stop calling me. We're done. Alright? You made your choice."

"It didn't mean anything. I-I was just saying goodbye to the single life."

"You've got a hell of a way of saying goodbye. But you know what? I have a better way. Goodbye, Pam." I hung up the phone and blocked the number she'd called from. With mixed emotions lying heavily on my heart and in my mind, I sighed when Al reentered the house.

He had a big smile on his face. "Great news. Gary's got a gun *and* handcuffs. He said you can use them both."

Resignation covered my face as I nodded. "That's good."

He looked at me and then looked at the phone in my hands. "Who squashed your grapes?"

"No one."

"Oh, come on, kid. I know squashed grapes when I see them. A second ago you were on an adrenaline high. I come back and you look like someone killed your dog. What happened?"

"Pam called."

Al made an O with his lips and raised his bushy white brows. He shuffled closer to me and patted my shoulder. "Bring back old feelings, did she?"

I stood up. "Hell no! I don't have any feelings for her." The extra-deep tone in my voice made me wonder if I was trying to convince Al or myself.

"It's alright if you do, you know. You were supposed to get married. I'm sure you loved each other."

I looked down at him, peering into the watery aquamarine abyss of his eyes. He was a smart old man. He'd been through a lot in his life. He didn't have to tell me that for me to know it. I could see it swimming around in there. But I wasn't in the mood to talk. My face was taut and my voice firm when I muttered, "You got a point in there somewhere?"

Al swatted the air with his gnarled hand. "Oh, fine. So be it. You don't wanna talk about it. Then we won't."

"Good."

He nodded. "Good." Then he turned on his heel and shuffled towards the front door, waving for me to follow. "Come on. Gary's got a gun. He's gonna meet us in the lobby. Lock the door, will ya?"

"Perfect." I followed Al, locking up his cottage behind me. I half-wondered if I wouldn't be better off going gunless. Maybe everything that had happened to me was God's way of saying I was a prick that didn't deserve to be on the planet anymore. Maybe it was my time to go. And if that was the case, in that moment, I felt like I had no cause to argue.

# 35

With Al, Eddie, Gary, and the ladies all at lunch together and Gary's Glock G17 tucked away in a concealed-carry appendix holster beneath my tank top, the hotel shuttle driver pulled away from the resort. It was the same man and the same car that had driven Al and me to the police station earlier in the week. He was a stocky man with cropped black hair and a patchy beard. He was quiet and didn't speak unless spoken to, but when he did speak, he was very friendly.

As the car drove down the resort's long driveway, my eyes immediately swung down to the GPS locator app on my phone. The little red flashing light on the map had moved from where it had been the day before when someone had unintentionally installed the app. That, in and of itself, had been faster than any of us had anticipated. No sooner had Big Eddie sent the message than someone had clicked the hard-to-resist link. Minutes later, Eddie, Al, the guys, and I were all staring with astounded smiles at a red blip on the computer monitor. Al and I had been happy to see that the blip was nowhere near the island's police station, meaning it was more than likely in the hands of the men who'd killed Jimmie and not in the possession of Sergeant Gibson.

But now that it was a day later and the signal had moved, I couldn't help but wonder if the phone was still with Jimmie's killers. I also wondered whether or not Nicolette Dominion was still following them. Would I actually manage to find her? Or would I only find trouble?

"Take a right, Akoni," I said to the driver, scooting forward in my seat. No sooner had we driven off the resort property than the little blipping light on my app stopped blipping and a white screen popped up that read Service Unavailable. I rolled down my window and held the phone out with one hand, searching for a signal, to no avail.

"What's with the internet on this island?"

"It is very limited, sir," he said. "On the resort property, you are connected to the Seacoast Majestic's wireless internet, but away from the resort, it is very difficult to get a signal."

I curled my lip as I looked down at my phone. "I see that." How in the world was I supposed to track Jimmie's cell phone without the internet? "Isn't that annoying?"

His onyx eyes glanced up to meet mine in his rearview mirror. "It is very annoying. Where would you like to go, sir?"

"Honestly, I'm really not sure. The place I wanted to go was on the map on my phone, and now my map isn't working."

"The island is not large. I do not require a map. You can just provide me with an address."

I stared at the blank screen. I had no address, and I couldn't even show him a map with where the little blippy dot had been. "Unfortunately, I don't even have an address without the internet. Isn't there somewhere else that has good Wi-Fi on the island?"

Akoni nodded. "Yes, sir. I will take you there."

"Thank you." With the window open, I leaned back and let the refreshing island air hit me in the face. It felt good to breathe it in and let it clear my head. I felt my shoulders start to relax slightly as my eyes closed.

I hadn't slept well at all that night. Unsure if those Aussie men would make an encore appearance, I'd once again slept on Al's sofa. Not only had Mrs. Al cranked the air conditioning up and nearly frozen me out, but I'd slept curled in a ball since, fully unfurled, my body was about twice as long as their sofa. Now every muscle in my body ached. I reminded myself that I should just be thankful that I didn't have a bullet hole in my head, and I tried to forget about my dull aches and pains.

With that out of my mind, the next time I opened my eyes, we were in the dusty parking lot of a large, nondescript dilapidated building. The vertically paneled siding was painted olive green, making it blend in with the vegetation skirting the parking lot. There was a long porch on the street side with a corrugated tin roof protecting a row of picnic tables from the sun.

"Where are we?" I mumbled, barely able to open my eyes. The sleep felt too good to want to leave it.

"Greasy's Taco," said Akoni. "Best Wi-Fi on the island. Best tacos too."

I lifted my head. It was heavy and didn't want to move, but I knew I had to press forward if I ever wanted to relax again. The spicy smell of taco meat wafted in through the open window and made my stomach churn. I was decidedly hungry. I adjusted my posture, sitting up straighter, and looked at my phone again. I found the Wi-Fi signal available and unprotected. After connecting to the Wi-Fi and refreshing the app, the little blippy light reappeared on my screen. I showed the map to Akoni. "Can you take me there?"

He looked it over and then nodded. "Yes, sir."

I took off my hat and scratched the top of my head. "Just call me Drunk, Akoni, please? Being called sir makes me uncomfortable."

"Yes, si—Drunk. We will go there now."

I nodded, pleased, and then held out a hand to stop him.

"Wait! Can we go through the drive-through first? I'm starving."

Ten minutes later, we drove away with three hard-shell tacos and a fountain Dr. Pepper for me and a pair of chicken fajita burritos, extra sour cream, for Akoni. "Thank you, Mr. Drunk."

"My pleasure," I said through loud bites of the best damn crunchy taco I'd ever eaten. I blew through my entire meal in less than the seven minutes it took for Akoni to drive me to the location of the blip on my phone app.

"This is it, Mr. Drunk," he said, pulling over to the side of the road.

One glance out the window had me hanging my head and sighing. It was an impound lot. Now there was exactly zero chance that I was going to find the Aussies or Nicolette. "Shit," I muttered. "You're sure this is the place?"

Akoni nodded. "Yes. I am sure."

I took one more sip from my straw and handed my cup to him. "Hold this for me? And don't go anywhere. I'll be back in a few minutes."

He took the cup from me and put it in his center console's cup holder. "No problem, Mr. Drunk." He grabbed the lunch I'd bought him from the passenger's seat and got comfortable.

The small impound lot was backed by a steep rock wall and surrounded on the other three sides by a chain-link fence with curled barbed wire on top. The front gate of the impound lot was swung wide open. I didn't see any security guarding the entrance, so I took it upon myself to go poking around the lot. Almost immediately, the sight of fog lights fixed to a roll bar caught my eye. I walked around the first row of cars to the second and stood up tall, with my hands on my hips.

"Well, I'll be," I muttered as I saw the black Chevy Silverado parked ten cars down. My brows lifted and my bottom lip plumped out. "Aww, get your truck taken away, did ya, fellas?"

I looked around. There still didn't seem to be anyone around, so I walked down to the truck. After the lax security at the entrance, I wasn't surprised to find the truck unlocked. I opened the door, and a handful of Greasy's Taco wrappers tumbled out onto the ground. "Ah. So you guys are fans of Greasy's too," I said, climbing into the truck. "I don't blame you. Best tacos ever." The first thing I found was Jimmie's phone, shoved between the seat cushions on the passenger side. I pushed a button to wake it from its slumber. It lit up, but I quickly discovered it had been wiped clean of any contact information and incoming or outgoing messages or calls.

I slid down and opened the glove compartment. I rifled through it, hoping to find a registration with a name and address. Anything to give me a clue as to where to go next. A small sheet of paper buoyed my spirits. I grabbed hold of it, just as I heard a voice call out.

"Hey!"

I looked up over the dash to see a tubby man in a white t-shirt, dirty jeans, and a baseball cap standing at the hood of the truck, staring at me.

"Hey! You can't just come on in here without checking into the office."

"Oh, I'm sorry," I said, pocketing Jimmie's phone. "This is my truck. I came to get it out of impound."

He made a face. "Oh, this is *your* truck? Well that was sure fast. We only impounded it last night."

I shrugged. "What can I say? I'm fast."

"Cops said it was stolen."

*Dammit.* That meant that the name and address on the registration I was holding would do me no good. But I had to play along anyway or risk getting myself impounded. "Yup. Stolen right out from underneath me!" I shook my head. "Damn kids. Parents don't teach their kids right from wrong anymore."

The man held a hand up over his face and squinted at me. "You live on the island?"

"Of course I do. If I was a tourist, you think I'd have a truck?"

He gave me the kind of look that said he knew I was full of shit, but he wasn't sure that he cared enough to call me out. "You just don't look or talk like an islander. What did you say your name was?"

"Umm..." I snuck a quick glance down at the registration I'd found in the glove compartment box. "Malakai Charles." I swallowed hard as I stared at him.

He pulled his ball cap off and scratched the back of his sweaty head. "Well, alright. I guess I'll just get the paperwork ready, then. You'll have to come into the office and sign some stuff."

"Sure thing, boss," I said with a nod as I began to climb out of the truck. "Say, where'd they find my truck at, anyway?"

"We towed it out of the Tally's Discount Liquor parking lot."

"Right." I scratched the side of my head. "And where's that at again?"

He puffed air out his nose. "You're an islander and you don't know where Tally's is at?"

I pointed at him like he'd gotten me. "Oh, *Tally's*! I thought you said *Bally's*. I was like, what? Yeah, no, never mind. I know exactly where Tally's is. Yeah. Yup. Good to go. Thanks so much."

He looked at me as if I were cracked and took off towards his office. "I'll meet you in the office," he threw back over his shoulder as he lumbered away.

I'd already slipped down out of the truck, through the aisle, and back towards the open gate. I heard the office door slam shut just before I jumped back into the resort's car.

"Akoni, do you know where Tally's Discount Liquor is?"

"Sure thing, Mr. Drunk."

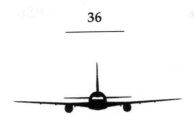

## 36

A LANKY MAN WITH A SLOUCHY RASTAFARIAN BEANIE AND dreadlocks sat behind the counter at Tally's Discount Liquor, watching a sitcom on an old tube-style television set with rabbit ears. It was one of those shows that were filmed before a live studio audience, because I could hear the laughter emanating from the box as I entered. The stale smell of cigar smoke hung in the air, and a purring fan on the counter did little to dissipate the smell.

The clerk paid no attention to me when I walked past him and down the far aisle to grab a bottle of Dr. Pepper out of a cooler and a Snickers bar from the candy aisle. I quietly browsed the gin section and then rounded the aisle and cruised down the tequila and bourbon aisle for a few more minutes, just to seem casual, and then finally I walked to the front, dropping the candy and the pop on the counter along with a five-dollar bill.

I'm pretty sure I could have gotten out of there without either of us exchanging a single syllable, but I had questions that needed answers.

"Hey, man."

Slouchy beanie man gave me a wassup nod but didn't utter

so much as a single pleasantry.

"You work last night?"

"Yeah."

*He speaks.* "Cool. You didn't happen to see a black Chevy getting towed, did you?"

"Mmm-mmm." The sound that came out of his throat, a sort of mumbled *I don't know*, was the same kind of sound I used to make when I was trying to lie to my mother without *actually* having lied to my mother.

"Just wondering if you happened to see who left it there?"

He pursed his lips and raised one thin eyebrow at me. "I'll tell ya what I told da cops. I didn't see anyting."

"Oh, come on, man. Help me out. It was my truck. Some guys, they stole it from me."

He shrugged one bony shoulder. "Tough break, but I don't know nuttin'."

I pulled my wallet out of my back pocket and dropped a hundy onto the counter. With one finger, I slid it over to him.

He picked it up and folded it neatly before sliding it into the front pocket of his shorts. "Green house, five blocks down on da right."

"Much appreciated," I said with a nod.

"Ya didn't hear it from me."

I grinned. "I've never even been in here before. How could I have heard it from you?"

Without another word, slouchy hat man sat back down on his stool and turned his attention back to the television, and I went back outside.

Unwrapping the Snickers, I sidled up to Akoni, still parked outside. "I guess I'll walk from here."

Akoni hung his elbow out the window and looked around. "I can't leave you here, Mr. Drunk."

"Just Drunk, and it's fine. I know some fellas down the street. I'm just gonna go hang out with them."

"This is a bad neighborhood. Mr. Balladares would not like

knowing I left a resort guest here."

I patted his shoulder. "I appreciate the concern, Akoni, but I'll be fine. I swear. I know how to handle myself."

"I can come back and get you." He looked at his watch. "In an hour or so?"

I shook my head. "I'm hoping I'll find my way back with someone else. But I'll call if I need a ride."

Akoni handed me a resort business card. "It has my cell phone number on the back. I do pickups anytime before ten p.m."

I winked at him and made a little clicking sound with my mouth. "Got it. Thanks, buddy."

Against his better judgment, Akoni drove away, leaving me to eat my Snickers bar alone in the Tally's Discount Liquor parking lot. I consumed it in three bites before turning around to face the street the clerk had gestured towards. I took a deep breath.

"What's your plan?" had been Al's final words to me before I'd gotten into the waiting car just before leaving the resort.

"Not to get killed," had been my only answer. I'd tried to come up with a plan on the ride over, but without knowing where I was going, who I was going to encounter, and what they were going to be doing, how could I possibly have a plan? I was flying blind.

I rolled my head and shoulders, trying to loosen up. "Don't get killed," I muttered to myself as my heart pattered in my chest. Oh, I wished I had a partner next to me. And as highly as I thought of Al, I still found myself wishing for a younger, less frail partner. I would've felt a whole hell of a lot better had Mikey been by my side.

Taking two big swigs of my Dr. Pepper, I started down the road. Old broken-down cars lined the narrow side street. The houses were in poor repair, with crumbling foundations and porches, broken windows, and decrepit fences that did little to offer protection. I couldn't see any people, but I could hear children playing in a nearby backyard. I didn't make a conscious attempt at staying out of the limelight until I was two blocks away from the location, at which point I ducked into the shadows on the other side of the street and walked lightly with my hand at the ready. I figured whoever had had the phone probably wasn't looking out their windows waiting for me to chase them down, but I did have a gut feeling that Nicolette Dominion wasn't far away. It was as if I could smell the spicy scent of her perfume riding in on the island air.

I took another couple of steps towards the green house and realized that my imagination certainly had a good sense of smell. It was as if that spicy perfume were really right next to me. I stopped walking, closed my eyes, and inhaled. Opening them, I shook my head as a light smile covered my face. It wasn't my imagination. The scent was real. Nicolette Dominion was nearby.

Stealthily, I slid over to the tree closest to me and clung to its shadowy cover. Carefully, I peeked around the trunk. Where was she hiding? I wanted to sing to her. *Come out, come out, wherever you are.* I still couldn't see her, but my nose could most definitely smell her. Was she sitting in a parked car? There were many of them, but only one had its window down. It was a four-door Chrysler 200. Two cars away, its dark grey paint job blended easily into the neighborhood. It was too dark inside to tell if anyone was sitting in the car. I had to get closer.

With my heart throbbing against my chest wall, I put my hand on my weapon and began to ease myself towards the open window. She had to be in there. Ever so slowly I crept towards it, trying not to make a sound. Just as I was about to draw my weapon, I heard a twig snap behind me.

"Hands up, nice and slow."

I closed my eyes and dropped my Dr. Pepper bottle on the ground.

*Fuck.*

## 37

"Nicolette," I said, turning around even though I hadn't been invited to do so.

"Nicolette? Well," she said, with an undertone of appreciation, "you've done a little research, haven't you Drunk?"

I looked down the muzzle of the same gun I'd seen only a day and a half before. This time, in the shade and behind my dark sunglasses, the gun was hazier and seemingly less threatening. Maybe it was because I'd seen it before and she hadn't pulled the trigger. Or maybe it was because Nicolette was looking extra sexy in her hiking boots, shorts, and white tank top with the trimmings of a lacy black bra peeking out.

Either way, I smiled at her. Like she was my best friend, and I was thrilled to see her. "Well, hey there, sugar. I'd done gone almost a full twenty-four hours without bein' harassed by you. I was just needin' myself a fix. Now come on over here and give Big Daddy Drunk a hug." I reserved my Southern accent for when I wanted to be extra cheeky. Whether women thought it to be charming or it got under their skin, I always managed to get a reaction out of them. I threw my arms out on either side of myself and lumbered towards her.

With the gun extended out in front of her, she didn't flinch. "Stay where you are. Don't move a muscle."

I made a face and froze. "Now, you know you don't mean that."

"I do mean that." Even behind my shades, I could see that Nicolette wasn't playing. "What do you want, Drunk?"

"Who said I wanted anything?"

"You're here."

"So are you."

She snuffed air out her nose. "I was here first."

I shrugged. "I was here second, and two's a bigger number."

Nicolette shook her head, but a small smile finally played around the corners of her mouth. "Oh my God, are you serious right now? How old are you?"

"Younger than I look." I gave her a smarmy grin.

"Obviously."

"So tell me, Nicolette. What's a beautiful lady such as yourself doing in a place like this?"

She cocked her hip out and rested the insignificant brunt of her weight on her right leg. "I can only assume you know exactly what I'm doing here."

"As a matter of fact, that's where the details get cloudy. I was hoping I might bump into you here and you might fill in the missing spots."

She squinted at me. "And why in God's name would I do that?"

"Because we're old pals, Nicolette. We go way back."

"Do we?"

I nodded. "We do. But you know, old pals generally know more about one another. I feel like we should take a moment to get to know each other better."

"You think so?" Sarcasm dripped from the corners of her mouth.

"I do. First of all, there's this little issue of your name. Now, if it were up to you, you'd have me still believing that your name was Natasha Prince, but lo and behold, I happened to find out that there was not a Natasha Prince on my flight in from Atlanta." I grinned at her then. "You remember that flight? The one where you throat-punched me?"

She rolled her eyes and groaned. "Are we seriously dealing with that again? You can't get over it? Maybe I should knee you in the balls just so you have some new material to talk about."

I took a confident step closer to her and pulled my sunglasses off. "Or maybe we should take this to a bedroom and you can give me something much more memorable to talk about?"

She reached a hand over the top of the gun and pulled the slide back. "Another step closer and I'm blowing your fucking head off, Drunk."

I stopped and put my hands up, my sunglasses dangling between two fingers. "Oh, come on now, sugar. Is that how you talk to an old friend? Back to what we were talking about. Imagine my surprise to find out that there wasn't a Natasha Prince on the flight, but there *was* a Nicolette Dominion."

Nicolette stared at me, unmoving.

"And then imagine my surprise to discover that Nicolette Dominion is ex-CIA cyber security. She gave up her job to work for a private company in Maryland of all places."

Nicolette rolled her eyes. "Oh, so now you think you know all about me, do you? Did you get my Social Security number and bra size while you were at it?"

"I'm pretty sure I can wrangle up your Social Security number, but you might have to help me with that bra size thing. What are you? A 34C?" I shook my head. "I mean, that's just an educated guess. You know, a *hypothesis*."

"Oh, look, Drunk knows a big word." Her tone was patronizing. Then she smiled at me. "What do you want, Drunk? A cookie? You solved the mystery of what my real name is? You think that's gonna make these fools inside there want to kill you any less?"

I folded my glasses and tucked them into my pants pockets and let my hands fall down by my side. "So they do want to kill me?"

"Of course they do. Did you think they wanted to play patty-cake with you?"

"I didn't know what they wanted."

She grunted. "As if I believe that. You're here, which means you know more than you let on before."

"Barely. I'm not an idiot. I put together a few pieces, but I'd like to know more. I'm being serious now." I took the smallest step towards her, making it look like I'd merely shifted my stance. "Can't we go somewhere that we can talk and you can tell me all about what's going on? The cops on this island think I killed Jimmie. They don't want me going back to the States until I'm cleared. I could use a little help."

She choked back a laugh. "You want *my* help? I knew you were crazy, but I didn't realize you were insane."

"Oh, come on, Nicolette."

"Stop calling me Nicolette, alright? It's Nico. Just call me Nico."

I smiled at her. "See? Look at us, getting all cozy and intimate with each other."

"Shut up," she growled, still holding the gun on me, though I could see she was starting to let her guard down a little bit the more we talked. "Listen, I'm not going anywhere. You need to leave."

"Leave? But I just got here!" I had my eyes trained on hers. She kept glancing over my shoulder at the green house across the street. She was getting more and more distracted. At any moment I was going to make my move.

"Listen, Drunk. I don't know what to tell you about the

island cops. It's really not my problem. But you need to go. We can't be out here talking like this. Those guys in there might see us, and then bang bang, we're both dead." She glanced over my shoulder again. This time she shifted her weight.

I took that as my cue.

Without hesitation, I pounced.

# 38

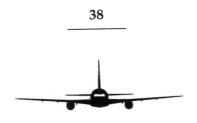

My pulse thundered in my ears, its rhythmic beat drowning out everything else when I made my move.

I lunged towards Nico.

Pivoting sideways on my left leg, I slid my head out of the line of fire. Then I shoved the gun away from me with my left hand while my right hand grabbed hold of the grip. My charm tactic had caught her off guard. She wasn't holding it as tightly as she had been, and it came out of her hand easier than I'd anticipated.

With a big smile on my face, I spun it around and held it on her.

She trained her narrowed eyes on me. "You think you're so smart, don't you?"

A cheesy shit-eating grin covered my face. "Like taking candy from a—"

Without warning, her own arms flared out, and before I could finish my sentence, one of her hands struck my wrist and the other struck the gun in the opposite direction, sending it flying out of my hands and clattering to the ground. She wasted no time in launching a jab intended for my jaw.

My hands went up defensively, blocking her shot.

She fired off a second jab.

I blocked it too and then leaned over and kicked out my leg, landing it squarely against the side of her knee.

She stumbled to the ground. Even though I had my own gun, I went for hers. I wanted to retrieve it before she could, but before I could reach it, she was back on her feet with the lid of a metal garbage can in her hand. She lifted it over her head, charging at me with a howl emanating from her throat.

"What the *fuck*, Nico?" I hollered, ducking out of the way. The lid grazed the back of my neck and shoulders but did little damage.

"You started this, Drunk." Circling me, she held the lid in front of her like a shield.

Breathing heavily, I reached for the weapon under my shirt. "Yeah, well, I'm about to finish it."

I'd just lifted my shirt when she rushed me. Ducking behind the lid, she put her weight into plowing into my body, forcing me backwards to the edge of the curb, where she pinned me against the side of a grey Honda Accord parallel parked along the street. The jolt knocked my hat off my head, and it rolled onto the curb.

Grunting, I shoved her off of me. "You're a crazy bitch, you know that?"

She dumped the lid and went for my legs. Plowing her shoulders into them, she swept me off my feet and body-slammed me down onto the hood of the Honda, setting off the car alarm immediately. I felt an immediate burst of pain in the back of my skull, and the impact knocked the wind out of me. I gasped for breath as the car horn blared and the lights flashed, lighting up the neighborhood.

"Oh, good going, asshole," she muttered, flicking her eyes up to check out the house she'd been surveilling.

"My fault?" I gasped through wheezes of air. I struggled to climb off the car, holding my chest.

"Oh fuck, they're coming," she murmured before falling to her knees behind the Honda.

Wincing in pain, I rolled off the hood of the car to the pavement, where I found partial protection behind the car in front of me.

I glanced over my shoulder to see Nico army-crawling for her gun, still on the pavement.

"What the fuck?" came an Aussie voice from across the street.

Once Nico had reached her gun, I pulled out my own gun and carefully peered over the trunk of the car towards the green house. The two men I'd seen breaking into my room were storming down the porch stairs of the green two-story house towards us.

Gunfire sounded over the car alarm behind me. I turned to see Nico with her gun trained on the Aussies, firing as she slowly eased towards the Chrysler 200. *I knew it was hers!*

The men fired back. A rapid hail of gunfire blitzed the side of the Honda and the car in front of it, and Nico fell to a low squat on the ground.

I popped my hat back on my head and duckwalked back up onto the curb and past the Honda, heading for her car. I knew she'd be trying to make a quick getaway, and if I let her leave without me, I'd be left in the hands of the Aussies. I knew if they got ahold of me, they certainly weren't about to show me the sights on the island.

We got to her car at the same time. There was a break in the gunfire as they reloaded. She stood up and popped off a few more shots before she ran out of ammo. She dropped beside her driver's-side door just as I'd reached an arm up to open it.

"Where the hell do you think you're going?" she hollered over the sound of the return gunfire and the car alarm.

"I'm going with you."

"The fuck you are." She shoved me over and opened her door.

*Fuck.*

Squeezing the grip on my gun, I ran around the front of the car as I heard her engine firing up. I got off a couple of shots at the Aussies before I got ahold of the passenger door handle.

It was locked.

*Fuck!*

Bullets bit into the side of her car, narrowly missing me. The car began to reverse. I noticed that the rear passenger window was open. It was my only chance. I felt the car shudder when it smashed into the car behind it. Nico was forced to put it in drive to maneuver out of her tight parking space. When she did, I took the last opportunity I had and dove into the backseat through the open window.

"What the fuck, Drunk? Get out of my car," she squealed as bullets peppered the side of her car.

With the lower half of my torso still hanging out the window, I felt something bite me in the ass. "Ahhh!" I screamed. "I think they shot me! They fucking shot me!"

Nico put the car in reverse again and now, finally free of the rest of the cars, she stepped on the gas and we drove down the street backwards as bullets shattered the passenger window and the right half of her windshield.

While she drove, I wiggled further into the car, reached across the backseat and grasped the door handle, dragging my lower body and legs in through the window. "Fucking hell, they shot me!" I screamed.

With her right hand on the steering wheel while still driving in reverse, she curled her left hand around her chest and aimed her gun at me. "What makes you think you're any safer in here with me?"

"Because you're out of bullets," I said, sitting up in the backseat despite the fact that my ass hurt like hell.

"That's only temporary," she assured me. I caught her eyes flicking inadvertently towards the car's glove box. When we got to the corner, in front of the liquor store, she peeled backwards into the parking lot, then, without coming to a complete stop, threw it into drive and took off like a shot.

Before she could go after more ammo, I flung myself head-first between the seats and unlatched the glove box. Sure enough, that was where her stash was.

She struggled with me while she drove, and in an effort to get me to retreat into the backseat, she drove her thumb into my bullet wound.

"Ohhhh!" I howled. "*Fuck!* You fucking whore!"

The pain was excruciating, but I didn't let it distract me from the fact that if she got her hands on the extra magazines, I'd either be promptly shot or deposited on the side of the road for the Aussies to handle.

I couldn't let either happen.

So I let her do her worst, biting my bottom lip between my teeth to manage the pain while I began to toss everything from her glove box out the shattered window.

"What the hell are you doing, Drunk?" she bellowed. I could feel the car swerving as she leaned over me, trying to stop me. "Are you fucking kidding me? You asshole!"

When the glove box was finally emptied, I dragged the rest of my body into the front seat. I sat up, wincing in pain, and aimed my gun on her. "Yeah, well, I'll say it again. You're out of bullets. Lucky for me, I'm not. I don't care where the hell you go, just drive."

## 39

It was almost six thirty when Nico finally pulled her car into the motel parking lot and shut off the engine. Dusk had colored the island streets with a gritty blue-amber haze, and an eerie calm had settled over the streets. I'd insisted that she drive around longer than necessary just to make sure that the Aussies weren't following us, and when I was sure we were safe, she finally took a discreet route back to the room she'd been staying in.

We hadn't talked much in the car. She was still salty about the fact that I'd drained all of her ammo and her rental car had gotten shot up. I, of course, was dealing with the fact that I'd been shot and she'd body-slammed me onto the hood of a car.

So not only was my head throbbing like a mother, but my ass burned like hell too. It felt like I'd been beaned by a fast-pitch baseball. I badly wanted something to take the edge off, and then I wanted to crawl into a nice comfy bed and sleep until my plane left for America.

"So now what?" she asked me as we sat in silence in the parking lot.

I flicked the tip of the gun towards the motel. "Now we're

going to your room. You're gonna take a look at my ass and see what you can do to patch me up."

She let out a chortled laugh. "Like hell."

I aimed my gun at her. "You were saying?"

She slammed the heels of her hands into the steering wheel and screamed. "Fuck you, Drunk! This is complete bullshit! You ruined everything, you know that? Now those halfwits know they were being watched. They'll probably move, and it'll take me a week to find out where they are. And by then it'll probably be too late!"

"Too late for what?"

Her dark hair fell back against the headrest. She shook her head gently and then turned to look out her window in weary resignation. "Ugh, just fuck you."

I lifted my brows. "Well, here's an idea. First of all, I just want you to know that I'm willing to take you up on that very kind offer. You know, take one for the team. And second of all, while we're talking about teams, how about you just let me in on whatever it is that you're working on, and we'll partner up and be on the *same* team?"

"Partner up? You think I need a goddamned partner?" she scoffed. "And if I did, why in God's name do you think I would choose you, of all people?"

My jaw dropped. I touched the gun to my chest. "I'm hurt, Nico. I'm really hurt. I'm a cop, you know. I'd make an excellent partner."

"You're a fucking moron is what you are. To come walking down the street like some braindead clueless asshat..."

I nodded, "Yeah, yeah, easy. I get the picture. You don't like me. Alright, well, I can't be everybody's favorite brand of cereal, you know. I already knew that. But that doesn't mean you gotta want me dead or locked up in some island shithole prison, does it?"

She let out a guttural groan as she threw her head back against the seat back. "Ughhhh!"

I sat back in my seat too, and when the echoing sound of her groan faded away, the car fell silent. After what seemed like minutes, she turned to me. "Listen, Drunk, I'll make you a deal."

I was too exhausted to move my body as I replied, "I'm listening."

"I'll grab a first aid kit from the front desk, and we'll dig out that bullet and patch up your ass good as new. Okay? Then I'll load you back into the car and drive you back to your cushy resort and drop you off, and you can get a good night's sleep."

I was silent for a moment, waiting for the rest of the offer. "And then?"

"And then?" she repeated. "And then you're not walking around with lead in your ass, and I get to go about my business cleaning up the mess that you just made for me."

I lifted an eyebrow as I turned to look at her. "You think I came out here just so you can get a look-see at my ass and then get me home in time for curfew? You're fucking crazier than I thought." I shook my head and pointed the gun at her. "No way, lady. I need answers. But, in all fairness to you, your plan started out on the right track with all that first aid kit stuff. So we'll start there." I gestured towards the door with my gun. "Now march."

---

NICO DOMINION DIDN'T HAVE A PARTICULARLY friendly bedside manner. In fact, quite the opposite. She seemed to take great joy in my yelps of pain. On a normal occasion, I might find a little pain in the bedroom to be kinky, but as I lay facedown on Nico's musty-smelling motel bed with my pasty white cheeks exposed, I couldn't help but cringe at every tiny touch.

"Oh, quit being such a baby," she said as she dug the

tweezers deeper into the fleshy mound of my cheek. "It's really not as bad as you make it sound."

I thunked the muzzle of the Glock against my skull and stared at her perfectly round ass in the mirror across from me. "Well, then, how about I shoot you in the ass and see how you like me digging for the bullet? I don't think you're actually trying to find the bullet, you know. I think you're intentionally pulling out tiny pieces of my flesh just to seduce me."

"Seduce you?" The words seemed to be spat out in the midst of a laugh. "Hardly."

I shook my head. "Yeah, I think it's all a part of your master plan. A little S&M before the main course. I already told you, no need for seduction. I'm willing to take one for the team."

"Listen, Drunk, if I were trying to seduce you, you'd know it, alright? I'm trying to find the bullet. It seems to have lodged itself in there pretty good."

"Sure it did," I said, winking at her as she looked at me in the mirror.

My phone rang then. "Hand that to me, will ya?"

She stomped her foot down on the floor. "Damn it! How the hell did I get reduced to being your fucking nurse *and* personal assistant?"

I grinned at her as she handed me my phone. "Just luck, I guess. Drunk here."

"Drunk! You're alive!" Al's voice poured out of the phone like fine whiskey, dignified and old.

"Barely." I grimaced as Nico returned to her role of mean nurse.

"Barely? What the hell happened?"

"Eh, I met up with the CIA lady and she blew our cover— got us shot at and nearly killed."

"Drunk!" I heard Nico suck in her breath behind me.

I waved a hand backwards to quiet her. "Shhh."

"Well, are you alright?" Al said over my silencing of Nico.

"Yeah, I'm fine. Nico's trying to get the bullet out now."

"The bullet! You got shot?"

"Don't worry about it. It's in my butt cheek. Nowhere serious. She thinks she's going to be able to get the bullet out."

"Drunk got shot," I heard Al say on the other end.

"Who you talking to?"

"The guys."

"Big Eddie and the guys?"

"Yeah. Gary wants to know if you still have his gun."

My head and arms were draped over the foot of the bed. I lifted the gun and gave it a once-over. "Yeah. I still have it. Tell him I said thanks. It probably saved my life."

"I told you it would."

"Yeah, yeah. You find anything out over there?"

"Lots of stuff," said Al. "Where should I start?"

"I don't know. How'd the date go?"

"How'd the date go, Eddie?" asked Al. I could hear him mumbling, then he came back on the phone. "Eddie said she was a whole lot of woman. He's not sure if he can handle her."

"He picked Gladys?"

"Yeah. Gary took Ginger."

"Figures."

"The lunch theme was Fiesta Caliente. Artie showed up. You know, making the rounds, so I invited him to join us."

"Oh yeah?" I was starting to feel like I was talking to my mother. She'd tell me all about her social events and who said what to whom, and I'd just throw out a few *oh yeah*s to make it sound like I was listening, all the while wondering if a person could be trained to say *oh yeah* in their sleep.

"Yeah, except Artie had a major allergic reaction to something in the food."

"Did he?"

"Uh-huh. He couldn't stop sneezing."

"Wow." I let out a yawn.

"Of course Gladys and Ginger thought they were big-time, you know, having dinner with the resort owner and all. That scored Eddie and Gary some extra points. Gary wants to go out again."

"That's nice."

"Yeah. Oh, and before we went to dinner, Eddie cracked the file on that flashy thing."

My mind, which had been slowly drifting into sleep mode, flittered awake. "What!"

"Yeah. He was able to open the file. It was encrypted, you know."

"Al, I think you coulda led with that information. So what was it?"

"Some kind of a code."

"For what?"

"Well, that's the thing, we weren't sure. Based on the software Eddie had to use to open the file, we have a sneaking suspicion that it was some kind of cryptocurrency code, but I had no idea. So after dinner, Artie sent Evie and the girls out with one of his employees on a private Jeep ride along the beach, and he, Eddie, Gary, and I all went back to the computer lab. We showed him the stuff."

My hand tore through my hair and I gave it a solid yank. "What the hell, Al!" I muttered. "You can't tell everyone on the fucking island about that!" Immediately, my eyes flickered up to the mirror to see if Nico had been paying attention. Sure enough, she looked at me curiously. I had to remember that I wasn't alone.

"Yeah, I know, Drunk. But I trust Artie, and he's working with the island cops on Jimmie's murder. If there's anyone that can get you out of this situation, it's Artie. Plus he knows a lot more about cryptocurrency than I do."

I had to bite the inside of my cheek to keep from screaming as Nico plucked something from my ass. "Ergh!" I growled.

"Drunk, you okay?" asked Al.

"What the fuck was that?" I asked, turning halfway around to look at Nico, who was wearing a smarmy grin.

She held a pellet between her tweezers. "I got the bullet!"

"That tiny little thing?" Then my head lolled forward. My face flushed hot and I felt like I might be sick. "Oh my God."

"What? What?" Al's voice called out.

"She got the bullet. Keep talking," I breathed, trying hard not to pass out.

"Okay, so, we showed Artie the rest of the things in the bag —and, Drunk, he knew what the other two things were!"

"He did?" My heart began to hammer in my ears then. "Quit playing around, Al. What are they?"

## 40

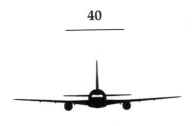

"HE CALLED THEM COLD STORAGE KEYS."

I glanced up at the mirror again. Nico didn't seem to be listening. Still, I couldn't risk saying much. "What's that?"

"I'm not exactly sure right now, but it's definitely cryptocurrency related. He said the flashy thing might be one too, but he didn't know for sure, so he called Ozzy over to take a look at it. You know he went to college for computers."

"Yeah, he mentioned that." I let my head fall into my hand. They'd fucking gotten Ozzy Messina involved. The dumbest fucking kid on the island now had information that, if let out of the bag, could wind up getting me killed. "Al, I can't believe it."

"I know, right? We're gonna get this figured out before you even get back."

I wanted to scream again, and not because of the literal pain in my ass, but because of the figurative one. "Listen, Al, you got any other information to share? Because I gotta go." I needed the stiffest fucking drink to cure the tension that was now racking my entire body.

"Oh, yeah. One more thing. Artie gave me that maid's address. You want it?"

Finally! A break that was *usable* information. "Yeah, I want it!"

"Okay. I'll have Eddie text it to you when I get off the phone."

I sighed. "Thanks, Al."

"Yeah. No problem. When are you coming back?"

I shook my head. I wasn't exactly sure. I still didn't have a clear plan. I'd been quite literally flying by the seat of my pants, and now my pants had a hole in them. "I don't know, Al. I'll have to be in touch, okay?"

"Yeah."

"Hey Al. Do me a favor?"

"Yeah?"

"Quit involving other people in this, alright?"

"Oh, yeah, for sure. We don't want any information falling into the hands of the wrong person."

"Exactly."

Al chuckled. "Alright, then. I'll let you go. Be safe, okay? Don't take any more bullets."

"I'll try not to." I hung up the phone and tossed it on the floor in front of me, perturbed that Al had gotten Artie and Ozzy involved. There were now nine people that knew that Jimmie had in fact left something in my suitcase, and I wasn't sure if I could trust a single one of them to keep the secret.

"What was that all about?" asked Nico the second the phone hit the tile floor.

I reared back and looked at my ass. She'd poured some antiseptic on it and bandaged it up with gauze, and now it stung as if she'd packed salt into the open wound.

"None of your beeswax," I muttered.

She rolled her eyes and began to clean up the mess.

I tried to roll off the bed in a dignified fashion, without springing Little Drunk on her.

"You know, you're such an asshole."

I pulled my underwear up and faced her. "*I'm* such an

asshole? Are you kidding me?" I stopped myself from refreshing her memory on the ass whoopings she'd inflicted on me since I'd met her.

She fired an arm out towards the window, pointing. "You skip down that street today like a kid licking a fucking lollipop and then blow my cover, get shot, get *my car* shot, make *me* pull the fucking bullet out of your ass, and then you get some kind of information and won't share it with me. You're an asshole, Drunk. I'm over it."

I shrugged as I tugged my shorts on. "Whatever. I don't need you anymore, anyway. It's not ten yet. The resort driver said he'd come get me. I'll sort this case out on my own."

"Ugh!" she screamed at me, pounding her fists down by her sides like a petulant teenager. Her face was red and her hair wild as she stood there next to me, panting slightly due to her little outburst. I found myself suddenly mesmerized by the way the outline of her black bra rose and fell behind her white tank.

"You're sexy when you get mad," I said with a cocky little grin and a tipped head. "But I'm sure you hear that from all the fellas, don't you?"

I had to duck then, so her jab didn't hit me. As I crouched, a searing pain shot through my backside, my bullet wound reminding me that it was still there.

"Okay, okay," I said. Chuckling, I held a hand over my head as she followed me to the motel door. "Mercy, mercy!"

"No mercy for you, Drunk," she bellowed, tearing a pillow off the foot of the bed and swinging it at me.

Her ineffectual efforts made me laugh. "You realize I still have the gun, right?"

"I don't care!" She hit me with the pillow again. "You're the most frustrating man I've ever met!"

I grabbed my holster off the small side table in front of the window and slid it into the front of my pants. "It's because you want to kiss me, right?" I holstered my gun and held my hands out wide. "There. Now there's nothing stopping you, sweetheart."

She stared at me then, dumbfounded. "Is that seriously all you ever think about?"

I couldn't help but nod. It was the truth after all. "Pretty much, yes."

"Okay. Then I'll make you a deal."

I rubbed my hand against my bristly chin and grinned. "I like the sound of this already."

"You tell me what I want to know, and I'll have sex with you." She said it bluntly, like a prostitute might. A simple exchange of information for sex.

Of course Little Drunk immediately liked the sound of that. Big Drunk wasn't so sure. I'd sort of expected better out of the ex-CIA agent standing in front of me, which told me she was probably lying. "You're lying."

"Maybe." She shrugged and sat on the bed, rubbing the spot next to her seductively. "Maybe not." Her voice turned sexy in what seemed to be the flick of a switch.

I rolled my eyes. "The CIA make you take a class in seductive reasoning?"

With her feet still planted on the floor, she fell backwards onto the mattress. "Fuck you." She'd had enough of me.

I stared at her torso then and wondered what she knew. Even though I knew I could probably find the maid and clear my name, another part of me realized I could probably do more than that. I could probably help find Jimmie's killer. And maybe, if we pooled our resources, she and I could do it together. I sat down on the bed next to her and leaned back, so our torsos lay side by side. I turned my head to face her. "Okay, listen. I have information you want, and you have information I want. Can't we just get along and work together?"

She covered her face with her hands. "But I don't want to work with you, Drunk. You're careless and stupid."

I winced. "Like I'm dying to work with you? You're egotistical and vicious. You're like a pit bull. Some people like them, but I'll never understand why."

"Shut up. I own a pit bull. Pit bulls are awesome."

I rolled my eyes. "Well, that figures."

She turned her head then. "Listen. Benny is full of energy, full of life. He loves to go jogging and has the best disposition. He's the most loyal animal you will ever find. So call me a pit bull. I have no problem with that."

I looked at her. If that was what a pit bull was like, she really was like a pit bull. The woman was full of energy, full of life. I could see her being loyal if anyone ever got past the rough exterior she liked to cling to. "Okay," I said quietly, looking into her serene blue eyes.

"Okay?"

I nodded as she stared back at me. "Okay, I'll shut up."

We stared at each other for a while then. Only the steady hum of the window air conditioner filled the room. Finally she gave me a half-smile. "I wanna know what you know."

"Same," I said quietly.

She rolled over onto her side and held her right hand out towards me. "Truce?"

"Truce."

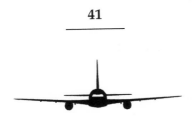

## 41

THE FULL MOON REFLECTED OFF THE OCEAN, PROVIDING JUST enough light to be able to see the surf in front of us as we strolled quietly along the beach barefoot. My toes slid through the sand while the ocean waves lapped gently against my ankles. The warm breeze coming in off the Atlantic felt good rustling my hair. I let out a relaxed sigh, quite possibly my very first of this trip. It was exactly what I'd pictured my honeymoon to look like.

Except, of course, the woman next to me wasn't Pamela.

She was Nicolette Dominion—a crazy CIA agent gone rogue. Whatever. I put that behind me as I moved the bucket of chicken to my other hip so that it was between us. "Another drummie?"

She rubbed her stomach. "Oh God, no. I couldn't. I'm stuffed."

I shrugged. "More for me." I took out another piece of the Colonel's Extra Crispy and gnawed down, savoring the crunchy taste of home. After calling a truce, we'd both agreed we needed food and booze before being able to properly relax enough to actually open up to one another. And imagine my surprise to discover that there was a Kentucky Fried Chicken on Paradise Isle, and it was located on a boardwalk, along a public beach.

I hadn't had to do any convincing when I'd suggested we leave our shoes in the car and take the bucket of chicken and the bottle of tequila down to the water. She'd actually been first to untie her hiking boots and pull off her socks.

Now our bucket of chicken was almost empty, there were no fewer than a dozen shots of tequila missing from the bottle, and we were *almost* starting not to hate each other.

"So she actually called you?" asked Nico. "Fucking brass balls, that one."

I nodded. "Right? I couldn't believe it either. I told her not to call me anymore, and I told her to stop harassing my folks."

"Want me to punch her in the throat for you?"

"Aww, Nico, you really do like me, don't you?" I slung an arm casually over her shoulder.

She didn't even let it rest there for a second before she shoved it off her. "Hey, hey, hey, let's not get ahead of ourselves. I just have a proclivity for punching people in the throat."

I eyed her out of my peripheral vision. "See? I knew it."

She laughed. "Joking. Joking. I just really think it's crappy what she did to you."

I'd told her the whole blessed story. Of course I'd left out the vow of abstinence part. I didn't need her to feel *that* sorry for me, and there was quite a lot of embarrassment that went along with admitting that I hadn't been sexually active for the better part of three years. "Well, thank you. I'm glad you understand why I came on to you so strongly on the airplane."

"I didn't say that, but—"

"Hey!"

"No, I get it." She laughed and laid a hand on my arm. "I get. You've been through a lot the last couple of days."

"I have! And it's supposed to be my honeymoon, but here I

am trying to figure out why everyone on this godforsaken island wants to kill me."

"I don't want to kill you."

"You don't?"

She shook her head. "I mean, I did. I just don't now. Now that I understand you really don't know what's going on."

"I'm kind of piecing things together. Okay, barely piecing things together," I admitted, swinging my eyes upwards.

She stopped walking and took a swig of the tequila.

I stopped beside her.

"Are you ready to talk about what you know?"

I took the bottle from her and took a swig myself. It burned on the way down, but I appreciated how the more my throat burned, the less my ass burned. I was almost starting to forget I was being chased around by a bullet wound. "Yeah, now I'm ready."

"Should we sit?" she asked.

I looked around. The choices were minimal. Beach or ocean. "I don't see a bench."

When I turned back around, Nico had already copped a squat on the sand. "Okay," I said, sitting down next to her and putting the bucket of chicken between us. I extended my long legs and crossed them at the ankles, leaning back into the breeze, I looked out over the ocean. "It's a nice night."

"Yeah, it is," she agreed. She wiggled herself around in the sand and scooted her butt so she was seated next to me and facing in the same direction. "I haven't had any time to sightsee while I've been here. It's been all work and no play."

"Well, at least there's no risk of Nico becoming a dull girl," I said honestly. "I don't think you could ever be a dull girl."

Nico giggled and leaned her head sideways over her shoulder, only inches from my own shoulder. "Aw, Drunk. Did you actually say something to me that was nice?"

"I didn't do it on purpose, I swear," I promised, holding up three fingers in a Boy Scout salute. "It was an accident."

"Well, I liked it. You should be nice more often."

"I am nice. Most of the time. You just happened to get off on the wrong foot with me."

She nodded. "Ditto that."

We were quiet for a few minutes. I don't know what she was thinking about, but I was pondering whether or not I still wanted to sleep with her. Nico broke the silence. "So, you've learned some new things about Jimmie's murder. You wanna share them?"

"I'd feel more comfortable if you show me yours first." I wasn't a complete idiot, after all.

"Fine," she sighed. "I work for a very wealthy man in Maryland, and Jimmie stole something very valuable from my client. In fact, I have reason to believe he was in the United States stealing similar items from other people as well."

"Ah. A cold storage key?" I asked, even though I had no clue what the hell a cold storage key was.

She spun around in the sand to face me. "All this time you knew what I was looking for?"

Playing it cool, I lifted a shoulder. "I figured it out."

"Drunk!" she breathed. "All this time I thought you were just a fucking numbnuts."

I swallowed hard. "Thanks?"

"You know what I mean. I bought your shtick. Hook, link, and sinker. Damn. I guess you're not quite as stupid as I gave you credit for."

I looked at her then. "Again, thanks!"

She giggled. "So. You've got the key. How many of them are there?"

"Two for sure. I'm not sure what the third is."

"What's it look like?"

"It's a thumb drive of some sort."

She nodded. "That's a key too."

"You wanna explain to me what a cold storage key is?"

"You don't know?"

"I mean, I…"

She giggled. "Drunk, you have no idea what any of this is really about, do you? You just know someone put something in your bag and now the bad guys are trying to get their hands on it."

My mouth opened, but no sound came out. I dropped my hand into the sand and then looked at her. It was time to just put my cards on the table. "Not a fucking clue."

She shook her head with a faraway smile. "Okay. Here's the deal as far as I can tell. Jimmie was hired by someone on the island to go to the US and steal these cold storage keys." She took a deep breath and another swig of tequila before she continued. "As cryptocurrency became bigger and more valuable, people began to hack them. Cryptocurrency isn't protected like a bank is protected. If someone robs a bank, you're still going to get your money. It's protected by the FDIC. If your Bitcoin is hacked, you're out the money. There's no tracing it. It's just gone. So lots of people started storing their Bitcoin fortunes offline, where they can't be hacked. They store them on what's called a cold storage key. Then, in order to hack it, the thief would quite literally have to come find your key and steal it."

"Okay, so you're saying Jimmie stole your boss's key."

"Exactly."

I nodded. "Okay, well, that makes sense. I'm shocked your boss sent you all the way down here to retrieve the key, though. How much was it worth?"

"I don't know about the other two keys, but as of the current price of Bitcoin, my boss's key is worth seventeen million dollars."

The blood drained from my face as I looked at Nico. "S-seventeen *million*?"

"Yup. That's why I have to get it before Jimmie's Aussie friends get their grubby hands on it. Once they've gotten the key, they can transfer the money to their own accounts and the money's gone. Then there's not a whole hell of a lot I can do about it."

"So if those guys were friends of Jimmie's, why'd they kill him?"

"I assume because when they met up, he didn't have what they wanted."

"And he told them who did," I said knowingly.

"Exactly." She crawled in front of me with a smile on her face. "But, Drunk, this is amazing news! *You've* still got the keys! Now all of this can be over."

I tilted my head sideways. "I do still have the keys, and they're hidden in a very safe place. I wish it could be so easy as to just give yours back to you, but that doesn't change the fact that these guys want the keys too. And Sergeant Gibson thinks I killed Jimmie."

She slumped down into the sand. "Oh."

"Yeah, *oh*. So if you want your keys back, I'm gonna need your help proving my innocence."

"Proving your innocence...but, Drunk—"

I held a finger to her lips. "Please, Nico. I know you don't want to help me, but—"

She pulled away and took my hand down from her lips. "No, I want to help you Drunk."

"You do?"

She nodded and kneeled up in front of me. "I do. I'm in. First thing in the morning, I'll help you. Okay?"

I looked at her skeptically. The moonlight glowed behind her head, giving her hair a shining halo, like an angel. "Is this the alcohol talking?"

"No, not the alcohol. I wanna help you. You deserve it. None of this is your fault. Alright?"

I nodded and sat up straighter in the sand. "Alright. Thanks, Nico."

She smiled and then crawled forward so she was kneeling over the top of my lap. Wordlessly, she dropped her head towards mine. Her silky black hair poured across my forehead. And then I felt her lips brush over mine softly.

My breath dammed in my lungs, and the steady staccato in my chest drummed faster. I hadn't expected her to kiss me.

Nico's lips wrapped around my bottom lip, and she gave a gentle suck. When I felt her tongue invade my mouth, I wrapped my arms around her waist and squeezed her tiny frame against me. It felt good to feel the heat of a woman against me again. Every instinct in my body told me to flip her over into the sand and quench my thirst.

But I resisted.

I knew she was probably just trying to pull one over on me, and I didn't have the heart to get played yet again. I snaked one hand into her hair and gave a gentle tug while I pulled my head back slightly.

Our mouths parted.

She looked down at me. Wanton lust filled her eyes.

I slid my hand off her waist and down the front of my pants, where I retrieved my weapon. I held it out to her.

Nico took one long look at the gun. My silent offer of surrender. The ball was in her court now. "I don't want it," she murmured. Her blue eyes swung up to look over my head. She glanced in both directions down the boardwalk before leaning over me again. This time she whispered in my ear. "Not here."

# 42

---

I REALIZE THAT WHAT I'M DOING HERE IS TELLING YOU A STORY about my life, and it would be wrong of me to leave out some of the juiciest, most relevant parts of the story. With that being said, some things should be left to the imagination. So I'll just let you imagine the amazingly epic moment when my three years of celibacy came to a dramatic and awe-inspiring grand finale. I could have given you every detail about how smooth Nico's skin felt pressed up against my bare chest and beneath my fingertips, and I could have expounded on how she moved on top of me like a bucking bronco rider, but I won't. This isn't a porno, after all, and I'm a gentleman.

I will say this, however. Waiting three years to have sex is stupid and makes absolutely no sense. While the buildup is epic, the grand finale is over far too quickly to make up for the previous three years of celibacy. It's like cooking dinner for a hot chick. It takes you all day to clean your apartment, go grocery shopping, do the prep work, and the cooking, and then you're done eating in ten minutes and on to the bedroom. And then you're left wondering why you'd gone to all that trouble in the first place, when you could have just taken her out to dinner and gone back to her place instead.

But it is what it is.

I hit the note.

I popped the cork.

And then I did it all over again, two more times that night and one more the next morning. Just to make sure my shit was still on point.

And by the way I had her singing, it was.

So the next morning, I rolled off her and headed naked to the shower. The bandage she'd used to patch up my bullet hole still clung to my backside, but now the white gauze was pilly and the tape curled at the edges—a byproduct of the friction between my ass and the bedsheet.

"Drunk! That. Was. Amazing," she breathed, her glistening breasts heaving in the sliver of morning light that poured through the shades of the scuzzy motel room. "You might be the worst cop I've ever met, but you certainly make up for any inadequacies on the street in the bedroom."

I stuck my head out the bathroom door and winked at her. "You're welcome."

I heard her throaty laugh as I shut the door, locking it. I started the shower water running and turned the fan on. Then I grabbed my shorts off the bathroom floor and retrieved my gun. I pulled the bottom towel off the little rack above the toilet, set it on the bathroom counter and carefully unfolded it. Safely ensconced inside was the magazine I'd hidden there the day before.

Yes, I know we'd called a truce. And, yes, I'd wanted to believe her. But I wasn't stupid. You really think I'd have handed her a loaded gun?

Come on! The woman had punched me in the throat just a few short days ago! And then she'd pulled a gun on me the day after that. She'd fooled me once, shame on her. She'd fooled me twice, shame on me. But I was not about to let her fool me a third time. I had much more self-respect than that.

Once I'd showered, dressed, and reholstered my now-loaded gun, I emerged from the bathroom. "Shower's free," I said, giving her foot a nudge with my hand. "Hurry up. We've got work to do."

---

NICO LOOKED at me as we drove away from her motel room later that morning. Her hair was down, but she had the sides pinned back just below her ears. She looked beautiful.

"What?" I asked.

The apples of her cheeks ripened as I looked at her. "Nothing."

I poked her underneath her rib cage and she jerked the steering wheel. "Drunk!"

"Then tell me. What?"

She shook her head and then turned to stare out the window as she pulled the bullet-hole-ridden car out onto the street. She sighed. "You just surprise me, that's all."

I leaned back in my seat and smiled. Letting my elbow rest on the car's windowsill, I looked out the window. I'd heard that statement a time or twelve in my life. "It's all about being underestimated."

"Yeah? Get underestimated a lot?"

"Damn straight," I said with a puff of air and a nod. "Story of my life. You know, when I was a kid, I was a little guy."

"You? You're huge."

I shot her a lopsided grin. "Yeah, I wasn't always huge. There was a time when I was scrawny. I had these little spindly arms and these knock-kneed bird legs. I was one of the shorter kids in my class too."

She shook her head and laughed. I could tell she didn't believe me.

"Yeah, my buddy Mikey was always having to take up for me because at that time he was bigger than I was." The thought of Mikey as a child brought a smile to my face. He was a tubby bastard back then. So fat that his own mother had called him Butterball until he'd reached the sixth grade and begun to stretch out. "You know, thinking about it, it's crazy now, because Mikey hit his peak sophomore year, but I kept growing well through my senior year, and now I dunk basketballs and he can only dunk donuts." I laughed.

"The funny thing was, I knew how to fight. My pops taught me. He called me scrappy or wiry. But my mom didn't believe in violence. So while I knew how to fight, I also knew that *getting in fights* meant getting in trouble at home. So I let Mikey take up for me. That's how my whole life has gone. No one has ever expected much out of me, and therefore, I haven't had to give much. In school, the teachers knew me as Danny Drunk, the little awkward kid with the stupid name. My pops worked hard, but he wasn't much of a social guy. So I don't think he ever went to a single school event. Not parent-teacher conferences, not Christmas concerts, not bring your father to school days, nothing. I think my teachers made some kind of assumption that my father was an alcoholic, and that I was being raised by a single mother. So they floated me."

"Aww, poor Drunk." She patted my leg. Maybe she was being sarcastic, but it sounded sincere.

I shrugged and looked out the window again. "Not poor Drunk. I don't feel sorry for myself, and I'm not saying any of that to make you feel sorry for me. I had a great childhood. I had great parents. I didn't give a fuck that Pops didn't go to my Christmas concerts. I was a shitty singer, and what good did it do to have thirty second-graders standing on risers dressed in navy-blue dress pants and red sweaters? Not a damn bit of good if you ask me. I was saying all of that to highlight the fact that I've been underestimated my whole life. And after a while, you kind of don't try very hard. Especially in my case. I'm a pretty likable guy. I'm friendly. I'm easy on the eyes. I'm not a bully. I like beautiful women, and beautiful women like me. People let me slide."

"Even as an adult? I find that hard to believe. At some point, you have to give things your all."

I lifted a noncommittal shoulder. "Maybe, but I haven't gotten to that point yet. Think about it. You're a teacher and you have two guys. One's an unattractive asshole who misses an assignment and blames his fucking dog, and the other's a good-looking suave fella who apologizes and brings you a snack and says it'll never happen again. Who you gonna cut a break?"

She laughed and turned the car down a side street. "I got it."

"Yeah, exactly. I'm not a bad guy. I think I've just become a bit lazy over the years. At least that's what my mother says."

"You ever gonna change?"

I shrugged. "I dunno. Maybe. Maybe I'm being forced to now. Maybe this is some kind of cosmic karma that's happening."

"You believe in karma?"

"That's a hard fucking yes. Everyone gets what's theirs eventually."

"Not everyone."

I looked out the window again. "I'm a cop. I have to believe that justice will prevail. Otherwise, what am I doing? Look at Jimmie. While I don't think he deserved to be murdered, he certainly caught karma right between the eyes."

"Yeah," she said with a quiet nod.

I turned to her and rubbed her arm. "I'm sorry. Was that too cold-hearted?"

"Maybe a little graphic. But I agree, he didn't deserve to be murdered."

"Yeah, so the way I see it. Someone else has some karma coming to them. You know, for taking Jimmie's life. Worthless as it might have been. I mean, I know he stole from your boss, but I don't know what else he's done in his life. Maybe he was a rapist before he turned into an international thief."

"Maybe he was a priest."

My head bobbed up and down. "Or maybe he was a goddamned monk. Exactly. We don't know. It's not our place to judge."

"So we're going to go talk to this Cami Vergado, and then what?"

I sighed. I wished there was a clear answer to that question. It would make my day go so much more smoothly. "And then we get her to talk to the cops, tell them what she knows, and then they find the bastards that killed Jimmie and I'm in the clear."

"You make it sound so easy."

"Let's hope it goes that easily."

"And then how are we going to celebrate?"

I reached a hand over to caress her cheek. "I think you know the answer to that question." I smiled. My life of celibacy was officially over.

# 43

THERE WERE PARTS OF PARADISE ISLE THAT WERE BEAUTIFUL. Large parts. The beaches were gorgeous. The ocean views continued to amaze me. Fenced estates sat pristine, likely worth a mint. The touristy shops downtown, which ran the length of the harbor, were kept immaculately groomed to accommodate cruise ship day-trippers. And the resorts, at least mine, anyway, were little slices of heaven.

But then there was the rest of the island. The urban parts. Those parts of the island looked much like an impoverished inner city or a third-world country. Not having been on the island long enough, I had no direct knowledge of the crime statistics. I only knew what I could see. The buildings were all in poor repair and looked as if one big tidal wave could obliterate the better part of the island's infrastructure. The schoolchildren, dressed in uniforms, played ball in the streets. Produce vendors lined the sidewalks, and men selling bottled water out of cardboard boxes stood on the street corners. Goats, chickens, and domesticated animals ran amok, and the traffic buzzing by seemed not to notice.

Cami Vergado lived in what might be considered an upscale neighborhood to an islander, though in many cities around the United States, it still would have been considered "on the wrong side of the tracks." Her home was in a three-story apartment building. Painted a sun-faded yellow, the stuccoed exterior crumbled around the foundation.

Nico parked her car along the street.

"Let me do the talking," I said quietly as we walked up the front sidewalk. I gave a nod at two women sitting on a bench six feet away, smoking cigarettes.

"Are you sure? She hasn't been to work all week because she's scared. Do you really think *you* talking to her makes the most sense? I'm a woman. Women feel more comfortable with other women."

"Clearly you're underestimating me once again," I said with a smirk. "I make women feel very comfortable. I got you to ease up, didn't I?"

Nico rolled her eyes. "Not at first! At first you were like a bull in a china shop!"

"I admit, I might have come on strong at first, but that was because you called for it. I mean, look at you! You're not just any woman."

"Fine. I'll give you the benefit of the doubt. You go ahead and do the talking, and we'll see where that gets us. Alright?"

"Thank you," I said, holding the door for her. The dank, musty smell of wet sheetrock hit us immediately.

"Ugh," groaned Nico, holding her nose.

Just as repulsed by the smell, I tried not to show it. I pointed to the stairs. "Second floor. Cami's in apartment two ten."

We launched ourselves up the stairs, taking them two at a time. Apartment 210 was the last door at the other end of the hallway. I knocked while Nico peered out the square window that faced a narrow alley and a matching apartment building on the other side of the alley. I stood in front of the door, holding my breath, willing her to answer. When she didn't come to the door after several additional knocks, I looked at Nico. "Now what?"

"Come back?" she suggested with a half shrug.

"We could get a key from her landlord."

"You know which one is the landlord?"

"Not a clue." I looked at the door then and wondered if I could break it down. It looked flimsy enough. Maybe one kick would do it. I held a hand up to Nico. "Stand back. I'm gonna kick it."

Just as I reared back to give it a solid kick, she grabbed my arm. "Hello? You can't be serious. Bull in a china shop?" she reminded me, lifting her brows. "You are not going to kick the door in, Drunk. Why would you kick it?"

"What if she's in there and hurt or something?"

"Again. Why would you kick it?" She rolled her eyes and put her hands in her hair. "I realize you've *got* brute force, but that doesn't mean you have to use it. Sometimes things can be handled with a much lighter touch." She held up two bobby pins she'd pulled out of her hair. "Step aside, sweetie."

I let her push me out of her way and watched as she gnawed off the rubber end of one of the pins. She straightened it and bent the tip, then bent the second pin into an L shape. She squatted down in front of the door and began to work her magic. It took her less than two minutes before she was able to turn the handle and the door opened.

She stood up and smiled at me. "See? Light touch." She handed me the pins. "You're welcome."

Nico strutted past me. "Hello! Anybody home?" she called out, announcing her presence in the apartment while I stood in the doorway, observing the sexy confidence she exuded, seemingly without effort.

It was hot.

I removed my hat and tucked the pins into the inner hatband. I'd keep the pins as a memento. I guess I was sappy like that. Buried somewhere in my old room at my folks' house, I still had the panties from the woman who had taken my virginity. Yes, woman. I was sixteen, and she was Mikey's twenty-five-year-old cousin, Alexis, visiting from Topeka. She'd tucked her panties into the waistband of my Nike athletic shorts as she'd kissed me goodbye, and I'd learned that older women really were a beautiful thing. Nico would now live in infamy as the second woman to have taken my virginity, and her bobby pins would be my constant reminder.

Replacing the hat, I followed her into the apartment. "See anything?"

Nico returned to the doorway with her weapon drawn in front of her chest defensively. "No. She's not here. Close the door."

I laughed at her. "What's the point of holding the gun? You don't have any ammo in it."

She shoved it into the holster she wore on her hip. "Yeah, because of you I don't," she barked. "Thanks again for that."

I shrugged as I pushed the door shut behind me. "Better safe than sorry."

"Yeah, well. I'd rather carry it and look scary than not carry it and look like a pushover."

"Oh, trust me. You're plenty scary without the weapon," I said with a chuckle. I threw my arms up. "So, she's not here. Now what?"

"Think like a cop, Drunk."

"Right." I hadn't had my morning dose of Dr. Pepper. My brain felt like a watch with a stuck second hand. I walked to her fridge and peeked inside. She had a six-pack of diet soda inside. I pulled one out and looked at it with a wrinkled nose. "Diet, ugh," I said as I cracked open a can. Something was better than nothing.

"Are you seriously stealing this woman's soda?"

"Did we seriously just break into her apartment?" I retorted before taking a big swig of the nasty-tasting sludge.

All I wanted was the caffeine to infiltrate my veins. I'd suffer the taste just to get my brain to turn on.

Nico rolled her eyes and walked towards an open door. "I'll check her room for any clues as to where she might be. You check out here."

I nodded and strolled around the kitchen. It was tiny by American standards. One small white cupboard hung over a four-foot-long counter with a sink. A miniature gas stove and a refrigerator flanked the counter. No microwave. No toaster. Her coffeemaker was a teakettle on the stovetop, and the filter was some sort of sock attached to a wire. There was a small wooden table and two chairs in the middle of the kitchen area. I poked through the unopened pieces of mail on the table. It was just bills and junk mail, nothing that looked like it might offer any clues to her whereabouts. I sucked down another slug of the sugar-free soda and walked to a small stand in her living room area where a phone and answering machine sat. I pushed the blinking button. The machine beeped then spit out an assortment of messages.

"*Camila, es mami. Llámame cuando llegues a casa del trabajo.*" Beep.

"Hello, dear, it's Mrs. Acosta. Are you coming into work today? Call me when you get this message, please." Beep.

"*Camila, es tu madre. Llámame por favor.*" Beep.

"Cami, it's Mrs. Acosta again. Are you okay dear? I'd really like to hear from you. Give me a call." Beep.

"Cami, it's Mariposa at work. Is everything alright? Are you coming in today?" Beep.

"Yo, Cami, it's Freddy. Just checking on you. Mari said you haven't been showing up at the resort. Everything okay?" Beep.

"Cami, it's Mrs. Acosta. I'm really getting worried. It's not like you not to show up for three days in a row. Please call me." Beep.

"*Ahora estoy preocupado por ti. ¿Estás bien?*"

The machine beeped again as Nico reentered the room. "Sounds like lots of people are worried about Cami."

"She hasn't checked her message in days." I shook my head. Even *I* was beginning to get worried about her. "This isn't a good sign."

Nico poked her head into Cami's bathroom.

"Maybe we need to get ahold of someone who knows her," I suggested. "Mrs. Acosta, Freddy, or her mother."

"Yeah, unfortunately, how are we supposed to find any of those people? This place is pretty sparse. I didn't find any clues in her bedroom. But I did discover that the woman enjoys a decent pair of high heels."

"You wouldn't think it would be that hard to find out who Mrs. Acosta is. Obviously Cami was working for her. So we ask around."

Nico nodded. "Let's try those two women out front."

I locked her apartment door as we left, and Nico and I rushed outside to fresh air. The women who had been sitting on the bench smoking were now gone.

"Great," said Nico, shoulders slumped forward.

A loud banging on the side of the building caught our attention. "I'll check it out." I sprinted to the far end of the building to discover a maintenance man unloading garbage into a dumpster. "Hey!" I hollered at him.

He looked up at me. "Yes?"

"You work here?"

"Yes."

"Do you know any of the people who live here?"

He nodded. "Of course. I know them all."

Nico caught up to me.

I pointed towards the building. "We're looking for the woman that lives in apartment two ten. She hasn't shown up for work in a few days, and we're worried about her."

"Her name is Camila Vergado. Cami," added Nico.

"Yes, I know Camila," he said, his furrowed brow telling of his concern.

"Have you seen her lately?" I asked.

He looked thoughtful for a moment. "Maybe a week or two ago was the last time I saw her. She works a lot."

"Two jobs, right?" said Nico.

He smiled. "Yes, she's a very hard worker."

"We're coming from the Seacoast Majestic," I said. "Do you know where else she works? Maybe I could check with them and see if they've heard from her."

"We know she works for a Mrs. Acosta," Nico added for authenticity. "We just don't know how to get ahold of Mrs. Acosta."

"Oh, Mrs. Acosta. Yes. She is an apartment manager. Camila cleans apartments for her a couple days a week, in the mornings, before she goes to the resort."

"Do you know how we could get in touch with Mrs. Acosta?" I asked.

"Sure. She has an office downtown. Sapphire Rentals."

"Thank you," said Nico, extending her hand to him.

"You're welcome."

As we began walking away, he shouted back at us. "Good luck. I hope that Camila is alright."

I grimaced. It was my only hope at the moment as well. "So do we."

# 44

WITH LITTLE TO NO STREET PARKING AVAILABLE DOWNTOWN, WE had to park several blocks away in a public parking lot and walk the three blocks back to Sapphire Rentals. It was midmorning, and tourists swarmed the downtown shops.

"Looks like a cruise ship just docked," said Nico, pointing across the bay to the most enormous boat I'd ever seen in my life. It looked to be the size of a small island floating in the water. Even from the distance, it was huge.

"Wow. That's impressive. I've never seen a cruise ship in person before."

"They don't have those in Kansas?"

"Missouri, and nope, no cruise ships in Missouri."

After leaving Cami's apartment complex, we'd stopped and gotten specific directions to Sapphire Rentals from a street vendor and were now following his instructions. Turns out, they worked out of an office above a jewelry store with a similar moniker, Sapphire Jewelers. The entrance to the rental company was a black door in a narrow, cobblestone alley behind the jewelry store. The staircase was narrow, and the wooden stairs creaked as we climbed them. At the top of the stairs, the landing split. A door on the left just had a number on it, but the door on the right had a small black placard engraved with gold lettering that said Sapphire Offices.

I pushed the door open to find a desk with a woman behind it talking on the phone. She smiled at us and held a finger up as if to say she'd be right with us while she finished her phone call.

Nico and I stood awkwardly while she described an apartment for rent to what sounded like a potential lessee. Finally, she hung up and looked up at us, shining a beaming smile. "Hello, may I help you?"

"Are you Mrs. Acosta?" I asked, even though I was fairly confident that that had been the voice I'd heard on Cami's answering machine.

She beamed even harder. She seemed like a sweet woman, with greying hair piled on top of her head in a bun and old-fashioned cat-eyed glasses perched on her nose. A string of pearls hung around her neck and attached to the back of the glasses. "Yes, I am. Are you looking for an apartment?"

"No, ma'am," I said, pulling my hat and glasses off. "We're actually looking for someone. We thought that maybe you could help us."

She sucked in her breath almost immediately. Then she lowered her chin and pulled off her reading glasses. "You're looking for Cami, aren't you?"

Nico nodded, narrowing her eyes slightly. "Yes, how did you know?"

"I've left her message after message. She won't return any of my phone calls, which is completely unlike her. I've just been worried sick about her."

"Have you tried calling the police?" I asked.

"No," she admitted reluctantly. "I haven't. I thought she might get upset if I got the authorities involved in her business. She's a very private woman. She doesn't like drama. But I was going to, I swear. If I hadn't heard from her by the end of the week, I planned to call. Has something happened to her?"

"We don't know what happened to her," I said. "She's not shown up for her job at the resort for several days. When was the last time you saw her?"

Mrs. Acosta pulled out a blue day planner and flipped it open. "She cleaned an apartment for me six days ago. She was scheduled to clean another one for me on Tuesday morning, but she didn't show up."

I nodded. That was the morning after she'd left the resort. I was starting to wonder if something hadn't happened to her. "Mrs. Acosta, do you have any emergency contact information that might help us locate Cami?"

She smiled, like she was happy to have some way of helping us. "Yes! I do. Let me get her file." She disappeared through a door.

"This is not looking good," said Nico under her breath.

"Maybe she's staying with family," I suggested. "You know, she's scared that there are a pair of killers on the loose, so instead of going back to her apartment, she decided to go stay with them."

Nico patted my arm. "I'll keep my fingers crossed that you're right."

Mrs. Acosta reappeared, holding a manila file folder. "Her mother lives in Puerto Rico. I've got her phone number if you'd like it. She's also got a brother Freddy Vergado that lives on the island."

"Can you write down his address and phone number for me, Mrs. Acosta?" I asked.

"Of course! Freddy should be able to help you. He's given Cami rides to work before. He's a nice man."

"Do you know where he works?" asked Nico.

"I believe he does auto repair or something."

"You don't know where?" I pressed.

She swished her lips sideways. "Hmm. Perhaps at Steve Dillon's?"

"Is that downtown?"

"No, it's on Route 37. Follow the coastline north and get off on 386."

"Thank you, Mrs. Acosta," I said, taking the slip of paper she'd written Freddy's contact information on. "We really appreciate it."

"I just hope that Cami's alright. She's such a sweet woman. She works very hard to be able to send money to her mother in Puerto Rico. If you would please tell her to call me when you find her, I would greatly appreciate it."

"We will," Nico assured her as I opened the door.

---

Sitting in Nico's car ten minutes later, we stared out at the road ahead of us. We'd both agreed that going to Freddy's place of employment was a better plan than going to his apartment. At midday on a Friday, it was very unlikely that a working man would be home.

The silent drive along the coastline with windows down was peaceful, but cloaked with a heady layer of unease. Neither of us had to verbalize our suspicions. The fact that Freddy had left Cami a message on her answering machine made us feel fairly confident that she hadn't been staying with him. Our only hope was that he knew someone else she might be staying with or, best case, that he'd heard from her after he'd left the message.

As the ride up the coastline progressed, we began to see billboards for Steve Dillon's Automart. Traffic was busy, but we made the drive in under a half hour. We parked the car and headed inside, unsure of what we were going to tell Cami Vergado's brother.

"Hello, may we please speak with Freddy Vergado?"

"Freddy?" asked the front desk woman.

"Yes, please."

She got on her phone and requested someone send Freddy

Vergado to the front counter. It took almost ten minutes before a side door opened and a stocky Puerto Rican man in his late twenties, early thirties, appeared in denim coveralls, wiping his hands on a shop rag. "You need something?" he asked the woman at the counter.

She pointed at Nico and me. "You have visitors."

Nico led this time, which was probably better, considering her *attributes.* "Hello, Freddy. My name is Natasha, and this is my friend..."

Oh, we were giving aliases, were we? I held out my hand to him. "Columbo."

He shook it but looked confused. "I'm sorry, do I know you?"

"No," said Nico. "We're from the Seacoast Majestic..."

"Oh, man," he sighed, shaking his head before Nico could finish her sentence. "Cami still hasn't shown up for work?"

"No," I said, feeling the wind rushing out of my sails. I felt like holding my hand up and saying, *Say no more, you don't know where she is either.* "We were hoping that maybe you'd seen her."

"No, I haven't. I've tried calling her apartment and her cell phone all week."

"When's the last time you spoke to her?" asked Nico.

"Sunday. We had supper together," he said.

"Does Cami have any other family on the island, or friends that she might have decided to stay with for a while?"

"Stay with?" He furrowed his brow. "Not that I know of."

"No boyfriend?"

"Nah."

"She would have told you if she did?"

He nodded. "For sure. We're pretty close. That's why it's so odd that she's gone this long without getting in touch with me."

"Is it also odd that she's not shown up for work all week?"

"Absolutely. My sister's a workaholic. The whole

family is."

"Yeah, that's what we've kind of heard," I said. "Does your sister drive to work, or does she walk?"

"She drives."

"What kind of car?"

"A little red two-door. A Nissan Sentra." He gestured with his hands. "It's old, I wanna say it's an eighty-seven. It's real boxy. You know? And it's got a black bumper."

"So, do you have any ideas on where we might go to locate her?"

Freddy sighed. "No, man. But now you got me extra worried. I thought for sure I'd hear from her by tonight or tomorrow. We usually catch up on the weekends."

The realization that the last time anyone had seen or heard from Cami Vergado was at the resort on the night of Jimmie's murder worried me, and I hated having to be the one to pass that worry on to her brother, but it was clear he hadn't heard about the murder. I flashed back to Al showing me the article in the newspaper. It was a small article. The death of a tourist hadn't even been worthy of making the front page of the *Paradise Isle News*. What were the chances it had been a big deal on TV? But the fact of the matter was, we needed his help if we were going to find her.

"Freddy, can you think of anywhere that Cami would go if she were scared someone was following her?"

Nico looked up at me sharply. My own words even made me wince, but I had to ask.

"Scared that someone was following her? Are you serious? Do you know something that you're not telling me?"

I fidgeted in place. This wasn't going to be easy. "There was a murder at the Seacoast Majestic on Monday night. Did you hear about it?"

Freddy shook his head, his eyes big. "Nah, I don't read the papers. I—I don't even have a TV. I work such long hours it's not worth it. Who was killed?"

"An Australian man. A tourist, I guess," I said, rubbing a hand around the back of my neck.

"Okay?"

"Cami was the one who reported hearing the gunshots."

"What!"

"She said she saw two men fleeing the scene," I added.

"Oh my God! You think they knew she saw them?"

"It's definitely a thought," I admitted grudgingly. "You know, at first, I think the resort thought she was just scared to come back to work, but now that we've been trying to find her and we can't... I'm not gonna lie, Freddy. It's concerning. Like, where would she go if she were scared?"

"Well, did you check and see if anyone saw her at the sandwich joint around the corner from her apartment?"

Nico frowned. "No, why would we check there?"

"She always goes there after work to grab dinner. Whether or not she thought someone was following her, she probably went there. I don't think she'd go home, you know. She wouldn't want to lead them to her place. My sister's not dumb. She'd try and go somewhere with lights in the parking lot. Gino's is all lit up. I bet she went there to eat dinner and then wait out whoever might have been following her."

"Okay, we'll go check it out."

"I'll go with you," said Freddy, shoving the rag he carried in his back pocket and heading towards the counter. "I'll just tell my boss."

I held a hand out to stop him from moving. "Listen, Freddy. We've got your number. There's no need to go getting all excited yet. It's very possible she's staying with a girlfriend or something until they get an arrest made in the resort shooting. You hang tight. We'll call you if we find something. Okay?"

"You promise?"

"You have my word."

## 45

WE DROVE THE HALF HOUR BACK TOWARDS THE DOWNTOWN AREA and then headed in the general direction of Cami's apartment. Just before we got to her place we came across a small strip mall on a busy road. It had lots of streetlights in the parking lot, and a sign out front read Gino's Deli. It had to be the place Freddy was talking about.

We went inside. The smell of warm, freshly baked bread snaked into my nostrils and went straight to my stomach, making it growl almost on impact. We'd had a long night and morning of lovemaking and then a long couple of hours tromping around the island with no food. I needed to eat.

I ordered a pastrami on Italian and a Dr. Pepper. Then I pulled out my wallet and looked back at Nico. "What are you having? I'll buy you lunch."

"I didn't realize we were eating. I can get my own," she mumbled, taking a half-hearted step towards the door. "I've got some cash in the car."

"Oh, quit," I said. After she'd returned my manhood to me, the least I could do was to buy the woman a hoagie. "Give the man your order."

"Fine. I'll have a turkey and cheese with lettuce and mayo and a bag of chips. On Italian," she added.

"You want anything to drink?"

She wrinkled her nose, and I was reminded just how perfectly adorable of a nose it was. "We've got too much to do right now. I can't drink a whole soda. Can I just have a sip of yours?"

I shook my head. "I don't share drinks with people. That's not happening."

"You can't be serious."

"I'm dead serious. You want me to get sick?"

"I'm not sick, Drunk. And if I were, you'd already have whatever I have. You realize that, right? We exchanged spit all night and all morning."

"Yeah, that's different. I don't share drinks. She'll take a soda too," I said to the pimple-faced kid behind the counter, who had gotten a smile out of the fact that Nico had essentially announced to him that we'd hooked up the night before.

"You're weird," she whispered as we walked away after I'd purposely let the kid behind the counter keep the change out of a twenty. He'd been stoked to get such a large tip, but what he didn't realize was that after I consumed my sandwich, I was coming back for information.

"Yeah, I suppose I've got my quirks. Doesn't everyone?"

"No."

"You have 'em too. You just don't see them as quirks," I explained with a smile before shoving a giant portion of my footlong sandwich into my mouth. "Everyone else sees them as quirks."

She curled her lip, which in turn wrinkled her nose. "Didn't your mother ever tell you not to talk with food in your mouth?"

I shrugged. "She told me lots of things. She also told me nice girls don't have sex on the first date. So there's that."

Nico shot me a dirty look as she opened her chips then and shoved a barbecue chip in her mouth. "Asshole."

I was so hungry, and the sandwich was so amazingly delicious, that I wound up going back up for another hoagie and a cookie. When we were done, we went back up to the counter armed with little more than a name.

"Hey," I said to the guy that had waited on us.

He looked surprised to see me up there for the third time. "Need another sandwich, sir?"

I smiled. "Not exactly. I was wondering if you've seen my friend. She lives around here and eats here a lot. Her name is Camila."

He looked at me blankly.

"Vergado. She goes by Cami. She's Puerto Rican."

"I don't know, sir. We have a lot of regulars that come in here. I really don't know their names, though. And there are a lot of Puerto Ricans on the island, so that doesn't narrow things down. What does she look like?"

I glanced over at Nico. I didn't have a picture, and I suddenly realized that I'd never asked anyone what Cami looked like. What a detective I was.

Nico shrugged.

I looked at the guy again. "We think she might have been in here Monday night. Did you work Monday night?"

The kid thought about it for a minute, then he shook his head. "No. I don't work on Mondays. Sorry."

"Anyone else here work Monday night?" asked Nico.

He looked through the window into the kitchen behind him and then hollered. "Hey, Rick, did you work Monday night?"

"What?"

"There are some people out here. They wanna know if you worked Monday night."

"Yeah, why?"

"Can you come out here?"

We heard the man groan, but he appeared a minute later. "May I help you?" the words were meant to *sound* helpful, but his face clearly told of his annoyance at being interrupted in whatever he had been doing.

Nico cocked her head sideways and smiled at him sweetly. "Hi, Rick."

He looked her up and down curiously. "Who are you?"

"My name is Natasha. My friend and I are looking for a woman who we think might have come in here on Monday night. She's a regular. Her name is Camila Vergado. She goes by Cami. Do you know her?"

Rick didn't seem very excited about answering our question. "Maybe."

"She drives a red Nissan Sentra. An older model. You know, the boxy kind with a black bumper," I added.

A light seemed to go off in Rick's mind. Now he actually looked interested in talking to us. "Kind of a beat-up junker?"

I could play along. "Yeah, sure. You seen it?"

He curled his finger. "Follow me." Rick led us around the counter, through the small commercial kitchen and out the back door into the alley. Next to a dumpster was a beat-up red Nissan Sentra with a black bumper. "It's been sitting here all week. I put a sign up in the break room that it needed to be moved by close of business today or I was having it towed. I thought it was one of my employees', but no one's claimed it yet."

I couldn't believe it. Finally, we had a break in the case. Her car! It had to be. I nodded at him. "Yeah, this is her car. Thanks man."

He frowned. "You gonna take care of moving it, or do I need to call someone to have it towed?"

"No, no," said Nico. "We'll take care of it. Thanks a lot for your help."

"Yeah, no problem."

He went back inside, leaving us standing in the alley

staring at Cami's car. Nico and I looked at each other uneasily. This was definitely *not* a good sign. We approached the car trepidatiously and peered inside. It was empty. I heaved a tentative sigh of relief.

"Check the door," said Nico across the top of the car.

I looked down at the driver's door. Hooking the hem of my shirt around the door handle, I gave it a tug. "It's unlocked."

"Good. Pop the trunk," she said, walking around to the back of the car and waiting.

I leaned down and hooked my shirt around the trunk latch and pulled.

I heard it pop and then squeak as Nico lifted it open. Immediately she sucked in her breath. "Oh my God."

I closed my eyes. I didn't even need to ask. "She's in there?"

"Yup."

*Fuck.*

"Now what?" asked Nico, slamming the trunk shut.

While I felt thankful in that moment that I hadn't had to see Cami, I felt my heart drop. Not only would I now have to tell Freddy Vergado and Mrs. Acosta that they weren't ever going to see Cami again, but finding Cami had been my last chance at getting the only eyewitness to relay to the island cops that I was *not* the one she'd seen fleeing my motel room.

I leaned backwards against the dumpster and crossed my legs out in front of me. "I don't know," I sighed.

"Well, Jimmie's killers obviously knew that she saw them."

"Yeah." I nodded absentmindedly. My mind had already wandered off to think about what life would be like inside an island prison. Would it be worse than an American prison? I shook my head. *Oh man, this is going to kill my mother.*

"Drunk?"

"Yeah."

"Are you with me?"

"Yeah." The muttered word came out without conviction.

269

She heard the resignation in my voice as I looked up at her blankly. "Come on. We can't quit now."

"I know, I know." She was right. I had to push past the feelings I was having.

"So Jimmie's killers followed her. Who knew that there was an eyewitness?"

I shrugged. "I'm pretty sure that everyone at the hotel knew. The front desk employees heard us talking about it that night, the valets knew, Ozzy—he's the head of security—and Artie, the resort owner. Obviously they both knew."

"Yeah. Who else?"

I shrugged. "I don't know. Maybe even some of the guests. The police obviously knew. Plus if any of the employees knew, they all knew. Gossip like that spreads like wildfire."

"Okay, well. Let's think about this logically. If after killing Jimmie, the killers came out of your room and saw Cami watching them. Then what?"

"Bang, bang. She'd be dead on the spot."

"Right. So, it's more likely that they didn't even known she'd seen them until after they'd fled."

"Makes sense," I agreed, thankful that Nico's cooler head was prevailing. Mine was still spinning.

"So, it's more likely that they'd found out later that she saw them. Right?"

"I suppose."

"That means someone told them there was a witness. It could have been any of those people you just listed. It could have been an employee, a guest, or even the cops that told those men about Cami."

"You think it could have been the cops?"

She shot a raised eyebrow at me. "You've met the island cops, right? They don't like American tourists much, do they? Would you put it past them to do whatever it took to blame this on an American?"

"And kill an islander to do it? I don't know." It seemed too far-fetched to believe, but there were definitely crooked cops in the US too. We couldn't rule anything out.

"It wouldn't just be about framing you, Drunk. Look at the bigger picture. Whatever's going on is worth millions. Dirty cops have killed innocent people for far less. If they're involved in this international cryptocurrency crime ring and Jimmie's murder, then of course they're going to take out an innocent islander just to keep their secret safe."

Dirty cops? International crime ring? I lifted my hat so I could run a hand through my hair. How in the world had I gotten wrapped up in this mess?

Nico continued. "The point is, we don't know what to believe and we don't know who is trustworthy. To me, this means that we can't call the cops. They'd be quick to pin Cami's murder on you. You were the one that found her, after all."

"Can't call the cops? So are we just supposed to let Cami rot out here in the car?"

"No. We can call in an anonymous tip after we're long gone," she suggested.

My head rolled back on my shoulders. The thought sickened me.

"Unless you've got a better idea?"

A light went off in my mind. I lifted my head and smiled at Nico. "As a matter of fact, I do."

## 46

With her hands on her hips, Nico shot me a confused look as a Paradise Isle police cruiser pulled up in the alleyway, just in front of the dumpster. "I thought we agreed not to call the cops?"

"Yeah, well, I have faith in this one," I said, shooting Nico a wink as Officer Francesca Cruz opened her car door and stepped out.

Nico took one look at the woman, with her long hair bound up in a ponytail, her impressive physique, and her perfectly made-up face, and turned to me, rolling her eyes. "Of course you do."

"What?" I said with a smile. "She told me she wanted to help me in any way she could. I thought she'd be a safe bet to call."

Officer Cruz walked over to me and Nico. "What's going on, Drunk?"

"Officer Cruz, we really appreciate you coming so fast."

She smirked. "Trust me, it's my pleasure. Sergeant Gibson had me behind a desk again, typing up some paperwork for him. I couldn't get out of there fast enough."

I pointed at Nico. "This is my friend, Nicolette Dominion. Nicolette, this is Officer Francesca Cruz."

The women cast critical eyes on one another. Nico's raised eyebrow and pursed lips told me she was annoyed. I wasn't sure if she was annoyed because I'd called island authorities, or if she was annoyed because the island authority just happened to be a beautiful woman.

Officer Cruz extended a hand to Nico. "Ms. Dominion." Her tone was stiff, and she dipped into a lower, throaty register to speak Nico's name. I couldn't help but smile at the female equivalent to a male's puffed-out chest when greeting another dominant male.

I could tell Nico wanted to roll her eyes, a gesture she seemed comfortable with, but she restrained herself. If Officer Cruz was going to be professional, Nico was going to be twice as professional. "Just Nico is fine. Right this way. Drunk, pop it."

I gave a curt nod and spun around to walk over to the car and pop the trunk. I made sure to once again hold my shirt over the door handle and the latch to avoid leaving fingerprints and being tied to the scene in any way. "We found Camila Vergado. She was the maid that saw the two men flee the scene at the resort."

Officer Cruz took one look at the body and sucked in her breath. Perhaps we should have prepared her before springing Cami's dead body on her. "Oh my God."

"Yeah," I said, hanging my head.

She held a hand to her nose and mouth. The smell was putrid. Cami had been in the hot trunk for the better part of a week, but she'd been next to a dumpster, so it was more than likely that any odor that had leaked out of the trunk had been attributed to the garbage. "How'd you find her?"

"Long story short, her brother, Freddy, told us to check Gino's. He said she always stopped here for dinner after work at the resort. We think she was followed after the murder. Her car's been parked back here all week. The restaurant owner thought it was an employee's car."

Officer Cruz's jaw dropped. "This doesn't look good for you, Drunk. You being the one that found her."

Nico made a face. "See? I told you we shouldn't have called the cops."

I swallowed hard. "Yeah. I knew it wouldn't look good. I hope you know that's why I called you. After our little run-in the other day, I could tell that you were in my corner. Probably one of the few people on the island that is. When we found her, we could have just left her in there for someone else to find or not find. But I'm a good guy. I couldn't do that. She's got a brother and a mother that are worried sick about her. I figured if I was going to report it, I would report it to someone that would believe my story."

Nico took one look at Officer Cruz's gaping jaw and shook her head. "Save your breath, Drunk. She doesn't believe you."

Officer Cruz looked at Nico and then at me. "Alright, well, I didn't say I didn't believe you. I just said it looks bad for you."

"I know it does. That's why I'm going to need you to just say that you got some anonymous tip about a bad smell coming from an abandoned car."

"You want me to lie to Sergeant Gibson?!"

I looked at her with pleading eyes. "Yes."

"Drunk—"

"I'm sorry, Officer Cruz. Francesca. I'm not trying to get you into any trouble here, but I didn't kill that guy in my room. I swear. And Nico and I are going to prove it. When we do, I'll make sure that you get the collar."

"I don't know, I—"

"She's not gonna help us, Drunk," said Nico, clearly not impressed by Officer Cruz. "We'll have to figure something else out."

Officer Cruz held up her flattened palms and tipped her

head forward slightly. "Now hold up a minute. I didn't say I wouldn't help you."

"Well, you also didn't say that you would!" snapped Nico.

I spun to face Nico. "Nico," I growled. "You're not helping any!"

"Listen. You asked for *my* help, Drunk. Not this... *secretary's*!"

Officer Cruz's eyes widened. "Secretary!"

"Nico!"

Nico threw both of her arms out by her side and stomped off, growling under her breath.

Officer Cruz watched Nico disappear around the corner of the strip mall, an equally annoyed look on her face. "What's *her* issue?"

I sighed. "I'm sorry about her. She's just upset. We spent all day looking for Cami, just to find her dead. And then we agreed we wouldn't call the cops, and I called you. But I called you because I really felt like I could trust you and we could help each other."

Officer Cruz put a hand on her hip and looked down at the ground while she mulled over my request. Finally, she looked up at me. "You'll let me make the collar when you find the guys who did this?"

"A hundred percent!"

She poked a finger into my chest. "You better not make me regret this, Drunk."

I raised my right arm to shoulder height and held up three fingers. "On my honor. You will *not* regret this."

She sighed. "Fine. I'll handle this."

I wanted to hug her. I gave her one of my winning smiles instead. "Thank you, Officer... can I call you Francesca?"

"No."

"Frankie?"

"No!"

"Okay, okay," I said, holding out a hand to shake hers.

"Officer Cruz it is. Thank you, Officer Cruz. I will forever be in your debt."

"You better not forget it!"

Just then Nico reappeared in her rental car around the corner of the alley. I waved at Officer Cruz as I began to walk towards the car.

Nico held my phone out the window as she drove. "Drunk! Your phone's ringing!"

I jogged faster and took it from her. "Drunk here."

"Drunk?"

"Al?"

"Yeah. Where are you?" His rough voice sounded panicked.

"In town. What's up?"

"Uh, we've got a situation."

I felt the blood drain from my body. "A situation? What happened, Al?"

"Artie's been abducted."

"Artie?"

"Yeah."

"How do you know he's been abducted and didn't just go somewhere?"

"Ozzy said he saw him leave with two men. I think it's the guys that broke into your room."

"*What!*" I bellowed into the phone. I rushed around to the passenger's side of the car and got in, gesturing for Nico to start driving.

"Don't yell, will ya? I got my hearing aids in."

I winced. "Sorry. Did Ozzy call the police?"

"Not yet."

"Good. Tell him not to. We'll handle this."

"Okay. There's more, Drunk."

"*More?*"

"Yeah. The cold storage keys. You know, those things that Jimmie hid in your bag?"

"Yeah?"

"They're gone too. I think the men got those too."

"Don't fuck with me, Al."

There was silence on the other end of the phone. Then finally, "I'm really sorry, kid."

I buried my head in my hands and sighed. Finally, I sat up straighter. "Don't move, Al. We'll be there as soon as we can. Meet me out front."

"Okay, Drunk. We won't do anything until you get here. Be careful."

I hung up the phone and glanced over at Nico, now behind the wheel and maneuvering back onto the busy street.

"Where are we going?"

"The resort."

"What happened?"

"Those two Aussies kidnapped Artie Balladares and took off with the cold storage keys."

Her jaw dropped. "Are you kidding me?"

"I wish I was. Just step on the gas, okay?"

# 47

NICO FLOORED IT ON THE RIDE BACK TO THE RESORT WHILE positively fuming. "I can't believe we've been fucking around in town all day, chasing a dead girl, and now the key's gone."

"Correction. The *keys* are gone. There are three of them," I pointed out.

"I'm only concerned about my boss's. Fuck the rest. If the Aussies get the money transferred before we get it back, we might as well kiss the seventeen million dollars goodbye."

Nico pulled up beneath the porte cochere, where we found Al waiting for us.

"Where's Ozzy?" I asked, jumping out of the car before it had even come to a complete stop.

Al's face looked pained as he followed me into the lobby. "He's in Artie's office. You don't think they're going to kill him, do you?"

I stopped moving and looked down at him. "Al, they didn't kidnap Artie because they wanted a new guy to hang out with. Of course they're going to kill him. But first they're going to make sure the keys are what they were looking for."

Al nodded, his mouth agape. Genuine fear floated in his eyes.

I squeezed his arm. "We'll find him, alright. I've gotta talk to Ozzy and see if he's got any clue as to where they might have taken him."

Al stopped walking as Nico came running up behind us, but there wasn't time for introductions now. "Come on. We need to talk to Ozzy before we run out of time."

"You go ahead." He waved us on and then pointed back to the lobby area. "I've gotta see a man about a horse."

I stared at Al incredulously. "Are you shitting me right now?"

"What?" he barked. "At my age, you never give up an opportunity to use the bathroom! Go, go, I'm not stopping you. I'll be there shortly."

Nico and I ran to the counter, where I found Anita working. "Anita. I need to see Ozzy. He's in Mr. Balladares's office. It's an emergency."

"Yes, Mr. Becker told me that Ozzy's expecting you. Go ahead."

I nodded and led Nico to Artie's office, where Ozzy was waiting behind Artie's desk. His usually neat office had been turned upside down. Drawers on Artie's filing cabinets had been pulled out and emptied, garbage littered the desktop, and the oversized portrait of the *Seacoast Majestic* that I'd admired just a few days before was now on the floor. I realized now that it had been hiding a wall safe, which now stood wide open and empty.

Ozzy stood up the second we entered the room. "Drunk, oh thank God you're here. I-I didn't know what to do." He looked up at Nico and his eyes grew round. "W-who's she?"

"Ozzy, this is Nico. Nico, this is Ozzy Messina. He's the head of resort security."

She looked him up and down and then lowered her chin as she turned to me. "Seriously?"

Even though I understood the ridiculousness of that statement, I furtively squeezed her ass as a silent gag order. We couldn't risk Ozzy taking offense and then deciding not to tell us what he knew as a result. "Okay, Ozzy. We need to know everything. Start from the beginning, and don't leave anything out."

Ozzy nodded and sat back down behind Artie's desk. "Well, I was in here, working on Mr. Balladares's computer. Earlier in the day, he said he was having some issues with his internet. I stepped out for a minute to check the settings on the equipment in the server room, and as I was coming back, I saw him leaving out the back with two men."

Nico leaned forward, putting her hands flat on Artie's desk. Her biceps smashed her breasts together, exposing her cleavage to Ozzy. "What did the men look like?"

Ozzy's eyes lowered to her chest. "T-they were *big*," he said slowly, unable to tear his eyes away from the pair of breasts within touching distance.

I snapped my fingers in front of his face. "Ozzy, focus. This is important. If we're gonna find Artie, we need to know who we're looking for."

"Oh, r-right," he stuttered. He closed his eyes and tried to gather his wits, then he looked at me and tried not to even turn his eyes back towards Nico. "They were big. One was a big bald black guy with tattoos on his neck. He had an eye patch. The other guy was white. He kinda looked like a cowboy or something."

Nico and I exchanged knowing glances. We knew them all too well.

"We were told they got the cold storage keys," said Nico, still leaning over Artie's desk.

Ozzy nodded, without taking his eyes off of me. "Yeah, Artie had locked them in the safe last night. T-they must have forced him to open it."

Nico slammed her hand down on the desk, then swiped a pile of trash onto the ground. "Shit!"

Something about that caught my attention. I leaned down

and plucked up one of the things she'd tossed off. "Is this a Greasy's Taco wrapper?" I asked, unfolding one of the crumpled wrappers.

Ozzy picked another one up off Artie's desk and turned it over. "Umm, yeah. Why?"

"I found Greasy's Taco wrappers in the truck those guys were driving," I said. I looked at Ozzy curiously. "Ozzy, do you think Artie was being abducted by those men, or is it possible that he left voluntarily with them?"

Ozzy made a face. "Well, now that you say that, it didn't seem like he was putting up much of a fight. He might have been leaving voluntarily. I-I really don't know."

My hands covered my face. It was all making sense now. Artie, Mr. Cryptocurrency himself, had set this all up! That's why Jimmie was staying at his resort. That's how Jimmie had figured out which room I was in the first night, and how the Aussies had figured out which cottage I was in later. He'd known about Cami seeing everything, so he'd sent them to follow and kill her. And then Al had just handed over the cold storage keys to him. I couldn't believe it. Al was going to be devastated to find out that his old buddy was the one that had ordered the hit on both Jimmie and Camila Vergado!

I looked up at Ozzy. "Can I see Artie's computer?"

"See it? Y-yeah, of course. Why?"

"I just want to check something."

Ozzy got up and moved out of the way. I took his place behind Artie's desk.

"What are you looking for?" asked Nico, coming up behind me.

I logged on to the internet and checked Artie's browsing history. Sure enough, he'd been on several cryptocurrency websites that day. I pointed at the screen. "I don't think Artie got abducted by those guys, Nico. I think he's the kingpin. Check this out."

She stared at the screen. Her jaw dropped. "No fucking way. He's been under our nose this whole time!"

"Exactly."

She gave me a little shove. "Move over. I wanna see if he cashed out the cold storage keys yet."

I got up and paced the room while she worked. "I can't believe this. Al's going to flip out when he hears that Artie's been behind this all along."

Nico suddenly sat up straighter and clapped her hands together. "He hasn't cashed them out yet!"

"You're sure?"

She nodded. "I'm sure."

I shook my head. "But that doesn't make any sense. Why would he not cash them out? Why wait?"

She shrugged. "I don't know. Don't shit where you eat, I guess. He's trying to make it look like he was abducted. He steals the keys and cashes them out off-site so if the cops check his computer, they won't have a record of him doing it here. That way he keeps the money and no one is the wiser. It'll just look like the bad guys got him and the keys, and then when he comes back to the resort, pretending to have escaped, it's business as usual."

"So if he hasn't cashed out the keys yet, then where's he going to do it at?"

Ozzy raised a nervous hand. "U-umm, excuse me?"

We both looked at him at the same time.

"What?" asked Nico, her voice clearly annoyed.

"D-do you think if Artie and those guys knew I saw them, they might come after me?"

My mind immediately went to Cami and what had happened to her. I couldn't help but nod. "Unfortunately, Oz, yes. I think until we get them arrested, no one's safe."

Ozzy's eyes widened. "U-mm," he began, clearing his throat. "I just remembered. I've got something really important to do. Ummm, in my room. Do you need me anymore, or can I go?"

Nico flicked her hand towards him as if she were shooing away a mosquito. "Go, go."

"We should go too," I said. "We can figure out where to start looking for them in the car. Come on."

We left Artie's office and headed for the lobby, where we found Al just returning from the bathroom. "Drunk! Sorry about that! Did you figure anything out?"

"Hey, Al. We've got a pretty good idea of what's going on," I said. "And you're not going to like it."

Al shook his head. "What are you talking about?"

I put a conciliatory hand on his shoulder. "Al, we think those two Aussies were working for Artie. We don't think he was abducted. We think he left willingly."

Al furrowed his puffy white brows. "What!" His head began to shake. "No way. You're crazy!"

"No, Al. He had all kinds of cryptocurrency stuff on his computer's history. We think he left the resort property to cash out those cold storage keys."

"There's no way Artie would have tried to have you killed, Drunk. Artie's a nice guy. H-he wouldn't do that."

"Al, I realize you're having a hard time with this. And I get it. The guy was a lifelong friend, but it's time to face facts. He got into some deep shit."

"Drunk, we gotta go," said Nico as she edged towards the glass lobby doors, tugging on my arm. "We're going to get there too late if we don't hurry."

I nodded. "We're going to try and find Artie."

Al's eyes widened. "B-but I have to tell Evie what's going on. Wait for me. She's in the dining room having lunch with Eddie, Gary, and those two women."

Nico tugged harder on my arm. "We don't have time for this, Drunk. We have to go."

I looked back at Al. The thought of taking him on such a

dangerous mission worried me. All I could think about was Mrs. Al's face when she'd told me to keep her husband safe. I smiled at him. "Go ahead, Al. We'll wait here for you. Just hurry up."

He gave me a smile and then turned and hobbled away.

"You can't be serious, Drunk. We're waiting for that old guy to ride along?"

As soon as Al was out of earshot, I shook my head. "No. I can't have him getting hurt. Let's go."

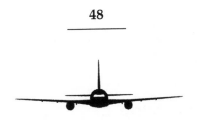

## 48

"They've got to have a base of operations on the island. Where would it be?" asked Nico as she drove back in the same direction from which we'd just come.

"Hell if I know," I grumbled. "You know more about this island than I do."

"Maybe they took Artie to the house we were staking out the other night?" suggested Nico.

I lifted a brow. "You don't think the shooting might have put a big red target on that place?"

"Ugh," she groaned. "That was your fault, by the way."

"Not my fault, and must we point fingers? You started shooting at them first."

"If I hadn't, we'd both be dead right now. You're welcome."

I waved a dismissive hand at her. "I'll say thank you when I've got something to be thankful for."

"You're a real pain in my ass, Drunk. You know that?"

"Can we stop arguing? We've got to figure out where they would go." I massaged my temples with the pads of my fingers. "We need to think like criminals. That shouldn't be too hard for you, right?"

She rolled her eyes. "Well, we're dealing with computer hacking, cyber security, so you know they're going somewhere that they can get online. I definitely think they're headed into town. Lots of the places out here in the rural areas of the island aren't wired for internet, or even phones."

"Oh man, the internet on the island definitely sucks," I agreed.

"So, where would they go for decent internet?"

Decent internet. Suddenly, Akoni's words were replaying in my head. *"Greasy's Taco. Best Wi-Fi on the island. Best tacos too."* The image of the wadded-up Greasy's Taco wrappers in both the Aussies' impounded truck and Artie's office rolled around in my mind. Then it clicked. Their base of operations was somewhere near Greasy's Taco! "We've got to get to Greasy's Taco!"

"Oh my God, Drunk. You literally just ate two footlongs two hours ago. There's no way you can be hungry already!"

I chuckled. "I'm not hungry, Nico. I think that's where they're using the internet. Greasy's has the best Wi-Fi on the island, and both the Aussies and Artie had Greasy's wrappers. I think their base of operations is somewhere close by."

Nico threw her hands up. "What the hell? We've got no other leads."

My phone rang then. "Hey, Al."

"Drunk! Where in the hell are you? I'm waiting outside."

"We left. We couldn't wait around any longer. I'm sorry."

"You left without me?" I could hear the hurt in his voice. It was like a knife to the chest. "But I'm your partner!"

"I know, Al. It's just that—"

"Just that what? That you don't have faith in me? You underestimate me, Drunk."

The knife twisted. "I'm sorry, Al. But I promised your wife I'd keep you safe when things got hairy."

"She isn't my boss. Artie's my friend. I'm not going to just hang him out to dry."

"Al, I swear to you. Artie's involved in all of this."

"Where are you now?"

"We're headed downtown. We think they might have their base of operations somewhere near Greasy's Taco. It's a fast-food joint."

"I know what it is," he snapped.

"Listen, we'll get it all figured out. Alright? I swear, I'll—"

The line went dead before I could finish my sentence. I'd offended him.

"Shit."

Nico looked at me. "What?"

I let out a heavy sigh. "Nothing."

"Who is that guy anyway?"

I put my elbow up on the windowsill and peered out at the palm trees flying by. "Oh, no one special," I said with a heavy heart. "Just my partner."

---

NICO PULLED the car into the Greasy's Taco parking lot and we went inside. Greasy's was a small, grungy diner situated in the front end of a large warehouse-style building, well deserving of a name such as Greasy's Taco. The spicy, pungent aroma of chilies and cilantro made me cough upon entry. There was a salsa bar beneath a sneeze guard by the door and a small one-register counter beneath a hand-painted menu board. The small dining room was divided into two distinct sides by a wall running down the middle. On one side were two rows of booths separated by a narrow alley of square tables, and on the other side, there were two rows of tables with only a walkway between them. In the back of the dining room, there were small half-tables attached to the wall, each with a barstool so singles could sit and eat while looking out the window facing the covered front porch and the street.

Nico and I paced the length of both sides of the dining

room before meeting back up at the counter. "They're not here," she said through a clenched jaw.

"I see that." I turned to look at the girl working a piece of gum behind the counter.

She was probably all of sixteen years old. Her long black hair was wound up in a pair of braided space buns on either side of her head. She had long, fake red fingernails that looked incompatible with her position at the register.

"Can I take your order?"

I leaned on one elbow on the handmade wooden counter. "Actually, we're looking for a friend of ours. It's kind of an emergency. His name is Artie Balladares. We think he might come here a lot. He's hard to miss. He's a really big guy. Like *really* big." I gestured with my hands to describe Artie's girth.

The girl blinked. I was fairly confident she was wearing fake eyelashes too, as I'd never seen eyelashes that long before. "I dunno," she said with a shrug.

"You dunno?" Nico repeated.

"Nope." The girl snapped her gum, telling us exactly what she thought of our emergency situation.

I glanced over at Nico. Her face was red and her fists balled by her thighs. It looked as if she was working very hard at suppressing the urge to leap across the counter and strangle Little Miss Gum Chewer. I stood up straighter and put a hand against the small of Nico's back, hoping the touch might calm her. "How about two big Australian guys? One's white. He wears a cowboy hat and boots, and the other is black. He's bald and wears an eyepatch. They used to drive a big black truck," I suggested.

She lifted a brow. "You talking about Colin and Bruce?"

I stared at her. "Do Colin and Bruce look like the guys I was describing?"

"Yeah."

"Okay, then, yes, I'm talking about Colin and Bruce. Have you seen them lately?"

"Yeah."

I had to let out a steadying breath. "When's the last time you saw them?"

"Just a few minutes ago, they pulled into the parking lot."

"Did they come inside?" asked Nico anxiously.

The girl shrugged. "I'm not really sure."

I frowned at her. "How can you not be sure if they came inside? Wouldn't you notice?"

"No, because they work in the back," she said as if that was the dumbest question ever. "There's a separate entrance back there, so I wouldn't know."

"In the back?" said Nico.

"Yeah. Around the corner." She kind of pointed with one of her long blood-red nails.

I nodded. "Thank you."

"Hey, don't you want a taco?" she asked as we began to walk away.

"Don't worry. I have a few more days on the island. I'll be back later for one," I promised.

Outside, I looked at Nico. "Now what? We just go barging in?"

"We have no choice. It'd be nice if we had more than one gun with bullets." She shot me a dirty look.

"Why are you looking at me like that?"

"Because it's your fault that we don't have any lead for my gun. If you hadn't tossed all my ammo—"

"Are we still keeping score? Because I'm pretty sure you're still ahead in the fault game." I held up a hand and began ticking off fingers. "First there was the throat pun—"

"Shut it, Drunk," she said, pulling out her empty weapon.

I pulled out mine and together we stalked around the side of the building. The dilapidated back door had a window in it, but the inside had been covered with paper.

I tried the door handle. "It's locked," I whispered and then removed my hat. "You wanna pick it?"

"You really think now's the appropriate time for picking a lock, Drunk? I think now's more like the time for brute force, don't you? You don't see the difference?"

I threw up my arms. "Women." Then, popping my hat back on my head, I reared back and plowed my foot into the door. The jamb splintered and the door sprung open, and Nico and I rushed inside, guns blazing.

# 49

THE UNFINISHED AREA WE BURST INTO WAS LARGE, WITH HIGH ceilings. It was kind of a cross between an oversized garage and a small warehouse. Artie Balladares was seated stiffly on a wooden chair facing the doorway. Only his hat and the top of his head were visible from behind a row of computers. At the far end of the building, there was an overhead garage door with a black Jeep Cherokee parked inside.

Artie's eyes widened when he saw me. Immediately, he glanced around furtively before whisper-hissing at me, "Drunk! Oh, am I glad to see you! How in the world did you know where I was?"

I pointed my gun at him. "What the fuck, Artie? How could you?" My booming voice echoed, bouncing off the empty corners of the room.

His eyes scanned the room once again. "Shh! What are you doing? They'll hear you!"

Nico disregarded the warning and slowly approached him, her gun drawn on him too. "Where are the keys, Artie?"

Artie shook his head. "The keys? I don't have them." He jerked his head backwards towards a set of wooden doors in the wall. "They have the keys. And they're going to hear you if you don't keep your voices down." Then his face crinkled and he let out a loud "AACHOO!" He wiggled his nose, like he was trying to stifle another sneeze. "Can you get over here and untie me so I can itch my nose?"

I made a face. "Untie you? You're tied up? Why are you tied up?" I walked towards Artie, still holding my gun defensively. I wasn't about to look like an idiot and fall for his trap.

"Well, that's generally what bad guys do when they abduct you. They tie you up," said Artie. He raised his eyebrows. "Are you new at this cop thing or something?"

I grimaced. "Oh, please. We know damn good and well this isn't an abduction, Artie."

Artie looked confused. "It's not an abduction? Then what exactly would you call it?"

"I call it you trying to double-cross your friends."

"You're not making any sense, Drunk. Now get over here and untie me before they come back." He looked over his shoulder again. "I'm not really sure where they went."

I was standing right next to Artie now. His hands were indeed tied behind his back, and his feet were tied to the chair. I tipped my head sideways. "I don't understand why you're tied up."

Nico approached me. "I'll tell you why he's tied up. He knew we'd come looking for him, and he's still trying to make this look like an abduction."

"*Look* like an abduction!" snapped Artie. "Why in the hell would I need to make it *look* like an abduction? It *is* an abduction."

"Shut up, Artie," I growled. "We've had enough. We just want the keys back."

"I don't have the keys! I'm telling you! *They* have the keys."

Without warning, a noise sounded behind us. I turned to see Ozzy Messina coming in through the door I'd just kicked down. My eyes widened. "Ozzy!"

"Drunk."

"What the fuck are you doing here? I thought you were hiding in your room."

Ozzy lifted a shoulder. "I decided to follow you. I was worried about Artie, and I thought if I was ever going to be a good security guard, I should probably start taking lessons from a real-life cop."

I rolled my eyes. This kid was something else. "Ozzy, now's not the time for a ride-along. These guys aren't playing around. They killed Jimmie, and they killed Cami. You need to get out of here before you get hurt too."

Artie sucked in his breath. "Oh my God. They killed Cami?"

Nico groaned. "Oh, please. You were the one that tipped them off that there was a witness. Quit acting. We already know you're the kingpin of this whole operation."

"I'm the—" Artie's eyes widened and he sneezed again. When he recovered, he tried speaking again, "What the hell are you talking about? I'm not the kingpin of this operation! Whatever gave you that idea?"

I smiled at him. I couldn't believe he was still trying to sell the act. "Do you seriously want to go over everything?"

"Yes!" boomed Artie. "I do! Those men barged into my office, forced me to get the keys out of my safe, then forced me at gunpoint to get into their vehicle. And then they brought me here, tied me to this chair, and then disappeared. Then you three show up. It's like a three-ring circus around here, and I have no idea what's going on!"

Ozzy wagged his finger at Artie. "You know, I trusted you, Artie. All these years of my father working for you and then me working for you. I thought I could trust you. I can't believe you'd go to such elaborate lengths to fool us all."

Artie shook his head. "I really wish I knew why you all think I have something to do with kidnapping myself. Why would I do this?"

"So you can steal the cold storage keys and hack the funds

for yourself," hollered Nico. I could tell she was sick of the games. I didn't blame her, I was too.

"Why would I do that? I have my own money! I'm a self-made billionaire. I had a prosperous business, and I invested in cryptocurrency in its infancy. I don't *need* to steal anyone else's money. I have my own!"

"The fact of the matter is, Cami Vergado is dead. Someone tipped off those two goons that there was a witness to their crime," I said.

"And you automatically assume that was me? I love all my employees! Why would I want Cami to be killed? It breaks my heart to hear that she's been killed! It could have been anyone that tipped off these guys."

"Well, it's pretty coincidental that you're so big into cryptocurrency and that's what's involved in the crime right now, don't you think?" asked Nico.

Artie puffed air out his nose. "Not really. If I had to guess, I'd think that these guys thought they could get money out of me in some way. I mean, I don't know how else to explain that coincidence."

I shook my head. "We saw your computer history, Artie. You've been on a bunch of cryptocurrency websites."

"Well, yeah! I'm an investor. I check my accounts several times a day. There's nothing wrong with that!"

I let out a dry laugh. "You know, you would have gotten away with it all if it hadn't been for the mess in your office today."

"The mess in my office? What are you talking about?"

"The Greasy's Taco wrappers."

"What?"

I nodded. "That was when all the pieces finally came together for me."

He shook his head, scoffing. "I have no idea what you're talking about."

"I found Greasy's Taco wrappers in your two friends' truck yesterday."

"I assume you're talking about Bruce and Colin. They're not my friends, but okay?"

"And Greasy's Taco just happens to have the best Wi-Fi on the island."

Artie curled his lip. "This is cop logic?"

I ignored him and continued. "So when we found Greasy's Taco wrappers in your office after you were abducted, I finally *saw* the connection. You all had the wrappers because you were working out of the building!"

"I certainly didn't have any Greasy's Taco wrappers in my office," said Artie in a huff.

"We saw them, Artie!"

He shrugged. "Believe what you want, but I don't eat Greasy's Tacos. For starters, I'm allergic to cumin. And greasy foods don't sit right with my stomach. I've literally *never* eaten a Greasy's Taco in my life."

My eyes widened. "But I saw the wrappers! We all did!"

Artie shook his head and shrugged. "They weren't mine, then."

I narrowed my eyes at him. "Well, then, who else would have been eating Greasy's Tacos in your office?"

"I don't—" He stopped talking and looked at Ozzy then. "Wait. Ozzy, were you still working in my office after they took me?"

All eyes turned to Ozzy then.

The kid's mouth hung open, and he slowly started walking backwards, towards the two doors behind Artie. "I—"

My mind swirled. "Ozzy?" I said the word like I didn't believe it, mostly because I didn't. Ozzy was a joke. There was no way he'd be able to pull this off and somehow manage to frame Artie!

Ozzy lifted his hands defensively as he slowly backed up.

"Now, I don't know what you're talking about, Artie. Those were your wrappers. I saw you with them!"

Artie's eyes narrowed in on Ozzy. "You little weasel! So it *was* you! You were trying to frame me for this?" Artie struggled to get up out of the chair so he could go after Ozzy.

Ozzy reached a hand around his back.

Nico aimed the gun at him. "Freeze!"

But it was too late. He pulled a gun out of the back of his pants. Then he leaned his head backwards and let out a whistle.

I trained my gun on him. "Put the gun down, Ozzy."

"You put the gun down, Drunk," he said. When the doors behind him didn't open immediately, he hollered backwards, "Bruce! Colin!"

We could hear thumping, and then the two Aussies appeared in the doorway. As soon as they saw the scene in the warehouse, they both drew their weapons.

"Drop your weapons!" I yelled. My heart pulsed in my ears, and my head spun. I was stunned to learn that Ozzy was *actually* the one behind everything that had happened.

"No, you drop your weapon, Drunk. It doesn't have to end like this. I don't have to make these two shoot you," warned Ozzy. "I mean, I actually thought you were a pretty cool guy. Of course, you hurt my feelings a little by underestimating me. I mean, I get that I don't look like your average evil genius, but isn't that the beauty of all of this? What does an actual evil genius look like these days? And why *can't* it look like me?"

"Ozzy, your father is going to be so disappointed in you. Why would you do this to him?" asked Artie, still tied to the chair in the middle of the room.

"You really have to ask, Artie? Really?"

"Yeah, I really do, Ozzy."

Ozzy shook his head. "My father was your right-hand man for all those years. He helped you get rich. Richer than either of you could have ever imagined! And then you went and sold the business, and you didn't even ask him if he wanted to buy it from you. And then you went and got richer on what he called fake money. He couldn't believe it. None of us could when you actually cashed out the money and left to buy a resort on an island!"

Artie's eyes widened. "Ted wanted to buy my business?"

"See! You didn't even know!"

Artie looked stunned. "No, I didn't know! There's no way he could have afforded it."

"He might have been able to get loans, or maybe you two could have worked out a deal. The point is, he missed out because you didn't even give him a chance."

"So you decided to go into cryptocurrency theft and kidnap me to take out your frustration?"

Ozzy shrugged. "I decided to go into cryptocurrency theft after I saw you bankrolled for life. This really isn't about avenging the diss you bestowed upon Dad. I mean, yeah, it's a perk. But I only had Colin and Bruce kidnap you because I needed someone to pin the thefts on. I figured you were the logical suspect. So, I figure, by this time tomorrow, we'll have cashed out the millions, we'll be safely back in the US, you'll be dead, and everyone will have blamed all of this on you. And no one will be the wiser."

"Except you forgot about one thing," I said.

Ozzy swished his lips to the side. "Hmm. One thing. What's that, Drunk?"

"You forgot about me. And her. We're not going to let you get away with this." I cocked the gun.

Ozzy laughed. "Well, yeah, there's you two. Of course, now that we've had the big denouement, and the mystery's been solved, I can't allow there to be any witnesses to my crimes. So, unfortunately, the three of you will all have to go." He smiled sadly before hanging his head and sighing. "You know I hate to do this, Drunk. Like I said, you're a pretty cool guy, but dude! Money talks. I'm really sorry." He held his hand out to the cowboy. "Colin, the keys?"

"Sure thing, boss." Colin dropped the baggie of items into Ozzy's hand. Then he started towards the Jeep parked in the garage. Right before he got to it, he held up a hand and snapped his fingers. "Take 'em out, fellas!"

And then, before either of us could get a shot off, the wall behind me imploded.

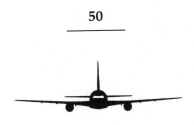

## 50

Instinctively, I leapt to the left, pulling Nico along with me. Wood and debris blew past our heads as a very familiar sky-blue Toyota Land Cruiser blew past us into the garage, knocking over the row of computers and getting within an inch of Artie, now lying on his side, but still attached to his chair. Gunfire peppered the passenger side of the vehicle.

The driver's-side door opened, and Al slid out.

I was hunkered down behind the vehicle when I saw him. My eyes widened when I saw him. "Al!"

"Drunk! Looks like I came at the right time. You appear to be in a bit of a predicament."

"No shit! We just found out that Artie doesn't eat tacos. I guess he's not the bad guy after all."

Al looked at me like I was crazy. "Well, no shit, Sherlock. I could have told you that. In fact, I *did* tell you that. Remember?"

"No, I don't remember."

"Do we really have to talk about this right now?" asked Nico, snatching Gary Wheelan's pistol from my hand. She stood up and fired several rounds at Ozzy and his men over the hood of the Land Cruiser.

"At lunch the other day. I told you that Artie was allergic. The theme was Mexican food."

I looked at Al. "Well, now, how in the hell was I supposed to know that?"

"Well, if you'd included me in the conversation, I could have told you!" snapped Al. "Instead you left me high and dry at the resort, and I had to come save your ass!"

"I'm sorry, Al. I didn't want you to get hurt," I hollered over the return gunfire.

"Dammit, I'm supposed to be your partner, Drunk. You can't treat me like I'm fragile. I'm not fine china. Okay?"

"But what about your wife? She'll kick my ass if you get hurt."

Al pointed at me. "Well, now the truth comes out. You're the big baby here. Scared of Evie."

I groaned. "I'm not scared of your wife, Al."

"Can you two shut the hell up? Artie's about to get his head blown off if we don't get over there and help him!" shouted Nico.

She pointed at Artie, who was lying on his side behind the computer tables that had flipped over when Al had blown through the side of the building. His white safari hat had fallen off, and his completely bald head was drenched with sweat as bullets flew over his body in both directions.

"Shit," I muttered as gunfire rained down on the side of the Land Cruiser. "I'll try and get him."

But Ozzy and his men were already strutting towards Artie. Ozzy had his gun trained on the Land Cruiser. "On your feet, Artie," I heard him say.

"You're going to have to untie me, then. I can't get up like this."

Ozzy groaned but nodded at his men. Colin and Bruce leaned over and freed Artie's hands from the ropes and then helped him to his feet while Ozzy covered them. "Get him in the Jeep."

Artie refused to move. "I'm not going with you, Ozzy."

Ozzy thunked his gun against the back of Artie's head. "Get in the fucking Jeep, Artie."

Artie winced in pain. "Hell, Ozzy. At least give me my hat."

Ozzy bent over and picked up the hat and handed it to Artie. "Here. Now get in the Jeep."

"Your father is never going to forgive you for doing all of this."

"Oh, no, no. Now that's where you're wrong. My father is going to be *proud of me*. He's going to love it when I come home with loads of cash. Of course he'll have no idea how I got it." Ozzy let out a maniacal laugh. "Oh, wait. I know. Maybe I'll tell him you left it to me in your will." Then he turned to face the Land Cruiser, where Nico, Al, and I were still hiding. "We're leaving now. Wish us well. And if anyone dares to follow us, I'll make sure Artie eats a bullet. Got it?" He whistled. "Bruce, Colin. Let's go. I got a plane waiting for me."

Colin and Bruce shoved Artie into the Jeep, and before we knew it, the overhead door opened.

"What now?" asked Nico. "We can't let them get away!"

I leaned back against the Land Cruiser. "They're headed to the airport. Let 'em go. I've got a plan."

With the taillights disappearing out of the warehouse, Nico stood up and turned to me with her hands on her hips. "Let 'em go? What the ever-living fuck, Drunk? I can't believe you just let them get away with my key!"

"I can't believe you let them get away with Artie!" added Al.

"Listen, it's obvious they're headed to the airport. Both of you need to calm down. I have a plan. Get in the vehicle. We'll sort this out on the way. Just don't follow them too closely. I don't want them to know we're following them."

We loaded into the Land Cruiser, with Al in the driver's

seat, me riding shotgun, and Nico in the back. "I can't believe Gary let you use his Land Cruiser. I thought this thing was like his baby."

"It is," said Al. "I didn't exactly tell him I was taking it. I know where he keeps his keys."

I stared at Al incredulously. "What?!"

Al navigated the Land Cruiser around the debris in the garage and pulled out the back garage door. "He said I could use it anytime I wanted. I thought this was an emergency. It's not like we can't fix it."

"Al, the passenger side is covered in bullet holes. He doesn't need a patch job, he needs an entirely new vehicle now!"

Al shrugged. "Trust me, if we save Artie's life, I think he'll be okay with buying Gary a new vehicle."

Nico leaned forward, propping her elbows up on either headrest. "So what's your plan, Drunk?"

"Well, first, we need to stall any plans they have of leaving the island." My phone hung onto the signal from Greasy's Wi-Fi, and I managed to find the Paradise International Airport's phone number before we got too far. Then I asked for the only name I knew there.

"Yes, may I please speak to Lola?"

"Her last name, sir?"

"Hmm," I said. "I guess I didn't catch her last name. She helped deboard a plane I rode in on earlier in the week. She maybe works for the Delta counter. Brown curly hair. Pencil skirt."

"Oh, yes, sir. Just a moment."

"You've got to be kidding me, Drunk!" snapped Nico.

"Shh," I hissed as I heard a voice on the other end of the phone again.

"This is Lola." Her voice was soft and feminine, just as a woman named Lola should sound. I was definitely going to have to give her a call when this was all over with.

"Hi, Lola, my name is Danny Drunk. I was on a flight you deboarded from Atlanta earlier this week."

"Officer Drunk, yes, you gave me your card. I remember you."

"You do?" I suddenly wished this was a personal call.

I could almost hear her smiling through the phone lines. "I do. I'm sorry I haven't called…"

"Oh, no, no, it's no problem. I still have a few days on the island."

She giggled.

"Listen, I was wondering if you could help me out with something?"

"Help you out? I can do my best!"

I proceeded to give Lola a brief rundown of how a friend of mine had stolen something that belonged to me. I told her his name, and I told her that he'd be heading back to the States on their next flight out. She informed me that there was a Delta flight to the United States leaving within the hour, but she promised she'd delay the departure as long as possible and do her best to make sure that no one boarded the plane until we got there.

"I can't believe you, Drunk," snapped Nico when I hung up the phone. "You just use women, don't you?"

"*Use women?*" I shouted, turning around. "I've never used a woman in my life! Women *use me!*"

"Puh!" spat Nico. "You're incorrigible!"

"Well, at least I got the plane stalled. What have you accomplished?"

Nico groaned and threw herself backwards against the seat.

I turned back around again to face the windshield. "Now, I've got one more call to make."

## 51

WE TORE INTO A PARKING SPACE IN FRONT OF THE AIRPORT. Ozzy's getaway vehicle was parked outside too, but we found it empty. Neither Artie nor the cold storage keys were inside. A Delta plane sat on the tarmac several hundred yards away behind a tall chain-link fence. A luggage cart filled with luggage sat underneath it, but there were no men loading it. I could only hope that was Lola's doing.

A siren wailed in the distance.

Nico looked back at me. "I can't believe you fucking called the cops again."

I shook my head. "Only one cop. I promised her she'd get the collar, remember?"

"You and her have a thing or something?"

I grinned. Back in the alley at Gino's, I'd thought it was possible that I'd seen a spark of jealousy, but now I was sure I saw it. "Jealousy doesn't look good on you, Nico."

"Jealousy?" She slugged me. "Don't get it twisted, you ass-napkin. I just want my fucking key back. And all the cops are going to do is fuck it up."

Al lifted his brows at Nico. He hitched a thumb towards her. "This is the girl that pulled a gun on you in your room?"

"Yes! This is the girl."

"I mean, don't get me wrong or anything. She's a good-looking dame, but she's got a mouth on her like a drunken sailor."

I stifled a laugh.

Nico rolled her eyes at him. "Oh, the dinosaur's got jokes. Fabulous. Now come on, let's get in there. We need to find Ozzy and get my key back."

I held her arm, preventing her from moving. "No. We can't go in there half-cocked. They've got security guards all over the place. They'll take us down in a second. We need to wait for Officer Cruz so she can go in there with us and take control of the situation."

Al nodded. "I agree with Drunk. Without island law enforcement, we won't be able to stop anyone. And we'll all wind up in jail."

Nico threw her arms up and began to pace while the sounds of the siren got louder. "You know, this would all be a helluva lot better if I had a gun that fucking had bullets in it." She shook her empty gun in my face.

"You were trying to kill me with it, so ex-fucking-scuse me for trying not to get shot." I was sick of hearing about how I'd tossed all her ammunition.

Al pointed at Nico. "You need a gun? Gary's got another gun in his glove compartment box."

I palmed my forehead. Gary was going to flip when he saw what had been done to his vehicle, and now Al was just casually handing out his guns like they were Tootsie Rolls.

"Yeah, I need a gun!" said Nico excitedly.

"Gary's not gonna like you giving his gun to a perfect stranger."

While Al crawled inside Gary's vehicle to retrieve the gun, Nico reached a hand out and pinched my lips together. "Shut it, Drunk."

I swatted her hand away.

Al emerged with a handgun and a box of ammo. While Nico and I loaded up, the police cruiser pulled up behind our vehicle.

Officer Cruz emerged. "What's the 411?"

"The two guys who killed Camila Vergado and Jimmie Wallace are inside, and so is the kid who ordered the hit. They have a hostage. It's Artie Balladares, the owner of the Seacoast Majestic."

"You said the *kid* who ordered the hit?"

I nodded. "Ozzy Messina, probably in his early twenties. Brown spiky hair and oversized grey suit. He's carrying stolen goods worth millions."

"What kind of stolen goods?"

"Cryptocurrency cold storage keys. Each key is worth a ton. One alone is worth approximately seventeen million dollars," said Nico.

Officer Cruz nodded. "I've called for backup. I appreciate you giving me a heads-up, though. If we can get this collar made, it's gonna look really good for me in front of my boss."

"It's the least we can do. We really appreciated you helping us out with the Camila Vergado situation."

Nico shot us an overly fake smile. "Aw, look at you two, scratching each other's backs. Isn't this sweet?" Then her face sobered and the smile disappeared. "Now can we get the fuck inside and get these guys before they take off with my boss's money?"

"She's really charming, Drunk. Where'd you find this one? The gutter?" asked Officer Cruz with a half smirk.

Al couldn't help but laugh while Nico's balled fists shook by her sides.

With no time for a snappy comeback, I led the crew towards the terminal. "Let's go. We have to hurry. There's a flight back to the States boarding on the tarmac right now."

Officer Cruz led the charge through the small, crowded terminal towards the Delta kiosk, when all of a sudden we heard a commotion on the other side of the room. Travelers and employees alike screamed and ran for the exit. Many hid behind the airport's bench seats, in doorways, and behind counters.

We raced in that direction and found Bruce holding Artie in a headlock with a gun to his head. Colin and Ozzy flanked the two men with their guns drawn as well. Three security guards with guns drawn had cornered the four men. The four of us crouched behind one of the terminal desks.

"Drop your weapons!" hollered one of the security guards.

"Get any closer and I'll shoot this man!" Bruce shouted back.

Ozzy aimed his gun at one of the security guards. "Put your guns down!" When they didn't do immediately as he'd ordered, he screamed again. "Down!"

Slowly, the three security guards lowered their weapons to the ground. No sooner had they stood back up again, this time unarmed, than Ozzy fired off two shots. One hit a guard in the stomach and the other in the leg. The two men fell to the ground. Colin discharged his weapon next, shooting the third security guard and sending him to the ground. The sound of the gunshots ricocheted off the walls and new screams filled the terminal. They began to ease their way towards the exit door behind them.

Officer Cruz stood then and trained her gun on the men. "Freeze!"

Ozzy, Colin, and Bruce all fired at her as they kept walking.

She managed to get off a few shots, but then crouched back down as bullets whizzed past her.

More sirens sounded in the distance. Officer Cruz's backup was on its way. We just couldn't let Ozzy and his guys get to that plane, where they could force the pilot to take off.

Bruce shoved Artie through the exit while Ozzy and Colin covered him. Officer Cruz and I stood and fired at them, but Ozzy and Colin got out the door onto the tarmac.

"Let's get 'em!" shouted Nico, jumping over the counter and rushing the door.

Al stood up.

I held his shoulder. "Al, you don't have a weapon. You stay here. Get those security guards some help," I instructed.

"But..."

I looked at him seriously as Nico and Officer Cruz barreled towards the door. "This is no time to argue. I need you to help the security guards. Without a weapon, you could become a liability out there."

Al nodded. "Yeah, go, go. I wasn't going to argue, Drunk. I got these guys. You go help Artie!"

I patted Al on the shoulder and took off after Nico and Officer Cruz.

Outside, Ozzy led the way, with Colin hot on his heels and Artie slowing Bruce's escape. Nico and Officer Cruz both fired at Bruce. One of their bullets struck him in the back of the leg, and he fell to the ground, pulling Artie down with him as he went. I caught up with the women just as Ozzy and Colin were climbing the stairs and four police cruisers tore into the parking lot on the other side of the fence and several hundred yards away from where the plane stood.

Nico and Officer Cruz both fired at the two on the stairs. Ozzy stopped and fired one shot back and then promptly realized he was out of ammo. Even Colin seemed out of ammunition, and with us shooting at them, they didn't have the ability to reload. They struggled with each other for a moment on the stairs over who was going up first.

Officer Cruz took the opportunity to fire off another shot. That one sent Colin reeling backwards as Ozzy disappeared inside the plane.

"I'll get Ozzy," I hollered as I sprinted past her towards the airplane. "Make sure Artie's okay, and get cuffs on those two." By the time I got to the stairs, Colin was midway down with a bullet to the chest. I climbed over him and went after Ozzy with Nico hot on my heels.

## 52

A<small>T THE TOP OF THE STAIRS</small>, I <small>POKED MY HEAD INSIDE AND</small> breathed a sigh of relief to discover the cabin to be empty. I was sure that was Lola's doing. She'd been able to manage that, and help avert a hostage situation. When I was sure the coast was clear, I slid carefully into the cabin.

"Where is he?" Nico hissed in my ear as she caught up to me.

I shook my head and held a finger to my lips. I pointed towards her and then the cockpit, and then I pointed to myself and towards the back of the plane. I'd search the back. She could check all the nooks and crannies and the cockpit at the front of the plane.

She nodded and went left while I went right. I walked slowly with my gun drawn and my heart in my throat. Ozzy could be at the back of the plane, or he could be hiding in any seat. I was thorough as I moved from seat to seat. And then I heard a noise towards the back of the plane. I had him!

I rushed towards the back of the plane, and with my back against a bulkhead compartment, I raised my gun. Before I knew what was happening, the compartment burst open. Ozzy's feet came out first, knocking me across the narrow hallway and into the lavatory. He had a fire extinguisher in hand as he jumped out of the small space, and as I came out of the lavatory, he swung at me with it. I bobbed left and it narrowly missed my head, instead hitting the door frame with a loud smacking noise. I heard him curse and then rush towards the flight attendant station at the end of the short hallway.

"Give up, Ozzy," I hollered at him. "The cops are here. You're done, man."

"No way, Drunk. You ruined everything for me!" he hollered back at me like a petulant child.

I stood in the doorway of the lavatory. "Give yourself up now and you'll walk away from this. Keep going and you'll wind up getting sent home to your dad in a body bag."

"Fuck you."

I rolled my eyes. "No, fuck you, Ozzy. You fucking ruined my vacation, man."

"Yeah, well, you ruined my life."

I rubbed a hand against my forehead and then gave a glance over my shoulder. Nico was now standing in the center of the aisle, motioning for me to go after him. I sighed. I didn't want to have to shoot Ozzy. As much as he was a pain in my ass, he was a kid. I was over it all, but I nodded. I held the gun up again, and with my back pressed against the bulkhead compartment, I eased back the last few feet towards his hiding spot. When I stepped into the stewardess station, a serving cart came flying at me. It shoved me backwards into something hard. I winced as the cart handle dug into my stomach and the hard thing jabbed me in the bullet wound I still had in my butt.

"Fuck!" I growled through clenched teeth, even though I was thankful the handle was high enough not to destroy my ability to bear children someday.

I lifted my arm to shoot Ozzy, and that was when he rushed me with the fire extinguisher. He swung it at me again.

This time it struck my arm, knocking the gun out of my hand. I heard it clatter to the floor. My hand throbbed almost immediately, but before I could dwell on it, I heard a gunshot ring out inside the airplane. I looked over to see Ozzy looking down at his leg, his eyes wide. Blood poured out of his thigh.

"You bitch! You shot me!" Ozzy sounded surprised.

"Damn straight I shot you." Nico strutted up to him and shoved her hand into his pocket. Still wide-eyed, Ozzy looked at her as if she'd reached into his pants to grab his junk. She pulled out the baggie of cold storage keys and tossed them to me. "Hang on to these for me, will ya?"

I heard a commotion coming from the other end of the plane, and before I could even get to my feet, Officer Cruz was upon us. She pushed Nico out of the way and looked back at me. "Drunk, you okay?"

I nodded. "Just a crushed hand. I'll be fine." I lifted my chin towards Ozzy, who looked like he might pass out at any second. "You better get him some medical attention, though."

She holstered her gun and hooked an arm under Ozzy's armpit. Nico took the other side, and together they managed to pull him forward. Ozzy's eyes flickered closed for a moment, like he was having trouble not passing out at the sight of his own blood. "Stay with me, kid," said Officer Cruz.

Officer Cruz and Nico managed to get Ozzy to the back exit, where another police officer was waiting to assist. Once they'd gotten Ozzy's hands cuffed, Officer Cruz looked back at me and shot me a wink. "Thanks, Drunk. I owe you one."

"Yeah, you do, Officer Cruz," I said with a chuckle.

"Enough with the Officer Cruz. I think you've earned the right to call me Francesca."

"Have I?" I said with surprise. "How about Frankie?"

She pointed at me. "Don't push your luck."

I held up both hands. "I know when to say when. Hey, and good luck explaining this mess to Sergeant Gibson. Better you than me."

She gave me a little two-fingered salute and then shoved Ozzy ahead to the waiting police force on the tarmac, leaving Nico and me alone on the plane.

I suddenly felt a little light-headed. My ass hurt like hell, and my hand throbbed from being smashed. I stumbled backwards into the hallway.

Nico tried to catch me before I fell. "Drunk, you alright?"

I braced myself against the doorjamb of the lavatory. "Yeah. I think so. That kid had more spunk in him than I gave him credit for," I said, taking a heavy breath. I reached into my pocket and pulled out the cold storage keys. "Which one's yours?"

She pulled the key fob attached to the lanyard from my hand. "This one." She hugged it to her chest. "Oh my God, my boss is going to be so thrilled. Thank you, Drunk. Thank you for all your help!"

I let out a breath. I was starting to feel a little better. "Not a problem. I'll have Big Eddie help me figure out who these other two keys belong to."

Nico smiled and gave a little nod towards the bathroom behind me. "Hey, by any chance, did you happen to see any airplane keys lying around in there?"

I turned around, furrowing my brow. The only keys that were on my mind at the moment were the cold storage keys, so her question threw me for a second. When I turned to face her again, she had a sexy smile on her face. I couldn't help but smile back. "Nope, no keys."

She ran a hand along the side of my face. "You know, a little birdie told me that you were federally licensed to go down my landing strip."

"A little birdie told you that?" I asked with a smirk.

She nodded. "Yup."

"You didn't happen to throat-punch that little birdie out of the sky, did you?" I said with a chuckle.

She rolled her eyes.

That was when I made my move. My good arm shot out and wrapped around her waist. I pulled her to me and laid a kiss on her. Her lips parted beneath the pressure of mine. When we'd parted, I breathlessly whispered in her ear. "So, uh, how about you and me join the mile-high club?"

"We're on the ground, Drunk," she whispered back.

"There aren't any windows in the lavatory, and I have a vivid imagination. I won't tell if you won't."

She pressed me backwards into the bathroom and slammed the door behind us.

Maybe I didn't officially join the mile-high club that day on the plane, but I sure as hell got close.

# 53

BIG EDDIE, RALPH THE WEASEL, TONY SOPRANO, BOB HOPE, Elton John, and Gary the Gunslinger—a moniker I'd given him because I didn't think it was fair that he was the only one without one—gathered along with Al and myself in the Seacoast Majestic's clubhouse computer room the next afternoon.

It had been almost an entire week since I'd first flown to Paradise Isle. I'd decided that meeting Nicolette Dominion had been both a blessing and a curse. She'd been a big pain in my ass in more than one way, and had nearly ruined my vacation. And yet she'd also forced me out of my comfort zone, and she'd reignited my love life. Even though we'd gone out with a bang in the airplane bathroom, having to say goodbye to her had been more difficult than I thought it would be.

Having to say goodbye to Sergeant Gibson on the airport tarmac *hadn't* been difficult, however. When he'd told me that I was no longer a person of interest in the murder of Jimmie Wallace, Al and I had cheered, and then we'd driven straight over to the Paradise Isle Medical Center to check on Artie and get the hole in my ass sewn up properly.

Now, with less than a week left of vacation to enjoy, I was looking forward to spending some quality time on the beach with a never-ending supply of cold drinks in my hand.

"So what do you think about Paradise Isle by now?" Tony asked, clapping me on the back.

I let out an extremely heavy sigh. "Are you kidding me? I haven't even had a minute to relax since I've been here! Ask me a week from now, when I'm boarding the plane back to America!"

"We'll take good care of you," promised Al. "Won't we, fellas?"

The guys all nodded.

"Of course we will," agreed Tony.

Gary and Eddie were especially anxious to look after me. Because of my matchmaking prowess, they'd both managed to get lucky. Which was probably why Gary hadn't shat bricks when he'd seen the condition of his Land Cruiser upon its return. Of course, Artie had promised to fix it good as new, and he'd even agreed to spring for four new tires, so that had made the pill a little bit easier for Gary to swallow.

I pulled up a chair next to Big Eddie, who was seated behind one of the computers. "So, how's progress coming on finding out who those other two cold storage keys belong to?"

Eddie pointed at the flat-screen monitor. "Well, I was able to figure out who the flash drive belonged to. There was an IP address that I was able to trace back to its rightful owner. They'll be happy. It's worth a little over ten million."

"Wow," I said. I still couldn't believe people had that kind of money available to them on a simple little device. It literally blew my mind.

"Yeah," said Eddie. "But we're running into a snag with this other one." He held up the credit card sized pieces of metal.

"What kind of snag?"

"Well, it's literally just numbers and letters. There's absolutely no identifying information on it."

"None?"

Eddie and Al shook their heads as a smile played around both of their lips.

"What?" I asked, looking from one to the other. "What's that mean?"

Eddie lifted his brows. "It means that it can't be returned. We've literally got no way of knowing who the rightful owner is."

"You're kidding? Someone's just out that money? Fuck, I'd be crying right now."

Al nodded as he plucked the silver piece of metal out of Eddie's hand. "Unfortunately, that's exactly what the case is."

"So, what do we do with the key?" I asked.

Al looked backwards at the guys. "Well, the guys and I were talking about it, and you know what they say. Possession is nine-tenths of the law."

I lifted a brow. "But no one really possesses it."

"Someone does," said Al. He handed the piece of metal to me. "Jimmie gave it to you."

"To me!" My eyes widened as I took the key.

Al closed his eyes and tipped his head forward. "Yup."

"You think *I* should keep the last one?"

The guys all nodded. "We do," said Tony. "You're the one that got Artie out of the predicament he was in, and you solved the case. We think it's kind of like a finder's fee and a private eye fee all rolled into one."

My eyes were wide. "Well, how much is it worth?"

Al winced. "Well, that's the bad news. Unfortunately with today's Bitcoin rate, it's not worth near what it was in December, that's for sure."

"Okay? So, what's it worth now?"

"Oh, just a cool six point nine million dollars."

"Six point nine…" I felt the breath leaving my body and my head began to spin. "…million…"

Laughter filled the room.

"What's so funny?" boomed a familiar voice on the other side of the room.

I could barely see Artie as he entered the room.

"Artie!" said Al. "Good to see you! How're you feeling?"

"Feeling so much better now that I know that Ozzy Messina is where he belongs… behind bars!"

"We're all thankful for that!" said Tony. "I can't believe everything that kid put you through, Artie. The nerve!"

Artie shook his head. "I only hired the little shit because I was trying to help his father out. I knew Ozzy was kind of a problem, but I thought I could give him a professional job and maybe he'd gain some confidence. Apparently he got a little too confident."

"That's for sure!" agreed Al.

"But, if it wasn't for the two of you, I'd be dead right now." Artie laid a hand on both Al's and my shoulders.

"It was really all Drunk," said Al. "He's one hell of a great detective."

I smiled at Al. No one had ever called me a great anything, let alone a great detective. Hearing it come from Al felt good. "Thanks, Al."

"Al's right," said Artie. "I'm so impressed with what a great cop you turned out to be. You know, I need someone like that here at the Seacoast Majestic."

Tony nodded. "Yeah. Especially now, with Ozzy headed off to the big house on international theft and murder charges."

Al grinned from ear to ear. "Yup, a head of security position just opened up."

"Yes, it did," agreed Artie, nodding his head. He held one of his thick, squishy hands out for me shake. "And I'd like to offer *you* the job."

"Get the fuck out of here," I said, my mouth agape.

Artie laughed. "I can't get the fuck out of here, I own the place!"

The men roared.

"What do you say, Drunk?" asked Tony.

I looked at Al.

He was grinning at me like a proud father. "I would love for my partner to stay. What do you say, Drunk?"

I didn't know what to say. My head was still spinning. Six point nine million dollars and a job offer as a head of security at a Caribbean island resort, all in exchange for not going back to Pam and winter in the States?

In little more than a breathy whisper, I finally responded, "How can I say no to that?"

"You can't," said Al. "That's why you say yes."

I smiled at the guys. "Then I guess I'll have to say, *yes!*"

# HEY THERE, IT'S ZANE...

I'm the author of this book. I've got a huge favor to ask of you. If you even remotely enjoyed Drunk, Al, and their predicament, I'd be honored if you left a review on Amazon. It doesn't have to be much - or it can be a lot, whatever floats your boat.

I'd love to see this book reach more readers, and one way to do that is to have a whole bunch of feedback from readers like you that liked it.

Leaving reviews also tells me that you want more books in the series or want to read more about certain characters. Or, I guess, conversely, if you didn't like it, it tells me to either try harder or not to give up my day job.

So, thanks in advance. I appreciate the time you took to read my book, and I wish you nothing but the best!

Zane

# MANNY'S COOL AND DEADLY RECIPE

1 oz Spiced Rum
1 oz Jamaican Rum
1/2 oz Triple Sec
2 oz Pineapple Juice
1 oz Orange Juice
3/4 oz Grenadine

Mix all ingredients together and pour over ice in a tall glass.
Garnish with a pineapple slice and a maraschino cherry. Enjoy!

# SNEAK PEEK - DRUNK ON A BOAT

## THE MISADVENTURES OF A DRUNK IN PARADISE: BOOK 2

# 1

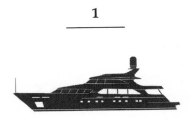

"DRUNK."

Facedown, I felt movement. The earth was shaking.

"Drunk, wake up."

A shrill sound blared in the distance, as if a sonic weapon designed to burst my eardrums and implode my skull had been deployed.

The shaking intensified. I gripped the surface beneath me tightly, afraid I was about to fall off the face of the planet. Panic surged through my body. My limbs were heavy, and my eyelids felt bolted down and unable to budge. A finger jabbed into the fleshy part of my shoulder, the skin-to-skin contact giving me the distinct impression that I wasn't wearing a shirt.

"Drunk!"

Was that a voice I heard?

"Hmm…" I groaned.

"Wake up. Your phone's ringing."

There went that damn sonic blaring again, drilling into my eardrums and making my temples throb. Even when the noise stopped, my ears rang with its distant echo.

I tried to swallow, but my mouth was turned inside out. My tongue was thick and heavy. I gagged a little.

"Should I answer it?" The voice was low, but feminine.

Rolling onto my back, I swiped a puddle of drool from the corner of my mouth. My foot slid sideways until I found a cool spot between the sheets. Spread-eagle, I stretched my arms out over my head. My hand touched a pillow.

I was in a bed.

A very comfortable bed.

But despite the bed's plushy comfort, the claws of death still knifed into my skull.

I pulled the pillow to my side and curled into it.

"Five more minutes," I mumbled around my lead tongue. Even to my own ears, the words were a garbled incoherent mess.

"It's Artie."

I shifted again, trying to find a way to lie that didn't press against my bladder. This time my foot made contact with someone else's bare leg. There was someone in bed with me!

The cogs in my mind suddenly clicked into place, and my eyes popped open.

Bright morning rays of sunshine streamed in from my open window, searing my retinas like death rays of torture. Squinting and throwing a hand up, I turned to look at the face behind the voice.

A woman lay in bed next to me. Young and fresh-faced with big brown eyes and a wild mess of curly brown hair, she had the better part of my bedsheet wrapped around her bare, voluptuous breasts.

I grinned groggily at the familiar face. "Mornin', Mack."

She responded with an easy smile, "Good morning, Drunk." She handed me my phone as it rang again. "Your phone's ringing. It's Artie. Hey, listen, I'm gonna use your shower. Do you mind? I have to get to work before Mari fires my ass for being late again."

I ignored the ringing phone and stared at her through squinty eyes. "Work? What? It's too early for work."

The husky undertones of her laughter softened the shrill sound my phone continued to emit. "It's not too early for work. It's almost eight." She eyed the ringing phone. "Aren't you going to answer that?"

"What? No! Don't go!" I yelled at her as she climbed out of bed, stealing my bedsheet right off of me, leaving me naked and now *fully* awakened. Mack was leaving? How was the night over already? It felt like it had just begun. "Oh, come on! No morning kisses?"

Pressed up against the bathroom's doorjamb, Mack shot me a sexy little pout. "Nope, no morning kisses."

"Rawck! No morning kisses. No morning kisses. Rawck!" The screechy echo radiated out from my bedroom window, effectively shooting a piercing dagger through my temples.

I blanched.

Mack giggled. "Sorry, Drunk. We both have to work today. You wanna hang out later, though?"

"Later? Oh, come on, Mack," I begged. I propped myself up on my elbow and patted the empty spot next to me. "You know what they say. There's no time like the present."

Smiling, she tipped her head backwards. The long tendrils of her curls reached down to sweep the curve of her backside. "Yeah, well, my aunt Doris always says better late than never."

I chuckled. "Okay, well, *one*, Aunt Doris is wrong. And *two*, I'm pretty sure the saying is better late than pregnant."

Mack rolled her eyes at me. "Oh my God. You wanna hang out later or not?"

My phone made the familiar shrieking sound again.

Every vein that delivered blood to my brain throbbed in unison.

*Fuck!* I needed to change that damn ringtone!

My bottom lip plumped out, expressing my disappointment that we weren't going to lie in bed all morning until the throbbing in my head subsided and I was ready to have another go of it. "Of course I wanna hang out later."

"Hang out later, hang out later. Rawck!" went the echo.

The sexy sound of Mack's laughter trailed behind her until I heard the bathroom door click closed.

"Ugh," I groaned, grabbing Mack's pillow off the other side of the bed and launching it blindly at my open bedroom window. "Shut up already!"

"Shut up already. Shut up already. Rawck!"

My phone trilled once more.

I clamped a hand on either side of my head and squeezed in an attempt to keep my head from rupturing and spewing splushy, vomit-inducing sludge across the room. Surely the resort cleaning staff wouldn't want to come clean up a mess like that.

I closed my eyes and sucked in a deep breath. The morning was not off to a great start. Slowly, I let out the breath, swiped the little green phone symbol, and put the phone to my ear. "Yeah, Artie, what's up?"

Pressing my thumb into my other ear, I almost couldn't hear the echo across the room: *"What's up, what's up, what's up."*

"Drunk, sorry to wake you so early. I know you probably had a late night, but listen, I need you to come in. We've, uh, got a bit of a situation."

I pulled the thumb out of my ear and ground the pads of my fingers into my eyes. I could hear the sound of the water turning on in the bathroom. "Hey, Artie, I got company this morning. Can't we do this later?"

"Yeah, I'm sorry about that. I wouldn't have called if it wasn't important enough to warrant you coming in."

I had no interest in going into work at this hour. All Little Drunk and I wanted to do was to go join Mack in the shower, knock off a quick one, and then crawl back into bed and ooze into unconsciousness. "Right now?" I pressed.

"Right now, right now. Rawck!"

I'd had enough. I bolted up in bed, sending a searing pain through my skull. My eyes met those of a yellow-bellied, blue-bodied, green-headed, zebra-faced parrot. "Shut the hell up!"

"*Drunk?*" Artie bellowed into the phone.

The parrot bobbed back and forth in the window, doing a little dance on the sill. "Shut the hell up, shut the hell up. Rawck!"

"Not you, Artie." I grabbed my own pillow off the bed and flung it at the parrot.

The bird ducked as my pillow sailed over its head and out the window. "Rawck!"

"It's this fucking parrot. Ever since you moved me into this cottage, it won't leave me alone."

"Oh. That's Earnestine."

"Earnestine? Fucking thing has a *name?*"

"Yeah. Hey, Drunk, how long before you can get here?"

I scratched my head and looked around. My quilt was twisted into a ball at the foot of the bed. Clothes were strewn all over the room. Empty shot glasses and tequila bottles lined my nightstand, and condom wrappers littered the floor. My head pounded—a memento of the wild night before. But oh, had it been worth it. My first night with Mack was everything I had hoped it would be and more.

It had been epic.

A real killer of a party.

I glanced back at the time. It wasn't even eight yet. I was pretty sure Mack and I had crawled into bed a little after two, but the festivities in my cottage had gone on well into the morning. I was guessing I hadn't gotten to sleep until after four or maybe even five. I wasn't sure. I didn't even remember falling asleep.

"Artie, it's not even eight yet, and I gotta work tonight. Can't whatever it is wait?"

"I'm afraid not. I've got a woman here who's demanding to see you. She's kinda making a scene, Drunk."

I slumped forward in bed and ran a hand through my

thick, unruly hair. If I had to guess, it was Alicia. Or maybe it was Gigi; I could see her being a vindictive one. Or maybe Mari had discovered I'd gone through her girls at the same speed I'd binge-watched *Breaking Bad*, and she'd run to Artie to tattle. I let my head fall into my free hand and groaned. They'd all been over eighteen and willing participants. I hadn't had to coerce a single one of them.

Charmed them, yes.

Coerced them, no.

*Fuck.*

"Hey, listen, Artie, I can explain…"

"No need to explain, Drunk. Just get in here ASAP."

Something in Artie's voice had me curious now. "Come on, man. You're not even gonna gimme a heads-up?"

There was a pause.

I could hear a woman screeching in the background. The voice sounded vaguely familiar, but it was too muffled to hear it well.

The phone crackled and then became suddenly hollow-sounding, as if Artie had wrapped his giant mitts around the receiver. "If I tell you, you're not going to want to come," he whispered breathily into the phone. His raspy voice made him sound like a stalker straight out of a suspense thriller flick.

I sighed. It wasn't like I needed this job anyway. After the $6.9 million windfall I'd received a few weeks prior, I was set for life. The head of security job at the Seacoast Majestic was as laid-back as jobs came, and in all reality, I was mainly doing it for shits and giggles, and so I had a reason to hide out on a tropical island instead of returning to the States and having to come face-to-face with my cheating ex-fiancée again. But if Artie wanted to fire me over sleeping with the help, he sure as hell was welcome to fire me. I'd get over it.

I groaned. "I need a shower."

"Fine. Shower and then come in."

"Have a Dr. Pepper waiting for me, will ya?" I was going to

need some caffeine if I was going to be worth a shit for the day.

"A Dr. Pepper?"

"Yeah, and a candy bar." I *had* saved the man's life, after all. The least he owed me was a damn soda and a candy bar.

"A Dr. Pepper and a candy bar?" repeated Artie like he was writing it down. "What kind of candy bar?"

"I don't care. Nothing with coconut. I fucking hate coconut."

"I fucking hate coconut. I fucking hate coconut. Rawck!"

## DRUNK ON A BOAT

*Drunk on a Boat* is now available on Amazon!

If you'd like to notified when new books in the series are released, then consider joining my newsletter.

I swear I won't spam you, I'm really not that ambitious.

I'll only send out an email when I write a new book or have something to give away that I think you might like.

So what is that?

A couple emails a year?

You can handle that, can't you?

Go to www.zanemitchell.com to signup!

# ABOUT ZANE

I grew up on a sheep farm in the Midwest. I was an only child, raised on Indiana Jones, Star Wars, and the Dukes of Hazzard. My dad was a fresh-water fish biologist and worked on the Missouri River. My mom was a teacher when I was young, and then became the principal of my school around the time I started taking an interest in beer. My grandpa, much like Al in my Drunk in Paradise series, actually owned a Case IH dealership, and I thought the world of him and my grandma.

I've been married twice. I'd say the first was a mistake, but that marriage gave me my four kids. Marriage numero dos came with two pre-made kids. So yeah, we're paying for Christmas presents for six and college for three. So buy my next book, *please*. I'd say that was a joke, but jeez. College is expensive.

In a former life, I was a newspaper columnist, and I actually went to journalism school but eventually dropped out. I did go back to school and eventually got a teaching degree, but let's face facts. I sucked at being a teacher. I was just as much of a kid as the kids were.

The love of my life and I live in the Midwest. We go about our boring lives just like you do. We parent lots of teenagers and twenty-something-year-olds. We watch superhero movies and Dateline on TV. We're a little obsessive in our love for the Kansas City Chiefs. We take yearly visits to the Caribbean because hey, tax deductible. And now, I write books - sort of a life long dream, to be honest.

So thanks for reading. You have no idea how cool I think it is, that you picked *my* book out of all of the choices you had to read and you made it to the end. You rock. Don't ever let anyone tell you otherwise.

Zane

Oh. P.S. I don't do Tweets. Or Insta. I do have Facebook and a website. www.zanemitchell.com. You're welcome to come over and hangout. BYOB.